the end of the road

true crime junkies

book six

Christy Barritt

one
Then

CHARLOTTE WATKINS PAUSED outside the glossy black door and suddenly second-guessed herself.

Was this really what she wanted to do?

She thought she knew the answer. And she thought that answer was yes.

This was the best option for her to make money now that her mom had kicked her out of their small apartment.

When her mom's new boyfriend had hit on her, Charlotte told her mom. She was certain her mom would make him leave.

Instead, her mom had blamed Charlotte and given her an hour to pack her things.

Now, Charlotte was on her own and questioning all her choices.

Pressing her eyes closed, she sucked in a deep breath.

Then she straightened and rang the doorbell on the

massive house located in the rolling New York countryside.

The house screamed money and affluence . . . everything Charlotte was not.

The door opened, and a woman stood there. She wore pearls around her neck. A tailored skirt with a creamy ivory blouse. Her blonde hair was cut neatly to her chin.

Charlotte had expected someone older. But this woman was maybe twenty-eight.

A tight, pointedly polite smile spread across her face. "You must be Charlotte."

Charlotte nodded, suddenly feeling underdressed in her jeans and pink sweater she'd purchased at Walmart. "I am. And you're Meredith?"

"That's right. I'm so glad you're here. Why don't you come inside, and I'll get you something to drink?"

When Charlotte stepped through the doorway, she sucked in a breath. The home was extravagant with its marble floors, leather furniture, and high-end trim work. It smelled like . . . what was that scent? Not the cheap candles her mom used. It was more like a fine wine or fresh leather.

At once, Charlotte knew she wouldn't be a good fit here. As soon as she started her interview with this couple, they would see there was nothing fancy about her. They would offer some flimsy excuse about why this arrangement wouldn't work.

But she was here now, so she needed to get through

this. When this plan fell through, she'd figure out something else.

A moment later, Meredith returned with a glass of lemonade and handed it to Charlotte. "Mark's waiting for us in the other room. Right this way."

Charlotte followed her from the foyer, past the massive kitchen, and into a cozy living area, where a man sat. Mark Wellington.

He was probably thirty-five, with a full head of dark hair, olive skin, and a movie-worthy profile.

Beautiful people in a beautiful house, she mused.

People had told Charlotte she was beautiful as well. But not like Mark and Meredith. Charlotte was beautiful in an ordinary way.

She had blonde highlights but not from a salon. Instead, they were from squeezing lemon juice in her hair on hot summer days. She bought her clothes from cheap department stores. Her face wore drugstore cosmetics.

She smoothed her hair, feeling entirely inadequate.

Mark rose and extended his hand. "Charlotte." His voice sounded rumbling and deep. "We're so glad you could come. Please, have a seat."

He nodded at a beige chair facing the couch. Windows outside displayed a pool and rambling countryside surrounded by trees. Everything around her screamed luxury.

She carefully lowered herself onto the plush cushion of a rolled-arm chair while Mark and Meredith sat on a tufted couch across from her to begin the interview process.

"We've been talking to several people, trying to find someone who's the right fit for us." Mark laced his fingers with his wife's as he started the conversation. "More than anything, my wife and I would like to have children, but we're unable to conceive on our own. Due to my wife's infertility, the process of starting a family has been challenging for us, to say the least."

"I can only imagine how difficult that must be." Truly. At nineteen—though Charlotte had told them she was twenty-one—she wasn't old enough to want her own children. But not being able to carry a child when that was your heart's desire had to be gut-wrenching.

"As you know, we're looking for a surrogate." Meredith's voice sounded thin, like she was unsure about this. But she proceeded. "But we need to make sure the woman we choose is a good fit. That she's someone who will take care of our baby while in the womb and not do anything foolish."

"Understandable." And responsible. Charlotte had always been responsible. She'd been forced into that role.

"I know most people go through an agency, so this is a bit unconventional," Meredith continued. "But so many of them have illogical rules. Mark and I really want to be more involved in the process."

"That's why we're requiring the woman we choose to carry our child to live with us for the duration of the pregnancy." Mark stared at Charlotte, watching her reaction.

She kept her face placid, not wanting to seem too eager or too put off.

She must have passed the test because he continued.

"We'll prepare the proper nutritious food and provide the best medical care available," Mark said. "Basically, we'll do everything within our power to ensure that the woman carrying our child is healthy and safe. Is that something that you would be open to?"

Charlotte didn't want to tell them she had nowhere else to live and no money for food.

After Charlotte had graduated from high school, she'd forfeited college in favor of working at a daycare. She'd never thought she was the higher education type, nor did she have money to pay for it. So she figured she'd work a few years, save some money, and then decide if she wanted to go for a degree.

But saving for her education hadn't been a reality—her mom had always needed more money to support her deadbeat boyfriend.

That had all led her to this moment.

Those facts would make her sound desperate. But she *was* desperate.

She swallowed hard, trying to maintain her composure, and then nodded. "I'm okay with those details."

Meredith's eyes narrowed as she openly scrutinized Charlotte—almost as if Charlotte were an outfit she was deciding on for an important event. Was the cut flattering? How would others perceive her in the outfit? Would she have any shopper's remorse?

"What makes you want to do this?" the woman finally asked.

Mark and Meredith were waiting for Charlotte to say something wrong that would mark her off their list. This was all a test, one most people failed. Only one woman would be chosen.

Why *did* Charlotte want to do this?

When she'd read about this opening through an online ad, she'd decided on a whim to apply. She'd never expected to hear back.

She supposed other women might go through agencies, but there was no telling how long that process would take. She really had no idea. She'd never considered doing something like this before.

"I love children." Charlotte rubbed her sweaty palms against her jeans, praying her nerves didn't get the best of her. "I'd love to help out a deserving couple who's unable to start a family on their own. I feel like it's a way I can give back, by helping others."

"Do you have a boyfriend and, if so, is he okay with this?" Mark asked.

Charlotte shook her head. She wouldn't call any of the men in her past her "boyfriends." Anything but.

She didn't want a boyfriend. So far, guys had only proven themselves to be jerks.

"I'm single," she finally said. "My only family is my mom, and we're not on speaking terms right now. So there are no relationships in my life that would hinder me."

"And you have no moral qualms about carrying someone else's child?" Mark continued to study her.

She swallowed hard. "No, I don't. I mean, there were surrogates in the Old Testament, right? If it was okay in the Bible, then it should be okay for me. More than okay. It should be honorable."

She'd been reading the Bible a lot more lately as she tried to find something to ground her. She only knew she couldn't find her hope in men like her mom had done.

She needed to believe there was something more to this life.

Mark and Meredith exchanged a look, an unspoken conversation passing between them. Charlotte couldn't read if they were pleased or not. She only knew that her entire life and worthiness was being judged based on this ten-minute conversation.

Her lungs froze as she waited.

If they said no, what would she do? Find a job at another daycare? Search for a roommate? Eat ramen every night?

Mark nodded at his wife, as if giving her the go-ahead to voice aloud their silent decision.

"I know this might seem rash." Meredith offered a hesitant smile. "But I feel in my gut that you're the one we want. I haven't gotten this feeling with any of the other women we've interviewed. Normally, I'd think about this decision overnight. In this case, I don't feel as if I need to. Charlotte, if you would like to be our surrogate, then we'd love to have you carry our child."

Charlotte's heart beat harder, but she tried not to show her excitement. She needed to keep her cool.

"I'd be honored," she started. "And I'd love this opportunity."

Smiles of relief crossed their faces.

"That's wonderful." Mark grinned, his voice suddenly warm and inviting.

"Truly wonderful," Meredith echoed. "You'll need a physical, of course. And there's paperwork. But if all that checks out . . ."

"Then you'll carry our child for us," Mark finished.

A smile spread across her face.

She was going to be a surrogate.

Charlotte could feel it in her bones . . . this job was going to change everything about her future.

Everything.

two
Now

"I **NEED** to get to the Lower 48. First flight out of here that doesn't cost an arm and a leg." Simmy Samuels shifted at the desk in front of the airline clerk as she waited, her desperation barely contained.

"Just give me a minute." The agent, a fortysomething brunette whose nametag read "Debbie," stared at her computer, tapping on the keys with her long pink manicured nails.

A minute? What if she didn't have a minute?

Despite that, Simmy nodded stiffly, trying to keep her patience. An Uber driver had dropped her off here thirty minutes ago, and she'd been waiting in line to speak with a ticket agent since then.

She had to get a flight out of Anchorage.

Now.

She didn't know where to go. She only knew she had to get out of Alaska before Knave found her.

As Debbie continued looking at something on the computer, Simmy glanced at the crowd of people waiting to check in for their flights. A flash of guilt shot through her for taking up so much time while there was a line behind her.

Part of her feared Knave was already here. That he'd already found her.

Yesterday, Simmy's name and photo had been released to the public. If Knave had seen that—and knowing him, he had—then he would have gotten the first flight to Alaska to find her.

That meant Simmy needed to leave the state.

She probably should have gone right away. She hadn't. She'd wanted to be a team player, to see the murder club's investigation through to completion.

Now she had to wonder if she'd pay the price . . . with her life.

In her pocket, she had six hundred dollars in cash. She needed to see how far away that would get her.

"Let's see here . . ." Debbie stared at the computer, her eyes skimming over the information.

The woman seemed too calm and patient for Simmy's liking. However, the agent couldn't possibly know everything Simmy was going through.

Once Simmy was on the plane, she'd have time to plan her next move.

She just needed to keep her cool for a little longer.

"How about Nevada?" Debbie glanced up at her. "I could get you there by tonight."

Nevada might work. Either Vegas or Reno.

She preferred Reno since it was smaller than Vegas. Maybe Simmy could find somewhere on the outskirts of town to start over.

She'd need to find a new name. Get a new ID. Secure a job to support herself. Finding housing probably wouldn't be easy.

"Let's see . . . it looks like I could fly you to Vegas, and then you could take a flight from there to Reno if you wanted." Debbie rocked her head back and forth in thought. "Although . . . it would probably be cheaper and faster to fly to Vegas and rent a car if you want to go somewhere else. Your choice, of course."

Simmy didn't have money to rent a car. Besides, she could only pay in cash. She didn't want her name to go into any type of system that could be searched. Even though she had a fake ID, she couldn't chance it.

She couldn't let him find her.

She forced a smile at the agent. "Straight to Reno please."

"Very well." Debbie turned back to the computer and called out a price.

Simmy's stomach sank.

The plane ticket would take up most of her money. And she'd still need to survive for a few days until she could find a job and a place to live in Nevada.

She was going to miss the beautiful state of Alaska. She'd thought working at the Almost Halfway Trading

Post off the Dalton Highway was about as remote and safe as she could get. But she'd been wrong.

If only she hadn't gotten involved with the Arctic Circle Murder Club . . . things would be different right now.

She should have known better. But her new circle of friends had been the first thing in so long to make her feel alive again. Especially Ranger. She'd come to deeply appreciate his friendship and support. His silent but constant presence. The way he always showed up at just the right moment.

Now all the security she felt with him was being ripped away.

Simmy pulled money for the plane ticket from her pocket.

As she began to count out the bills, she felt eyes boring into her back.

Goosebumps rose on her skin.

It was him, wasn't it? Knave?

Her lungs filled with cement as she slowly turned.

Had the man from her nightmares found her?

———

THE AIR LEFT Ranger's lungs.

He'd found her.

Simmy. Simmy with her slim build, her long, light-brown hair pulled back into a ponytail, and her slender neck.

Simmy, with her backpack strapped around her shoulders and a wad of cash in her hands.

Simmy, whose gaze showed both relief and irritation.

Ranger bypassed everyone in line and paused beside Simmy. He placed his hand—large and heavy—on the counter in front of her. He had to make his point, had to make sure she listened.

"You don't have to do this alone," he stated.

Her gaze fluttered up to him, her lips quivering and cheek twitching. "How did you find me?"

"It's what I do. I keep an eye on you." He hoped the words didn't sound creepy.

Simmy's expression remained panicked—but not from his words. "But you . . . you need to go after your daughter. You shouldn't be here right now."

That was just like Simmy—to always think of others.

And it was one more reason he loved her.

"I will find her," he assured her. "But I had to find you first. Don't get the plane ticket. Let me help you."

She stared at him, questions dancing in her gaze.

"Ma'am?" the desk agent asked. "Would you like me to proceed?"

Simmy stood there, cash still in hand as she stared up at Ranger like someone who had to make an impossible decision. A life-or-death decision.

Maybe that's what this was for Simmy. How could he make her see that he could help her? That he wanted to help her?

He took her hand and gently folded the cash back into her fist before quietly saying, "Let me help you."

She rubbed her lips together, the pensive expression still on her face.

"You don't know what you're getting yourself into." Her voice cracked.

"Whatever it is . . . I can handle it." He'd dodged guns. Survived being stabbed in the back. He'd even been chased by members of Russia's Foreign Intelligence Service.

"Ma'am?" Impatience tinged the agent's words.

Ranger glanced at the woman, fighting back irritation. "Just give us a minute."

"There's a line behind you."

Several people grumbled their agreement.

Ranger ignored them and stared at Simmy, waiting patiently for her answer.

She anxiously glanced at the line of people behind them. Tugged on the collar of her sweatshirt. Swallowed hard.

Finally, she turned back to him and nodded. "Okay."

The pensive look remained in her eyes as she jammed her cash back into her pocket and hiked her bag higher on her shoulders.

"So you don't want this ticket?" The desk agent sounded entirely too confused for her own good.

"She won't be needing it." Ranger wrapped his arm around Simmy's shoulders and led her away.

They had some serious talking to do.

He wasn't sure how much Simmy would tell him, and

he wouldn't push. He had secrets himself, so he understood Simmy's hesitation.

First, they needed to get out of here—before more danger found them.

Jeopardy seemed to be a theme lately.

Ranger didn't know exactly who Simmy was running from. But it didn't matter. He would protect her, no matter what.

He'd known from the moment they met that she had a troubling past. Most people who ended up near the Arctic Circle had a good reason for it.

Including him.

He glanced around as he led her outside, searching for anyone suspicious. Cars were lined up dropping off people. Picking people up. Vans from hotels waited for guests. A couple of taxis and Ubers lingered curbside.

People hurried to-and-fro, pulling luggage behind them. Talking on cell phones. Listening to their AirPods and clueless about life around them.

At least the sun was out, though obscured right now by a building in the distance.

All of that, and Ranger saw no one who made his guard go up.

They walked across the street. To the garage where he'd left his car.

With every step, he continued to scan everything around him.

Trouble could be anywhere, especially if his suspicions were true.

Simmy had never talked about her past. But the stark fear in her eyes when certain subjects were mentioned hadn't gone unnoticed. Subjects like leaving the trading post to travel elsewhere. Getting publicity or attention of any sort.

She was hiding.

Finally, they reached his rental SUV, and he ushered her inside, closed her door, glanced around one more time, and then climbed in himself.

Now he needed to figure out where to go from here.

————

AS SOON AS they were in the safety of Ranger's car, Simmy crumbled.

She didn't often let herself fall apart. She couldn't afford to. But the reaction felt out of her control.

Ranger reached for her, and she buried herself in his strong embrace.

He looked like a mountain man. Big and broad with a thick beard and curly dark hair.

Sometimes, he spoke in grunts.

Sometimes, he didn't speak at all.

Always, he seemed invincible. Like a rock.

Always, he had her back.

Without saying a word, he held her as she cried.

Simmy wasn't sure how much she could say. How much she *wanted* to say.

The realization that he'd dropped everything to come after her. To find her . . . it did something to her heart.

Something dangerous.

Matthew 18:12 filled her mind. *"If a man owns a hundred sheep, and one of them wanders away, will he not leave the ninety-nine on the hills and go to look for the one that wandered off?"*

She felt like the one sheep, and Ranger felt like the shepherd.

However, Simmy had vowed to never let herself have feelings for a man again.

Yet here she was, unable to hold back her emotions any longer. She was making herself vulnerable. That was always a mistake.

She finally backed away and wiped at her eyes with the sleeve of her shirt. "Let's get out of here."

Ranger started the vehicle and pulled from the parking garage, still not asking questions. She quickly leaned back and pulled on her seatbelt.

Simmy didn't talk about her history. She didn't want to be judged. Didn't want to relive those awful moments.

But she needed to tell Ranger. She couldn't avoid these conversations forever. Eventually, there were details that needed to be shared.

By both of them.

And Simmy wasn't referring to the growing feelings she had for the man. Because, yes, they were there, even if she tried to deny it. Neither had admitted their feelings.

But in their free time, they were nearly inseparable, drawn together by something invisible but powerful.

She hoped desperately Ranger might talk about his past also. So much about him remained a mystery.

Truthfully, almost *everything* about him remained a secret.

Even so, he'd proven himself to be trustworthy.

As they pulled onto a road that snaked through Anchorage, she asked, "Where are we going?"

She glanced at him. Noticed how self-assured he looked. Noticed his strapping muscles as he gripped the steering wheel. Noticed his intense gaze as he scanned the streets around him like a bodyguard protecting a priceless treasure.

"Anywhere in particular you want to go?" he asked.

Her throat tightened—burned, really. "Somewhere I can disappear."

"I know just the place."

She expected Ranger to head toward Fairbanks. There were only a limited number of directions they could go from Anchorage.

South to the Kenai Peninsula. North to Fairbanks. If they felt adventurous, they could catch a ferry to the Aleutian Islands or head east toward Valdez or Canada.

Simmy was no expert on Alaska. She'd moved north of Fairbanks, just outside the Arctic Circle. She'd rarely left the area once she arrived . . . until she met the other members of the Arctic Circle Murder Club. Since then, she'd been to Fairbanks. Salmon-by-the-Sea. Anchorage. Noorvik.

Every time she left, she knew she might be exposed.

Yet every time she left, she only wanted to get out more and more. Traveling caused something to grow inside her. A yearning to stop hiding. To start living freely again.

But she'd feared taking the risk.

And she'd been right to be afraid.

Now she would pay, probably with her life.

"Where is everyone else?" Simmy asked as they left the city behind. And by everyone else, she meant Duke McAllister, Andi Slade, and twins Mariella and Matthew Boucher.

"They were at the cabin when I left," Ranger said.

"I'm glad the guy was apprehended." The murder club had been working on their podcast and investigating the Lights Out Killer. Thankfully, the man had been caught and was now behind bars. People in Anchorage should be able to sleep better at night now.

"We all are."

Simmy glanced at Ranger again, her heart lurching into her throat. There was so much more at stake right now than her. More than her problems.

Ranger . . . he might not talk about it, but he was going through something also. He had things he needed to attend to. Things other than Simmy.

"I feel terrible." Her voice came out low, just above a

whisper. "I know you got that picture of your daughter and . . ."

He never talked about his daughter. But someone had decided to taunt each member of the murder club. Ranger had received a picture of his daughter on his phone, his daughter whom he believed had died in a drowning accident two years ago. In the photo, she looked older, which seemed to prove that time had passed and she was indeed still alive.

Ranger felt confident the photo was real and not AI generated.

Simmy couldn't imagine the shock Ranger must have felt at seeing the photo.

"Take me with you." The words slipped out before she lost her courage.

Ranger did a double take. "What?"

"You need to find your daughter. Take me with you. Let me help."

His jaw visibly hardened. "It's going to be dangerous."

"I'm already in danger."

He stole another glance at her. "You want me to put you in more danger?"

"Please, let me help you." Simmy's voice wavered with familiar desperation. "I want to do this. You've done so much for me. Now it's my turn."

Then she waited for his response.

———

RANGER CONTEMPLATED WHAT TO DO.

He didn't want to let Simmy out of his sight.

Yet he needed to search for his daughter.

His daughter whom he thought was dead.

Now that Ranger knew Anastasia was alive, he didn't want to waste any time finding her. Seeing with his own eyes that she was okay. Learning the truth about what had really happened.

But he knew what kind of guys he'd be running up against: dangerous men with no respect for human life.

Did he really want to put Simmy in that situation?

Absolutely not.

The decision jostled in his mind like a boat in a storm. Finally, unease anchored inside him.

As he headed down the road, Simmy remained quiet. Not pushing. Not begging.

She simply waited in that way she always did.

The woman was one of the most selfless people he'd ever met. Always taking care of others. Putting her friends' needs before her own.

That was what she did now also.

Which was part of what he loved about her.

But he also knew some people would take advantage of her kindness.

Ranger wouldn't do that. Ever.

After several minutes of silence, Simmy squeezed his forearm. A sizzle of electricity raced through his blood at her touch, and his throat went dry.

"It's going to be okay," she murmured.

It seemed like Simmy could read his thoughts. Like she knew how he struggled with what to do. Like she wanted to ease some of his burdens.

"I want to do this with you," she continued.

Ranger's throat tightened.

Whatever he did, there was no winning. Because he needed to find his daughter. He also needed to protect Simmy.

Doing both simultaneously seemed impossible.

three

I WAITED AT THE AIRPORT. As soon as I knew where Simmy was, I would approach her.

I couldn't wait to see her reaction.

I knew that, by now, she'd be running.

However, in Alaska, there weren't very many options for escape. She couldn't drive out of the state. Taking a boat would be complicated.

Flying made the most sense.

However, I didn't know if she would be in Anchorage or in Fairbanks. Numerous small airports were also scattered around Alaska.

Locating her in the largest US state wouldn't be easy.

But I had a plan.

I would find her if it was the last thing I did.

It had been my life's mission for the past ten years.

When I'd seen that article with her familiar face and

made-up name, I knew exactly what I needed to do. I'd dropped everything and packed my bags.

Finding her was all I had thought about for so long.

How dare she leave me?

Heat filled my veins at the thought of it.

She belonged to me—and to me alone!

My phone rang.

It was the private security group I'd hired. They were monitoring the airports.

"She was here," Chubby said—a ridiculous name for such a thin guy, but he had a solid reputation for being ruthless.

My heart skipped a beat. "In Anchorage?"

"Yeah, just saw her at the airport."

"Are you certain it was her?"

"Positive. She just left with someone. A man. He was also in that article. One of those murder club members."

My heart pounded in my chest. "Where are they now? What flight did they get on?"

"She was at the counter about to buy a ticket. Then that guy showed up, and she must have changed her mind. They left the airport together."

"And you just let them walk away?" My blood turned to lava. "Follow them! I can't lose her. Not again."

"I'm already on it."

"I'll get a ticket there and catch up. Don't let Simmy and this man out of your sight."

"Got it."

This woman had already gotten away from me once. I wouldn't let it happen again.

four

SIMMY GLANCED out the window as Anchorage disappeared behind her and mountains loomed all around.

One of the many things she liked about Ranger was she didn't feel like she always needed to talk when they were together. Being quiet in each other's presence was comfortable, and she deeply appreciated that.

As did she appreciate the fact that he never pressed her for answers about her past.

But if Simmy were honest, she'd admit she was curious about his past.

Ranger had mentioned his daughter was ten. That he'd thought she'd died at eight.

Had he ever been married? If so, what had happened to his wife? Who was his daughter's mother?

He'd also once mentioned something about Russia. That *really* perplexed her.

What kind of connection did he have with Russia?

As far as she knew, he'd worked for the National Park Service for the past couple of years. He was a survivalist. He knew the woods. How to live off the land.

And he was rugged and muscular, the type who could take care of himself in any situation.

Basically, he was unlike anyone she'd ever met before.

As the miles blurred past, she glanced at him.

He stared into the rearview mirror.

Then his hands tightened on the steering wheel.

Tension knotted her shoulders.

Something was wrong.

She craned her neck to look out the back window.

Several cars traveled behind them on the highway. Nothing unusual. As they got farther from Anchorage, traffic would ease.

But Ranger was anxious about something. Did he see something she didn't?

"Ranger?" She studied his face, searching for the truth. "What's wrong?"

He glanced in the mirror again before pressing his lips together.

Something was definitely wrong. Simmy waited for Ranger to share exactly what it was he saw that she didn't.

RANGER THOUGHT he'd seen a green Jeep following them.

He didn't want to be paranoid, but he couldn't let down his guard either. Not when Simmy's life was on the line.

He hadn't responded yet because he didn't want to get Simmy worked up for no reason.

Finally, he licked his lips. "The same vehicle has been behind us for the past several miles. I'm keeping an eye on it. The driver could simply be someone headed in the same direction. I want to be cautious, however."

Simmy let out a shaky breath and nodded quickly.

She turned back to the front, her entire body appearing more tense now than it had earlier.

That wasn't what he wanted.

He had failed Anastasia. He didn't want to fail Simmy also.

At the thought of Anastasia, his mind drifted.

He'd missed her every day for the past two years. He'd beat himself up. Thought about what he should have done differently in order to keep her alive.

She'd been the light of his life. His reason for getting out of bed every day. His hope for the future.

His beloved and only daughter.

And now . . . maybe she was still alive.

Maybe all his grief had been for nothing.

He cautioned himself against the hope.

He wasn't sure if he could find her.

But he would look for her, not stopping until he had answers.

He glanced in the rearview mirror again.

The car behind him slowed. He watched as the driver turned off the highway and onto a smaller road.

He released the breath he'd been holding.

Good. That was nothing.

But he knew better than to think he and Simmy were out of danger yet.

He needed to get her somewhere safe.

The only place he knew to go was back to where he'd last seen Anastasia.

It was on several acres homesteaders had owned more than fifty years ago. When Wrangell-St. Elias National Park was formed, this property was grandfathered in. The owners had sold it to Ranger.

Life had been good back then, back when those mountains had been his view every morning.

Then, with one phone call, everything changed.

Ranger's heart pounded harder at the thought.

He saw the sign for Glennallen. He'd been down this road enough to know the lodging options. They'd need to stop at a motel for the night. The second part of their journey was too treacherous to take at this time of day. He could do it but only if necessary.

They'd continue the rest of their trip tomorrow.

He'd need the time to prepare himself to return to the place he'd last seen Anastasia.

five

AFTER TAKING A LONG, hot shower at the motel, Simmy slipped from the bathroom to let Ranger use it. Then she sat on the edge of the bed to towel dry her hair and take a few deep breaths.

The two-story roadside motel was practically in the middle of nowhere. But at least there was a restaurant beside it, the outdated room was clean, and the back balcony had a glorious view of the mountains.

She'd stayed in worse places before.

Simmy knew that sleeping in the same room as Ranger was unconventional. But circumstances had dictated the choice. They had limited money right now, plus there were safety concerns.

The room had two beds, and she trusted Ranger. He'd never given her a reason not to. In fact, he'd given her every reason to believe he was the perfect gentleman.

But she'd fallen for that before. She constantly

reminded herself to be careful, to keep her guard up, and to not be too trusting. The other part of her thought—no, *knew*—Ranger was different.

What had she pulled him into? She'd tried to leave the state. To not involve her friends. She certainly didn't want to entangle anyone else in her mess.

Knave was one of the vilest men she'd ever met.

Her throat tightened at the thought of him, and Simmy reminded herself to breathe.

The water turned off in the bathroom, and she snapped back to the present.

She and Ranger would need to find some dinner. Although usually prepared, she hadn't brought any food with her.

That was what she did. She took care of people. Made sure they were comfortable and that their bellies were full. It was part of the reason her job at the Almost Halfway Trading Post had been perfect for her. Hospitality was her thing.

Several minutes later, the door to the bathroom opened.

Simmy sucked in a breath when she saw the stranger who emerged.

No, not the stranger.

It was Ranger. But he looked . . . incredibly different.

A face that had once been obscured by hair was now visible—and glorious. Ranger had shaved his thick beard and mustache. Trimmed the edges of his wavy dark hair and pulled the locks back in a ponytail.

He looked like an entirely different person. His face . . . it had all the right lines and angles. His green eyes were suddenly visible and clear.

And striking.

Everything about him was striking.

Ranger seemed to read her thoughts and shrugged, almost self-consciously—something he never seemed to be. "If I find Anastasia, I want her to recognize me."

Simmy nodded, still at a loss for words.

She'd always thought Ranger was handsome in a rugged way.

But right now . . . he could have stepped off the screen of her favorite action movie.

Jason Momoa?

Ranger could quite possibly pass for his body double. They both had the same tall frame, broad build, and dark hair. The same brooding eyes, edge of danger, and razor-sharp gaze.

Simmy cleared her throat and forced herself to look away before Ranger noticed her gawking.

Her thoughts quickly averted when Ranger paced toward the window.

He barely moved the curtain aside as he peered out.

Not surprising. Staying on the lookout was what he did, just like taking care of people was her gig.

As his back muscles stiffened, Simmy's easygoing thoughts disappeared faster than a rat in a drainpipe.

What did he see out there?

He turned to her, alarm flashing in his gaze. "We need to move. Now."

———

RANGER HAD CHOSEN this motel and requested this room on purpose.

It had a balcony in the back.

Just in case.

He'd been suspicious of that car behind them. Then he'd seen the vehicle turn off and had felt better.

But if the person following behind them had any type of skill, they would have known to be careful.

To pull off for a minute and then get back on the road.

That was the only way Ranger could explain the Jeep he saw outside. It was the same vehicle he'd seen following them earlier.

Two men climbed out—men he'd never seen before.

He glanced at Simmy and saw her face had gone pale.

By his estimation, they had about five minutes to get out before these guys found them.

"Get your bag," he barked.

"O . . . okay." With trembling hands, she stuffed her items back into the bag before pulling it over her shoulders.

Ranger grabbed his own bag and nodded toward the balcony at the back. "This way."

Her eyes widened. "But . . . we're, we're on the second floor."

He paused and locked gazes with her. "Do you trust me?"

Simmy didn't hesitate to nod. "I do."

"I've got this under control. Okay?"

She nodded again, but her pensive expression remained.

Ranger took her hand and led her toward the back. They stepped onto the balcony and closed the door behind them.

He turned toward her, not bothering to hide the urgency in his tone. "This is what's going to happen. I'm going to jump down first. When I tell you, I need you to jump also. I promise I'll catch you, okay?"

Simmy's breathing grew entirely too shallow as she looked at him. But she nodded.

Ranger hesitated before reaching for the railing.

Once he was on the ground level, he wouldn't be able to go back up to the room to prod her down to safety. Simmy had said she would jump after him, and he had no choice but to trust she'd do that.

He climbed to the other side of the railing, glanced at the grass stretching beyond the lower patio, and then lowered himself down, his hands gripping the metal barrier at the edge of the balcony.

The less distance to fall, the better.

He glanced below him at the grass. Swung his legs out. On the count of three, he propelled his body away from the building, let go of the railing, and his feet landed on the ground.

He straightened and looked up at Simmy.

Saw her staring down at him. Noted her wide eyes.

Then he prayed God would take away her fear.

To get through this alive, they would both need all the courage they could get.

six

SIMMY STARED at the ground below. Grasped the railing harder as she swayed.

She'd never been athletic, and all she could think about was breaking her leg. Then she and Ranger would *really* be in a heap of trouble. On the run while using crutches?

The thought only proved that things could get worse.

But she remembered Ranger looking into her eyes. Asking if she trusted him.

And she did.

"You can do this, darling," Ranger told her. "I promise you can."

Her entire body shook like porcelain in an earthquake.

But she followed Ranger's example. Climbed over the railing. Held on for a moment. Looked down below her to where Ranger stood waiting.

"I'm going to catch you," Ranger said.

Simmy swallowed hard, trying to work up the nerve to let go.

A noise pierced the air. The sound of wood splitting. It came from the motel room.

Had those men broken through the door?

Her heart rate ratcheted.

Sucking in a deep breath, she tossed her backpack to Ranger. Then she closed her eyes and jumped from the balcony.

As nothing but air surrounded her, her stomach dropped as if she were on a roller coaster. Wind whipped through her damp hair. Her limbs felt weightless.

She felt herself falling, falling.

Then she landed.

Not exactly like on a cloud.

Ranger's muscles were too hard for that.

But she was safe.

Unharmed.

And Ranger hadn't let her down.

Not that she'd thought he would.

He stared at her a moment as if assessing her mental state. "You good?"

She nodded. "Y . . . yes. I think so. But I heard the door to the room bang open."

Ranger set her down and grabbed her hand.

He scooped up their bags then they ran to the woods in the distance.

Simmy prayed her hesitation wouldn't end up costing them their lives.

———

RANGER PULLED Simmy into the woods and away from the motel as quickly as possible.

Once they were a good ten feet into the recesses of the forest, he tugged Simmy behind a tree. The branches and shadows should block them. But he'd need to keep his eyes open.

"Are you sure we shouldn't just keep running?" Simmy's voice trembled as she peered at the motel, her fingertips digging into the needles of the white spruce tree in front of her.

He placed a hand on her waist, trying to calm her. "Most likely, those men will think we're eating at the restaurant."

"How did they find us?"

"I have no idea."

He watched as the door to the balcony opened. As two men stepped out. Glanced around.

Ranger pulled Simmy closer, desperate not to be seen. Desperate to protect her. To calm her fears.

"Do you recognize them?" Ranger whispered.

Simmy stared at the men before shaking her head. "I don't. They could be hired, though."

Or these men could be linked to his past, Ranger mused. If someone had seen his photo in that article, they could have put the pieces together.

It was too early to say.

The men mumbled something to each other before

strutting back inside the motel room.

"What do you think they're doing now?" Simmy whispered.

"My best guess is that they'll hang out in the parking lot and wait for us to emerge. We can't chance going back."

"So are we staying in the woods all night?"

"No, I have another idea. But we'll need to wait a few minutes until it gets a little darker."

"Okay." The word sounded thin with fear.

Ranger wished he could take away Simmy's anxiety. But he couldn't. The situation was scary, to say the least.

But if he planned each of their steps just right, he and Simmy should walk away from this unscathed.

seven

THE ONLY THING that brought Simmy comfort was the feel of Ranger behind her.

She was keenly aware of his hand on her waist. She didn't mind his touch. In fact, it felt natural.

But seeing those men in their motel room only confirmed her worst fears.

There was nowhere she'd truly be safe.

How long could she keep running?

Ranger breathed softly behind her. She could smell the clean soap from his recent shower. Could feel his body heat. Was keenly aware of the weight and strength of his hand at her waist.

All the moisture left her mouth when she remembered him calling her darling. Remembered the tenderness of his tone.

Remembered how with that one word, she'd felt so loved. So connected.

Like she wasn't all alone in this world.

Thankfully, it was summer, so it wasn't bitterly cold like in the winter. Or in the middle of spring, for that matter. Alaska really only had a couple of months of truly warm weather.

Simmy glanced back at Ranger. Saw he still stared at the motel, not letting down his guard. He was clearly making sure these guys didn't come out back to check things out.

But his assumption was probably right. These guys most likely thought she and Ranger had gone next door to get something to eat.

At the thought, her stomach rumbled. What she wouldn't do for a nice juicy hamburger and some sweet potato fries. But food would have to wait.

For now, she needed to make the best of the situation.

She stared at the motel.

She would stay still and wait for Ranger to let her know that it was safe to move.

But another question lingered in her mind . . . she had to wonder if she would ever be safe.

Usually, she thought the answer was a resounding no.

———

RANGER KNEW WAITING WASN'T ALWAYS easy. But in this case, it was necessary. He couldn't take any chances, especially not with Simmy.

He remained frozen behind the tree, blocking Simmy from any danger.

Simmy . . .

His throat tightened.

She'd come to mean a lot to him. Ranger had vowed to remain single indefinitely after everything with Vivian. Yet he felt such protective instincts toward Simmy. All he wanted was to keep her safe.

Well . . . maybe that wasn't *all* he wanted. Sometimes, if he let himself, he imagined what it would be like to run his fingers down the side of her face. To tangle them with her hair. To feel her lips against his.

But as soon as the thoughts came, he quickly pushed them away.

Simmy was strong, but she was vulnerable. The last thing he'd ever allow himself to do was to hurt her or take advantage of a rough situation. He had a feeling that had happened one too many times already. He didn't want to add his name to the list of those who'd hurt her.

"Ranger?" Simmy turned.

When she did, he realized their faces were mere inches apart.

But he didn't move. Didn't want to risk it.

Her pupils widened when their eyes met. Then she licked her lips as if unable to find the right words. "I feel like you'd be better off without me. I don't want to pull you into my troubles."

Her selflessness was touching. Most people liked to

look out for themselves. But not Simmy. She thought of everyone else before herself.

Knowing Simmy, that was most likely how she'd gotten herself into the predicament she was in right now.

"I'm not leaving you," he told her.

"But—"

"There are no buts. I'm not leaving you."

She opened her mouth as if to argue but then shut it again. "Thank you."

As he stared down at her, his earlier thoughts slammed back into his mind again.

The thoughts about how soft her skin must feel. About what it would be like to lean closer. To get a whiff of her hair.

But he didn't. He couldn't afford the distraction.

Movement in the distance caught his eye.

Simmy also turned to look.

They watched two men stride across the space between the hotel and the restaurant. Based on their black clothing and militant steps, they were the same men who'd broken into their room.

They were looking for Ranger and Simmy.

If the men didn't see them inside . . . well, Ranger wasn't sure what that would mean.

As soon as the men disappeared inside the building, Ranger took Simmy's hand.

"We don't have much time," he told her. "We need to move. Now."

eight
Then

I COULD GET USED to this kind of life, Charlotte thought as she ran her finger down the marble countertop of the kitchen island. A life of luxury. A life where she didn't want for anything.

She was officially pregnant now. Almost three months along.

She poured herself some black coffee—she was allowed one cup a day—and sat at the breakfast nook to drink it. To marvel at how smoothly things were going. At how grateful she was she'd answered that online ad.

She'd been living with Mark and Meredith for four months.

The couple had been warm and inviting. Her meals each day were carefully laid out. Charlotte had a list on the refrigerator where she checked off how many glasses of water she drank every day. She also marked when she took her vitamins and how many steps she'd taken.

Moderate exercise was important for the pregnancy. That was what Meredith said.

This baby meant so much to them.

Charlotte had her moments of doubt about this whole thing. Wondered if surrogacy was mentally healthy. Wondered how hard it would be to give up the baby growing inside her in six months.

Doing this wasn't altruistic. It was practical.

She had no other options. She hadn't even talked to her mom in months.

Mom simply didn't care.

The thought made her throat burn.

If this child were hers, Charlotte would love the baby with everything she had inside her.

She'd never be like her mom.

But this child wasn't hers. She had to remind herself of that.

Despite the reminder, her thoughts shifted to the nursery Meredith was putting together.

The colors hadn't been picked out yet because Mark and Meredith didn't know if they would have a boy or a girl. But the furniture had been purchased and set up.

It was lovely with its oversized bassinet, a thick white changing table, and a white dresser already topped with stuffed animals and other trinkets.

She closed her eyes a moment and imagined herself taking care of the baby in there.

What if Mark and Meredith let her stay to be a nanny?

No . . . that would be weird. It would be crossing lines and cause confusion for all of them. She needed to get that idea out of her head.

But the thought of leaving this baby behind when she already felt so bonded with it . . . that was going to be heartbreaking.

"Charlotte . . . good to see you."

Her eyes flung open, and she jumped at the sound of the deep voice.

Mark strode into the kitchen, freshly shaven, hair still damp from a shower, and wearing a sharp-looking business suit.

Her cheeks warmed. "Good to see you too."

She'd never admit it to anyone, but she had a small crush on the man. Even though her mother hadn't taught her many virtues growing up, Charlotte knew that married men were off-limits.

However, she could feel attracted to Mark without acting on it. She could acknowledge he was good-looking while not letting her thoughts dwell on the subject. There were lines that couldn't—and wouldn't—be crossed.

She wouldn't be her mother—even if she could sense the strain in Mark and Meredith's marriage.

The longer Charlotte lived at the house, the more it became clear that Meredith didn't appreciate her husband. She made snide comments about him. When he touched her, she flinched.

Charlotte tried not to stare. But it was hard. How

could Meredith not appreciate a man like Mark? If Charlotte were in her shoes . . . she'd make sure Mark felt treasured every day.

Men like him . . . they existed only in her dreams. No handsome rich man would ever sweep Charlotte off her feet, even if some men did say she was pretty. She knew she wasn't ugly. But she was pretty in a very ordinary way, especially when compared to women like Meredith.

She shoved those thoughts aside and swallowed hard as she glanced up at Mark. "How are you doing today?"

"Just fine." He grabbed an oversized chocolate chip cookie from a glass-top pedestal, took a bite, and winked at her. "Don't tell Meredith. Breakfast of champions, right?"

She wouldn't dare tell Meredith.

Over the past few days, the woman had begun giving Charlotte side-glances and strange looks.

The only thing Charlotte could figure was that Meredith resented the fact Charlotte was carrying this baby when she couldn't.

Mark had told Charlotte once when Meredith wasn't around that his wife couldn't have a baby due to some medical issues that popped up several years ago.

That fact could very well be weighing on Meredith. Did it make her feel like less than a woman? It shouldn't.

Charlotte hoped those weren't Meredith's thoughts. She hoped that wasn't why Charlotte was getting weird vibes from her.

"Listen . . ." Mark stepped closer and lowered his voice. "I know you haven't been feeling well. I've heard you throwing up in the mornings. Are you okay? I didn't want to say anything around Meredith because she already worries so much. I don't want her to freak out."

Charlotte touched her throat, which still felt raw from vomiting. She hoped to hide that fact from the couple. She knew they'd be concerned.

But nothing got past Mark. It was probably why he was so successful in business, although Charlotte wasn't sure exactly what he did for a living. She'd asked once, and he'd said it was a boring office job that paid a lot of money. He didn't seem to want to offer more details.

"I'm fine," she insisted. "Just a little morning sickness. I don't want to worry you."

"I appreciate that, but you have to look out for your-self also." He quickly glanced over his shoulder as if about to divulge a secret. Then he stepped close enough that his breath brushed her ear. "I bought some cookie dough ice cream. I heard you say once that it was your favorite."

Charlotte practically salivated even hearing the words *cookie dough ice cream*.

She *did* love ice cream. But that wasn't on Meredith's healthy baby menu.

"When Meredith goes out today, you can have some if you want. I buried it deep in the garage freezer so she wouldn't find it. She never goes out there anyway."

Charlotte glanced at him sharply. Was he serious? Or

was this some kind of trap to see if she would follow their guidelines?

Based on the look in his gaze, the gesture was sincere. Mark didn't seem like a devious kind of guy.

After a moment, Charlotte nodded and then croaked out, "Thank you."

Mark straightened and gave her a smile that made her melt all the way down to her toes.

Mark grabbed his briefcase from the alcove near the back door. "I've got to go. Have a good day and remember what I said."

Charlotte nodded and watched him leave.

Six more months . . . six more months, and the baby should be here. Mark and Meredith would be parents. Their dreams would come true.

And Charlotte would get a nice payout. Enough that she could afford her own place. Put a down payment on a car.

She didn't know what she'd do after that. Another surrogacy? She was certain she couldn't jump into another pregnancy right away. Her body would need time to heal.

But she would figure things out.

She placed her hand on her belly.

A life grew inside her . . . but she couldn't get too attached. It would be too hard in the long run.

She glanced at the door leading to the garage. Thought about that ice cream in the freezer there.

Maybe she *would* try some later. Meredith usually

went to yoga class on Mondays and would probably be leaving in a couple of hours.

Some ice cream might be just the pick-me-up Charlotte needed to get past how sick and fatigued she'd been feeling lately.

She could get through this, she reminded herself.

In the end, it would all be worth it.

nine
Now

TEN MINUTES LATER, Simmy and Ranger headed down the road.

But not in Ranger's vehicle.

He'd managed to trade his SUV for an old white Nissan Frontier truck from the guy behind the front desk.

Simmy had watched in fascination as Ranger brokered the deal in record time. The clerk was probably in his early twenties. His old truck wasn't anything fancy, and Ranger's rental vehicle was newer and worth far more. So the guy had looked thrilled for the trade.

It was only once they were in the truck that Simmy asked Ranger why he'd done that.

"There's a good chance these guys put a tracker on the SUV," he told her. "It would have taken too long to search for it, so this was a safer bet."

"But that SUV was a rental," she reminded him.

"I'll figure all that out later."

She was amazed at just how clever he was. She would have never thought to switch vehicles.

"Get down in your seat," Ranger said as he put the truck into Reverse.

Simmy did as he instructed.

But as they pulled away, she peered up and glanced at the restaurant.

The men stepped out.

She sucked in a breath and ducked low again.

She hadn't recognized them. But they'd probably been hired by Knave. He liked to have other people do his dirty work. They'd probably been directed to grab her and bring her back to him.

That sounded exactly like Knave.

After several more minutes, she rose in her seat again and turned to Ranger. "Did we lose them?"

The look on his face didn't bring her the reassurance she'd been hoping for.

"Maybe." He glanced in the rearview mirror again. "But I wouldn't count on it."

"But they won't know what vehicle we're in."

"This road . . . it only leads one direction. Maybe they'll assume we backtracked. But most likely, they won't."

"So maybe we *should* have backtracked then."

His jaw hardened. "We can't. We need to keep moving forward. I have a plan."

Simmy studied his profile a minute—his handsome,

handsome profile. One that had been obscured behind facial hair and unruly dark locks since she'd known him.

Until less than an hour ago.

She still couldn't get over the change.

Hairy or not, he had always seemed so confident. Simmy had always been a sucker for self-assured men.

At one time, that had been her downfall. Even though she told herself Ranger was different, remaining cautious was still the best idea.

"What do you think those guys are doing right now?" Simmy's mind raced as she tried to put herself in their shoes.

Would they wait? Or leave to find them? How long would it take for them to realize she and Ranger had gotten another mode of transportation?

Ranger offered a stiff shrug. "Hard to say. Since we weren't at the restaurant, they probably went back to the room only to find it still empty."

"Maybe they'll assume someone picked us up."

"I suppose that's a possibility," Ranger said. "But we can't count on anything. We need to stay sharp."

Sharp.

If Simmy had been sharp, she wouldn't have made the decisions she'd made all those years ago. Decisions that had drastically altered her life and ultimately led her to this moment.

That was a fact she'd never forget.

———

IT HAD BEEN a long time since Ranger had seen this part of the state.

He'd tried to forget. But it was nearly impossible to leave the past behind—especially the most painful parts. Grief always showed up at the worst times, much like an uninvited guest outstaying his welcome.

Yet Ranger couldn't stop thinking about that picture he'd seen of Anastasia.

The innocence in his little girl's eyes.

He remembered the sweet sound of her laughter. The clean scent of her hair. The way she always asked him to twirl her around in circles.

Anastasia had given him a reason to live.

Then she'd died. Ranger had buried his little girl. His grief had almost done him in.

That was why the picture made no sense.

But it gave him hope.

His throat swelled with emotion.

If his daughter was alive, he would find her.

Did Vivian have something to do with this?

Her image flashed through his mind, followed by a rush of anger.

Would his ex really have faked Anastasia's death just to steal her from him?

Ranger didn't want the answer to be yes. But that was the only thing that made sense.

Vivian had been beautiful. Stunning.

Their romance had been exhilarating. Dangerous—and a whirlwind.

And a mistake.

Except for Anastasia. His daughter hadn't been a mistake. She'd been a beautiful blessing that came out of an ugly, regretful time.

As Ranger began to recognize landmarks, he glanced in the rearview mirror again.

The road still appeared to be clear.

He hadn't expected those men to be so persistent. Rather, he'd expected a jealous, scorned lover—not a jealous, scorned lover who hired professionals to hunt them to the death.

What exactly had happened in Simmy's past? There was more to it than he'd assumed.

He was going to have to unravel some of these secrets . . . soon.

For now, he needed to get Simmy far away.

ten

"WE LOST THEM."

"What do you mean you lost them?" I bit out the words as I strode through the airport. One more connection, and I'd be in Alaska.

Next time, I'd take a private jet. These commercial flights were ridiculous.

The lines. The delays. The rules.

The smelly people with no sense of personal space. I was ready to slap the man beside me on the flight here. With his large size, he encroached on my seat. He'd wanted to talk, despite the fact I wore headphones. He hadn't taken the hint.

"We don't know how, but they somehow managed to give us the slip," Chubby said.

My jaw tightened as more irritation stretched through my muscles. "Unacceptable!"

"I know." Chubby barked out every word, sounding more like a seal on the waterfront than a highly trained soldier. "But there's good news. This road only leads to one place."

I grunted. I supposed that *was* good news, but I didn't want to tell that to these two goons I'd hired.

I'd given them a lot of money for a simple job, and they'd failed.

"You need to find them and grab the woman," I growled, keeping my voice low so I wouldn't draw attention from any nosy travelers around me. "I want her—alive. I don't care about the man."

"Understood," Chubby said.

"I'm on my way, but still several hours away. I'll be in touch."

I ended the call.

I didn't deserve any of this. I'd taken care of Simmy when no one else had.

And what did I get from her in return?

Betrayal.

I should have known she wouldn't be loyal to the family.

She'd so easily replaced us.

I thought of the man she was with and clenched my hands into fists.

I needed to eliminate him.

I had too much invested in her.

And she knew too much. I wouldn't let her ruin me.

I *would* find her.
I'd kill the man she was with.
Then I'd bring her back home and keep her there.
She was mine.
And I couldn't wait to remind her of that fact.

eleven

FINALLY, Ranger and Simmy reached McCarthy, a town in the middle of the Wrangell-St. Elias National Park and Preserve.

There was no place like it. The paved highway had ended miles ago, and they'd had to travel on a gravel road through the winding mountains.

McCarthy itself was an old gold-mining town, and the neighboring town of Kennecott still had the old buildings from that time period preserved as a national landmark. Once the mines had closed in 1938, the old frontier town had become a skeleton of what it had once been. Only tourism had revived it—though revived seemed like a strong word.

At one time, Ranger had thought this area was the most isolated place ever. Then he'd moved to the Arctic Circle. He'd discovered that Alaska was the perfect place to hide.

Unfortunately, others thought the same. Others with more nefarious backgrounds. Others who didn't want to be found because of the terrible things they'd done.

People like Vivian.

He shoved the thought of her aside.

His friend Apollo Irwin lived nearby. Ranger hadn't seen the man in forever. But he knew Apollo always had his back. They'd been on so many treacherous missions together, missions that had bonded them for life. In his former line of work, it was detrimental to trust anyone except your team.

Sometimes, not even your team.

But Apollo was different. The two were like brothers.

Ranger put the Frontier in Park and glanced at Simmy.

She'd conked out an hour ago, and Ranger hadn't bothered to wake her. She needed her rest.

As her head leaned against the window, she looked like an angel—so innocent and full of love.

But he had to wake her up now that they'd arrived.

He gently touched her shoulder. "Simmy . . ."

She didn't budge.

He nudged her a little harder and said a little louder, "Simmy."

This time, her eyes fluttered open. She glanced around, blinked in surprise, and then turned to him, panic racing through her gaze. "Where are we? Are we . . . safe?"

"We're at a friend's house. We weren't followed."

Her shoulders relaxed, and she ran a hand over her face. "Good."

"Grab your bag, and let's get inside."

She followed him from the truck toward a small house with red wooden siding and a tin roof. Despite the fact it was summer, smoke rose from the chimney. A small porch displayed two wooden chairs, moose antlers, and an old gold pan that had been nailed to the wall.

Before they reached the front door, it flew open.

Apollo stood in the doorway, staring at them with a shotgun in his hands.

Simmy gasped, but Ranger placed his hand on her arm to let her know everything was okay.

Apollo was five-ten and thin. Beneath his unassuming frame were thick, strong muscles. He'd been trained as a fighter, and his instincts had been refined. He could slither in and out of a place without making a sound—a fact that had made him a very valuable asset to the team.

Though the man appeared ordinary, he was anything but.

Apollo lowered his gun, his shoulders relaxing. "Well, look what the cat dragged in."

"A rat, and I'm looking at the filthy beast right now."

The two of them chuckled then hugged, patting each other's back with a little too much force.

Apollo had been a good friend through the years. Had saved Ranger's life more than once. Ranger had saved his life on multiple occasions also.

That was the way they'd operated back when they

worked together.

They'd had to depend on each other for survival.

Apollo's gaze fell on Simmy, and he offered an approving nod. "Who's this?"

"This is my friend, Simmy. Simmy, Apollo."

Despite the dire circumstances, she managed to offer that winning grin of hers and extended her hand. "Nice to meet you."

"You finally wised up and found someone who makes you look good." Apollo gave Ranger a pointed look.

"It's true, but we're just friends. You know what people say about assumptions."

Apollo let out a skeptical, "Uh huh. Need I remind you that I'm a master at reading people?"

Ranger couldn't deny his words, but he didn't want to continue this conversation.

Instead, he asked, "You going to keep us out here all night?"

It was cold out, and Simmy was shivering. Plus, they were exposed. Though Ranger knew they hadn't been followed, he needed to operate as if they had.

"Of course not." Apollo stepped back. "Come in, come in."

Ranger and Simmy stepped inside his cabin, and warmth enveloped them. Even though it was July, at night the temperatures dropped into the forties in the heart of the mountains.

Ranger saw Simmy shiver again, although she hadn't complained.

She never did. She was always too busy looking out for other people. That was her greatest strength and her greatest weakness.

Apollo led them to a rough-hewn table in the corner.

A savory, smoky aroma filled the air, and the crackling fireplace lent a cozy feeling to the home. For a moment, Ranger felt safe. But he knew better than to believe that.

"You two have a seat." Apollo nodded at the table. "I made some iced tea. My mom was Southern, so it's sweet. Or I have coffee and water."

"Tea sounds perfect." Simmy offered a polite smile.

"For me too."

Apollo poured drinks and set them on the table in front of them. Then he walked into his small kitchen and lifted the lid from an oversized cast-iron pot. "Turns out you two arrived just in time to eat. Hungry?"

"I'd hate to impose," Simmy murmured.

"There's no such thing."

Ranger didn't know about Simmy, but he was starving.

Plus, they'd need to eat to keep up their energy.

Their journey had just started . . . and it wasn't going to get any easier from here.

———

SIMMY TOOK a sip of the salmon chowder and let the warm, savory liquid fill her stomach.

The soup was delicious and fresh with its potatoes,

herbs, and cream.

"Just caught those fish this morning." Apollo nodded at her bowl and pieces of pink salmon mixed among the creamy broth.

"I'm impressed." Simmy dipped her spoon into the soup again. "I'd love the recipe."

"Don't be impressed. I'm a one-trick pony. Really, all I cook is soup." He turned back to the stove and pulled something from the oven. "I suppose that's not the entire truth. There are actually two things I'm good at: soup and bread. Anybody want a slice?"

Ranger leaned closer. "You're definitely going to want to try his bread. It's delicious."

"Then I'm in," Simmy said.

Her mind had been racing ever since she stepped foot inside this place.

For starters, she wasn't sure she'd ever seen Ranger look so comfortable. The thought sounded terrible, and she didn't dare to voice it aloud. But she didn't see Ranger as the type who had friends.

Sure, she considered herself his friend. And the members of the murder club were his friends. But that was all in a very professional manner of speaking.

These two clearly had a history. However, Apollo didn't share the same rugged toughness as Ranger. So how did they know each other?

Later, maybe she'd ask and see if she could find some answers.

But for now, she would eat.

twelve

AFTER THEY FINISHED EATING, Ranger saw Simmy yawn.

Apparently, Apollo did also because he showed her to a spare bedroom, where she could turn in for the night.

Before Simmy disappeared inside, she called to Ranger. "Can we talk a minute?"

"Of course." He followed her inside the small room, one barely big enough for a twin-sized bed and dresser and closed the door.

His throat went dry as he turned and realized how close they were standing. Close enough for him to see the flecks in her eyes. To smell her flowery shampoo. To see the stray hairs popping from her ponytail and framing her face.

He had the sudden desire to smooth her hair back from her face. To lean in and immerse himself in her scent.

He quickly focused his thoughts and asked, "Everything okay?"

"How long are we staying here?" Simmy stared up at him.

"Maybe a night. Two, tops. We can't stay anywhere too long."

Her face paled. Ranger's words clearly hadn't lost their meaning on her.

"You think these guys are still tracking us?" Her gaze implored him. "I want the truth. Don't sugarcoat things for me."

He let out a quick breath before nodding and honoring her request. "Unfortunately, I think they might be. I'm sorry."

She continued to stare up at him with those big eyes of hers. She clearly still had some questions. "How about your daughter?"

"What about her? I'm going to keep looking for her."

"Good." She nodded again as if satisfied with his answer. "I guess we'll just talk more in the morning? Figure out more?"

Ranger nodded. But another question was on the tip of his tongue. "Is there anything I should know about the people following you?"

Her face paled again, and her expression stilled. "The man who hired them is sadistic, I guess you'd say. Ever since . . . well, ever since I made him mad, he's been obsessed with finding me so he can make me pay. He'll kill anyone who gets in the way."

Ranger's throat squeezed with anger at her words. More than anything, he wanted to protect her. She didn't deserve to be hunted. Didn't deserve to be running scared. To be living in fear.

If he had anything to do with it, that would end soon.

He lowered his voice. "I'm sorry, Simmy. Not every man is like that."

"I know." She licked her lips as if she wanted to ask more questions. To say more. But she didn't. "Good night, then."

"Good night." He stepped back.

Simmy slowly closed the door and disappeared from his sight.

Ranger felt as if she'd taken a piece of his heart with her.

But this was no time to think on those things. Instead, he joined Apollo in the living room. His friend sat in front of the fire waiting for him.

"I thought you'd disappeared off the face of the earth." Apollo took a sip of his coffee before glancing at Ranger.

"I tried." Ranger sat in the seat across from him. "It didn't work."

Apollo let out a deep chuckle. "I know you're not just here so I can meet your friend who's not your girlfriend. So what's going on?"

Ranger swallowed hard, wondering exactly how much he should share. "Two things brought me here. The first is the fact that trouble seems to be following Simmy, and I need to keep her safe."

"It seems like anywhere other than being with you would be safe." Apollo tossed him a pointed look.

Ranger let out a short chuckle. "You're probably right. But she has no one else."

"I presume there's quite a story behind that beautiful face of hers?" Apollo raised his eyebrows.

"More than I even know. Second reason I'm here . . ." Ranger found his phone, pulled up the photo he'd gotten, and showed it to Apollo.

His friend's eyes widened when he looked at it. "Is that . . . ?"

Ranger nodded somberly. "Anastasia."

"But . . ." He shook his head as if he couldn't find the words to say.

"John and Shannon told me she was dead. But she's clearly older in the photo."

Apollo continued to stare at the picture and ran a hand over his face. "I can't believe what I'm seeing. I . . . I don't know what to say."

"So you don't know anything about this?"

Apollo shook his head. "No, nothing at all."

"You haven't seen John or Shannon lately?"

He shook his head again. "You know they only leave their homestead if they have to. No news is usually good news. Is that where you're headed next?"

Ranger nodded. "I have to get some answers."

"I can't blame you for that." Apollo handed the phone

back to Ranger. "What can I do for you in the meantime?"

"I'm hoping you might let me borrow some equipment. I would have brought my own, but this was all last minute. Simmy and I have to get to their house. We'll need some supplies for the trip."

One never traveled in Alaska without being well-prepared. Nature was a beautiful but dangerous thing.

"Whatever you need, you've got it," Apollo said. "I have a side-by-side you can use as well as camping gear. In fact, the side-by-side is already loaded with supplies because I was going to go hunting tomorrow."

Ranger had known Apollo would come through for him. "You're a good friend, Apollo. Thank you. I'll pay you back somehow."

"Don't worry about it. I owe you from that time you saved me in Croatia."

"When you were dangling from the bridge and four gunmen bum-rushed you?"

Apollo chuckled. "That's the one."

"I thought for a minute about letting you fend for yourself." Ranger didn't hide the teasing from his voice.

"Everyone you've ever worked with knows that's not true. No man left behind. You were the epitome of that."

"Thanks, man." Ranger nodded and prepared to get some rest. Tomorrow morning, he would take Simmy with him to John and Shannon's place.

He prayed God would grant them safety in their

travels . . . because they were going to need all the help they could get.

———

SIMMY PACED THE BEDROOM. She knew she should lie down. Try to get some sleep.

She'd been so exhausted earlier. But now that she was alone in this dark room, her mind raced.

She'd always been aware that there was a lot she didn't know about Ranger. He hardly ever opened up. The man remained a mystery to her.

But who was this Apollo guy? How did Ranger know him? And what did all this have to do with Ranger's daughter?

At one point, she'd paused near the door. Pressed her ear to it hoping to hear some conversation and get some answers.

Then she'd felt guilty, so she pulled back and continued pacing.

She wished she hadn't slept so much on the way here. She wasn't even sure exactly where she was except the middle of nowhere.

How did Ranger even know about this place?

She paced to the window and gently nudged the curtain aside. It was too dark outside to see much, other than the shadows of the forest. She knew looming, glacier-capped mountains rose all around. They would be a sight to see—if she wasn't running for her life right now.

She squinted as something caught her eye.

Was that a . . . ?

She shook her head. No, she was probably seeing things. They were in the middle of nowhere. Why would she see a light bobbing in the distance?

Tension spread across her chest. She knew the answer to that question. She was just in denial.

She continued to stare. She needed confirmation before she cried wolf.

Then she saw it again.

It was *definitely* a light bobbing in otherwise complete darkness.

She dropped the curtain as her heart began to race.

She had to tell Ranger.

Now.

thirteen

RANGER STARTED to take a sip of his coffee when he heard Simmy's door open.

Then frantic footsteps rushed toward him.

He rose to his feet just as Simmy darted into the room.

"I saw someone outside." She sounded breathless, and her gaze filled with panic. "With a flashlight. Coming this way."

Ranger exchanged a look with Apollo.

In a split second, Apollo reached into his gun cabinet and pulled out a high ammunition rifle. "The side-by-side is out back, and the key is already in it. I can hold these guys off while you two get away."

"I can't leave you to handle this alone." Ranger paused, ready to argue.

"Sure, you can. You know me. I'll be fine. How many of them do you think there are?" He cocked his gun and glanced at Simmy.

"There were two men after us earlier." Simmy's voice trembled.

"Only two?" Apollo muttered, taking a step toward the window. "This will be easier than I thought. Hardly a challenge at all."

"Grab your bag," Ranger told Simmy. "We have to go. There's no time to waste."

She stared at him for only a second. But it was a second that seemed to convey eternity. Then she turned on her heel and darted back to the room.

As she did, Ranger pulled on his own backpack. Reached for the gun he kept at his waist.

Then he hurried to the window. Peered outside. Apollo peered out the other side.

"I see two," Apollo confirmed. "You?"

"Two."

The flashlights went dark as the men got closer.

Apollo got down on his knee, cracked the window, and aimed his rifle.

Before he could pull the trigger, glass shattered at the front of the house.

The men were firing on them.

Apollo fired back.

A cry of distress sounded outside.

One of the men had been hit.

Apollo could take out the other guy too. Ranger knew he could.

Simmy returned to the room, her bag over her shoulders and that same anxious expression on her face.

"The other gunman is still around front," Apollo called over his shoulder. "If you go now, you can escape out the back."

"Thank you for everything," Ranger said.

"You're cooking me a steak next time I see you."

"It's a deal." Meals were always proper payment for saving each other's life. It was the way Ranger and Apollo operated.

Ranger took Simmy's arm and pulled her to the back door.

———

SIMMY COULDN'T STOP TREMBLING. Could hardly catch her breath.

She had to get a grip, or she would pass out. That definitely wouldn't make this situation better.

Ranger reached the back door and motioned for her to stay back. Then, with gun in hand, he cracked the door open and peered out.

As he did, more gunfire filled the air.

Simmy covered her head as she ducked.

"It's time to go." Ranger took her hand. "Run!"

Everything blurred around her as Ranger pulled her through the darkness. She was grateful he held her hand. Otherwise, she wouldn't have kept up.

Where were they even going?

He hurried behind a stack of firewood.

A side-by-side was parked there.

"Get in," he told her quietly.

Simmy's entire body still shook as she climbed into the passenger seat. She tossed her bag in the back before whipping on her seatbelt.

Ranger started the engine.

As soon as the vehicle roared to life, Ranger zoomed away. But he didn't head toward the road.

He headed toward the dark, unknown wilderness.

A wilderness full of steep mountains, unexpected cliffs, and wildlife that could kill them in an instant.

In other words, they were leaving one danger behind . . . and diving headfirst into another.

fourteen

MORE GUNFIRE SOUNDED BEHIND THEM.

Ranger prayed Apollo was okay. It sounded like one of the men pursuing them had been hit. Apollo distracted the other one at the moment.

That should give Ranger and Simmy plenty of time to get away.

Plus, these guys had most likely driven here in that Jeep. The path Ranger planned to take right now wasn't one an ordinary vehicle could travel. The trail was all-terrain, requiring both an off-road vehicle and skills.

However, Ranger didn't like traveling this way at night. It had been a long time since he'd come out here, and things in the wilderness changed quickly. All it took was an overabundance of rain or snow melt, and his normal route could be compromised by mudslides, rock-slides, downed trees, a rerouted river.

He prayed that wasn't the case right now.

He continued to charge into the darkness. The path led up a sharp incline before reaching a peak.

He paused, his headlights illuminating the area in front of them.

Only, there was nothing there.

Almost as if they were on a cliff.

Then the vehicle teetered.

"Ranger!" Simmy gasped.

"I've got this." Ranger pressed the accelerator.

The side-by-side tilted downward.

Not on a cliff, but on a slope. The angle, if he had to guess, was probably a forty-percent grade. A river waited at the bottom.

But he'd expected all of this. If only he'd had time to explain everything to Simmy.

Just then, a motor sounded behind them.

These guys were coming after them in their vehicle, weren't they?

That would prove to be a mistake on their part.

But Ranger couldn't let down his guard just yet.

Simmy let out another gasp as they rumbled down the mountain toward the water.

The sight was probably terrifying, especially for someone who had no idea what was going on.

But there was no other way out of this situation right now.

Ranger gripped the wheel more tightly and prayed for the best.

———

SIMMY'S HEAD spun as she stared straight ahead.

At any minute, she felt like she and Ranger might topple over and roll down the mountain. Or that once they reached the river, the rapids would sweep them away. Or that a bear might appear in their path.

She couldn't think of one good outcome to this scenario.

The rumble of an engine sounded behind them. She knew better than to turn and look.

But how could she not?

The green Jeep from earlier appeared, the one from the motel.

The vehicle barely fit on the path. But it was there. Behind them. Seemingly gaining speed.

Then a bullet flew.

"Stay down!" Ranger yelled.

Simmy ducked in her seat. But the small vehicle didn't offer much protection.

"It's going to get rough for a minute," Ranger said as he jerked the wheel.

Another bullet sliced the air and wood splintered nearby.

She swallowed back a cry. That was too close.

Suddenly, the side-by-side lurched forward as the front wheels snagged on something.

Were they about to topple headfirst?

Nearly as soon as the rumble started, the vehicle lurched forward again.

Then she heard a splash.

Cold water sprayed up.

They were in the river, she realized.

A shiver captured her.

Would this lead to their escape?

Or their death?

fifteen

THE RIVER WAS DEEPER than Ranger remembered.
Maybe from the recent rain.

He didn't know. But they should be able to power
through. They had at least a fifty-percent shot.

He didn't tell Simmy that.

As water splashed on them and the current tugged
them downstream, he yelled, "Hold on!"

Simmy grasped a handle above her and another
beside her.

The water jostled them, and the side-by-side lost traction a moment.

Floated a couple more feet downstream. Farther from
the trail.

"Ranger . . ." Simmy gasped.

Unfortunately, this was far from being over.

But they could make it. Ranger knew they could.

As their wheels skimmed rocks below, Ranger hit the accelerator.

The side-by-side charged forward.

They splashed through more water. Small rapids doused them. Rocks jostled them as the wheels slammed into stones in its path.

Finally, they reached land on the other side.

They were almost home free.

The tires slipped again on the damp terrain. Turned. Turned.

Tried to move forward.

But didn't.

Finally, they found traction again.

The vehicle spun out of the water.

A similar slope waited for them on the other side. If Ranger hesitated at all, they wouldn't get up the incline. They needed all the power they could get out of this side-by-side right now.

The only comfort Ranger found in the situation was knowing this road narrowed up ahead. Even if the guys behind them managed to make it this far, crossing the river would delay them. Then it would be nearly impossible for them to make it through the opening in their Jeep.

"Here we go," Ranger said. "Brace yourself!"

Then he gunned it.

They bounced as they began their ascent.

They jostled over rocks and crevices. Tree branches swished by them. Mud made them slip.

But they climbed higher and higher.

They were halfway up now.

Ranger wanted to know how close those guys were behind them. But he didn't dare take his eyes off what lay ahead.

Just as the path began to narrow, the side-by-side lost traction.

The tires spun.

Kicked up dirt and debris.

Spun some more.

Simmy swung her head over her shoulder and glanced behind them.

"Ranger, they made it through the river." Her voice trembled.

He and Simmy couldn't get stuck now.

They were so close to escape.

But as he hit the accelerator again, the wheels continued to spin.

———

SIMMY'S LUNGS tightened until she could hardly breathe.

What if she and Ranger continued to slip down the slope? What if these guys caught up with them?

She and Ranger were practically sitting ducks right now, at the total mercy of this side-by-side.

She pressed her eyes closed. *Lord . . . be with us.*

"Ranger!" She glanced behind her again and saw that the Jeep had started upward.

Ranger hit a few switches before muttering, "Hold on."

He didn't have to tell her twice.

As he gunned it, they suddenly gained traction again. They charged up the mountain.

That should make her feel better. And it did. But only for a moment.

Then her heart continued to pound out of control.

Would they get stuck again? Next time, it could be a death sentence.

Instead, the side-by-side kept going. And going. And going.

Finally, they cleared the incline.

Simmy released a breath.

She glanced behind her one more time.

The men coming after them . . . they were now stuck. Two spruce trees physically blocked them from getting any farther in their wide vehicle.

That may just be the answer to her and Ranger's prayers.

"Are we good?" Ranger's voice pitched higher to be heard over the engine.

"Looks that way . . . " Simmy told him. "For now, at least."

sixteen

RANGER DIDN'T SLOW DOWN.

He knew from taking this trail before that the terrain would be flatter for the next several miles—flatter for the Alaskan mountains, at least. But there shouldn't be any more forty-percent grades to conquer.

However, he feared these guys would come after them on foot. It would be challenging for them to catch up. But if they were persistent enough, they might.

He looked at the gas gauge, barely illuminated in the darkness.

He probably had ten more miles before he'd need gas. He hadn't had time to check the side-by-side out before leaving, but it wouldn't surprise him if Apollo had put an extra gas can back there.

He hoped that was the case.

Ranger and Simmy were still at least forty miles from

John and Shannon's, the place he needed to reach. The people who might have answers about Anastasia.

Getting to their place probably wouldn't happen tonight.

He glanced at Simmy and saw her staring straight ahead, her body bouncing over every rock and crevice. But she hadn't complained.

She seemed to be holding up okay, even though Ranger knew this was a lot on her. It would be a lot on anyone.

When he saw her shiver, he reached behind him. He'd seen an old green army blanket back there.

He grabbed it and handed it to her. "Use this."

In their haste to leave, Simmy was still wearing a T-shirt and jeans. But the temperature had dropped, and the air had a definite chill.

Simmy wrapped the blanket in front of her, then tugged at one end. "Would you like to share?"

That was Simmy. Always thinking of others.

"I'm fine," Ranger told her. "But thank you."

The vehicle was loud, and it was hard to talk over the roar of the engine.

That very sound would easily alert people to their presence. Ranger was all too aware of that fact. But this side-by-side was still their best option.

He kept charging into the wilderness, into the darkness, knowing full well the risks ahead of them.

Eight miles later, the engine waned. Sputtered.

They'd run out of gas.

Before the side-by-side fully died, Ranger coasted into the woods.

When the engine choked out, he turned to Simmy. "The next part of this trip is treacherous. I say we set up camp here for the night and get some rest."

Her eyes widened. "But those men . . ."

"It will take them a few hours to walk this far—if that's what they even decide to do. My guess is that they'll backtrack and find a different way to travel the trail. It will take too long on foot. I'd say we have four hours, at least. It's probably a good idea to get a little shut-eye in the meantime. These mountains . . . they're rugged and unpredictable. It would be safer if we took the rest of the journey when it's lighter outside."

Simmy stared at him a moment, questions dancing in her gaze. Then she nodded. "If you think that's what is best."

"I do." He took his seatbelt off and climbed out. "Apollo said he had some camping gear back here. We can set that up."

She climbed out and joined him at the back of the vehicle. "Do you think he's okay?"

"Apollo? He's fine." Apollo knew how to handle himself in situations like that. Ranger had seen him in action plenty of times.

"How can you be so sure?"

"Because Apollo is tough, and he knows what he's doing."

More questions flashed through her gaze, but she didn't ask them.

Soon, Ranger would tell her the truth.

But right now, they needed to get things set up so they could get some rest.

———

SIMMY LAY in front of the small fire Ranger had started. The flames sent out warmth, and she welcomed the comfort from the chilly air around her.

Even though she was on the ground in a sleeping bag with only her arm as a pillow, she still felt grateful. She had covers and a fire to keep her warm, she'd survived unimaginable circumstances, and Ranger was here with her.

Ranger said he would get some rest soon. But right now, he sat by the fire, scanning everything around them.

He was still being cautious, and Simmy appreciated that.

Earlier, he'd given her some beef jerky and a bottle of water. She'd eaten it quickly, not realizing how hungry she was. Even though she'd had that salmon chowder and homemade bread earlier, the adrenaline rush from being chased must have kicked her metabolism into overdrive.

As she lay there, she stared at Ranger. He scanned the landscape in the opposite direction, so she took advantage of the chance to observe him unaware.

She soaked in his strong profile. Noted that just a touch of his beard and mustache had already started to reappear. Studied his intense gaze as he remained on guard.

The man fascinated her.

He had fascinated her since the first day they'd met.

He used to come into the trading post weekly to pick up supplies.

From day one, he seemed protective of her.

When a customer had gotten rough with her when their toilets had broken at the trading post, Ranger had stepped in. Had put the man in his place. Made it clear the guy was never ever to put his hands on a woman again.

Another time, her boss had talked down to her, and Ranger had come to her defense. Then he'd had a private chat with the man outside.

After that, her boss no longer talked down to her.

Ranger was a man of few words. In truth, Simmy didn't even know him well. Yet she felt as if she did. She felt as if they'd had hours of conversation every day.

He was so different than her ex. Her ex had been a talker. Had shared everything.

Except it had been lies. She couldn't trust a word that came out of his mouth.

Ranger . . . if he couldn't tell the truth, then he didn't say anything.

Nature sounded around them. The small fire in front of them crackled. Leaves brushed against each other with the slight wind. A stream babbled.

Her ex had loved camping. Said he loved being in nature.

The fact had surprised her because he didn't seem exactly like the outdoorsy type.

She'd gone along with him a few times, just to appease him mostly.

Right now, part of her was terrified.

But the other part knew that everything would be okay . . . because Ranger would do everything in his power to keep her safe, just like always.

With that thought in mind, she closed her eyes to get some sleep.

Before she could, a stick cracked in the woods, and suddenly she was wide awake again.

Was it a bear? A moose?

Or was it one of the men following them?

seventeen
Then

TWO MORE MONTHS HAD PASSED, and Charlotte's belly was definitely growing. She'd had to buy new clothes. Meredith had taken her shopping and let Charlotte pick out whatever she wanted. In theory, at least.

Meredith had made faces every time Charlotte picked up clothing she didn't approve of.

To appease the woman, Charlotte had put those shirts, pants, and dresses back on the rack. Then she'd waited for a look of approval from Meredith before choosing anything else.

After Charlotte had picked out several outfits, she and Meredith had gotten smoothies—the kind without any added sugar.

They'd walked around the shopping plaza, not for fun but so Charlotte could get her daily exercise.

The two of them hadn't necessarily bonded. Meredith

still had an edge of iciness to her. Still held herself at a distance. But at least it was a start.

It was better than that time Meredith had caught her eating ice cream.

Charlotte blanched at the memory. The confrontation hadn't been pretty.

Meredith had screamed at her. Insisted she throw the ice cream into the trash. She'd even watched to make sure Charlotte did so.

Mark had never said anything about it. Did he not know? Not want to get involved?

Either way, Charlotte hadn't sold him out. Hadn't told Meredith that Mark had bought it for her and left it there.

But there had been some animosity coming off Meredith like steam ever since then. In her downtime, Meredith furiously wrote things in a journal as she scowled at Charlotte.

Five months down, and four more to go.

This morning, Charlotte was in the kitchen having her coffee. It was better if she drank it before Meredith awoke. If the woman ever caught her, Charlotte received enough dirty looks to warrant a shower to cleanse herself of the disgust cast upon her.

The good news was that Meredith liked to sleep late.

But there was another reason also that Charlotte liked to wake up with the sun.

Mark was also an early bird.

Though she was attracted to the man, he was off

limits. He was married, and Charlotte often reminded herself of that fact. But he was pleasant to chat with, and he made her feel good about herself.

She got lonely out here sometimes on this secluded country estate. It wasn't as if Charlotte had any friends in the area anyway. She'd thought about trying to make some. But she'd be leaving in a few months, so it seemed like a wasted effort.

Instead, she spent her hours here. She tried to stick to her eating and exercise routine. When she wasn't doing that, she read. Even though Charlotte knew that knowledge couldn't be transferred to the baby, Meredith thought it was important. Meredith also felt it was important to listen to classical music and get fresh air at least thirty minutes per day.

She had a lot of opinions.

Sometimes Charlotte wanted to rebel. Then she realized that this was her job.

It was more than that. This was basically her life. Once the baby came, all the headaches and micro-managing would be worth it. The paycheck she'd received would help her get a good start with her future.

"You're glowing this morning." Mark stared at her a moment before turning to grab his own cup of coffee.

Charlotte felt herself flush as she stood near the breakfast nook. "Am I? They say women get a glow when they're pregnant."

He grabbed his coffee and stepped closer as he continued to observe her.

She willed her cheeks not to heat. But she felt them doing so anyway.

"Yes, you definitely have a glow to you." He nodded slowly. "You're stunning, Charlotte."

At his words, something fluttered in her belly, and she sucked in a breath.

"What is it?" Mark's eyebrows drew together with concern.

She reached for her stomach, waited a moment, and then she felt it again.

A smile spread across her face. "The baby . . . he or she is kicking."

"What?" The word sounded breathless.

The next instant, Mark reached for her belly and placed his hand near hers. His fingers were warm as they pressed into her, and Charlotte was entirely too aware of how close he was standing.

Her heart stammered.

This was his baby. Of course, he wanted to feel his child kick.

Yet the touch felt intrusive. Off-limits. Like a boundary that shouldn't be crossed.

"There it is," he murmured. "I felt it!"

At the sight of his smile, Charlotte's misgivings faded. He looked so happy, like someone who'd just experienced his dreams coming true.

In a normal pregnancy situation, he would feel his child kick—only it would be in his wife's belly. Maybe Charlotte shouldn't feel so weird about this.

"That's amazing," he murmured. "Absolutely amazing."

As he smiled down at her, hand still on her abdomen, Charlotte felt as if she couldn't breathe.

He was so handsome. So polite. So smart.

So perfect.

The longer Charlotte lived in this house, the more she'd realized Meredith was all wrong for him. She didn't appreciate Mark. Didn't act loving in any way toward her husband. It was sad, really.

"What's going on here?"

A shrill voice cut through the air, and Charlotte jumped back.

Meredith stood in the doorway, arms crossed and a scowl on her face.

Charlotte's heart stammered as she realized how this could look like an intimate moment, even though it wasn't.

She wanted to stutter out a response, but she glanced at Mark first.

He didn't look nearly as bothered.

In fact, he looked surprisingly *unbothered*.

He turned and reached for her belly again. "Come here, Meredith. You've got to feel this."

"Feel what?"

"Come here."

Meredith looked around cautiously before creeping forward.

Then Mark took her hand and placed it on Charlotte's

belly. "Feel this."

Charlotte glanced at Meredith, watching her expression.

Tears rushed to the woman's eyes. But were they tears of joy?

Or sadness? Sadness for herself that she hadn't been able to carry this life?

Mark had told Charlotte how depressed Meredith had become once she'd learned she wouldn't be able to birth her own children. The topic seemed to come up at least once a week during his and Charlotte's talks over breakfast.

He was clearly worried about his wife and her mental state. They thought the baby would fix things.

Charlotte hoped they were right.

"I can't believe it." Meredith's gaze caught with her husband's. "That's our child."

Mark used the back of his hand to gently wipe away his wife's tears. "I know. Our dreams are going to come true."

Charlotte's throat tightened, though she wasn't sure why. This moment felt too intimate. She felt intrusive. Intruded on. She wasn't sure.

Her place in this arrangement was strange . . . she carried this couple's baby.

Maybe procreation wasn't supposed to be this way. Maybe adoption was a better option for couples like Mark and Meredith. She didn't know.

But the bond between the three of them . . . it felt unnatural.

This was what Charlotte had wanted. This was what *Mark and Meredith* wanted. And this was what Charlotte had signed up for.

Get yourself in check, Charlotte, she told herself. This is just part of the deal.

But in her gut, something felt off-balance.

At times, she'd thought it would be better if she didn't live here with Mark and Meredith. There were too many opportunities for boundaries to be crossed. Not physical boundaries, like right now. But Meredith could be controlling, and it was starting to affect Charlotte.

She'd never in her whole life had someone dictate to her what she could eat. What she could do. How she could spend her free time.

Maybe it was the pregnancy hormones kicking in and making her overly sensitive. Charlotte didn't really know.

The doctor came to the house once a week now. She thought that was more often than necessary, but Mark and Meredith had insisted.

Dr. Matthews was older, probably in his sixties, and quiet with a standoffish demeanor. The man was a little strange, to be truthful. But Mark and Meredith seemed to trust him. She assumed the quiet conversation Dr. Matthews had with the couple the last time he came was about the process after Charlotte gave birth.

Charlotte swallowed hard and leaned back as Mark and Meredith continued to put their hands on her belly.

When the baby stopped moving, the couple finally dropped their hands and stepped away.

Charlotte's shoulders softened and her lungs loosened.

She hadn't been cornered, but she felt like she had.

Mark turned to Meredith, a new light in his eyes. "Go get dressed. I'm going to be late for work today."

"Why would you be late for work today?" Meredith stared at him, a knot of confusion on her brow.

"Because I'm going to take you to breakfast to celebrate. The two of us haven't spent nearly enough time together lately. This is what we need to do."

Meredith's entire countenance lifted as if those were the words she'd been wanting to hear, the words that made everything better. "Okay. That sounds perfect."

Mark planted a slow kiss on his wife's lips.

Charlotte glanced away, feeling as if she shouldn't witness the intimate moment.

Then Meredith scrambled down the hall to get ready as her husband had requested.

When Meredith was out of earshot, Mark turned back to Charlotte. "I'm sorry I touched you without asking permission. In my excitement, I didn't think things through. It was insensitive."

"It's okay." His acknowledgement *did* make Charlotte feel better. She could understand how he might have gotten caught up in the moment.

Mark continued to peer at her. "If you feel the baby move again . . . will you let me know? Feeling that movement makes everything so much more real." His voice warmed with adoration for his child.

Her heart softened again, torn between setting boundaries or finding delight in Mark's happiness.

"Of course," she finally said. "You're always welcome to feel your child moving."

She hoped she didn't regret those words. But, on the other hand, she'd never want to deprive this man of his child. She could get over her squeamishness.

His eyes warmed. "Thanks, Charlotte. I knew from the moment I met you that you were the one meant to do this. I haven't had a moment of doubt since then. There's no one else I would want to carry my child."

He must mean to carry *his and Meredith's* child. It was a slip of the tongue.

Charlotte did that sometimes also. She said something without being as clear as she would have liked.

That was what Mark had done too. No big deal.

But something about his words made her wonder what it *would* be like to carry his child.

Not his child with Meredith. But his child with *her*.

Charlotte chided herself. These were *not* the thoughts she needed going through her head.

She wasn't that type of woman.

And she refused to ever be.

She needed to get herself in check ASAP.

eighteen
Now

RANGER HADN'T SLEPT. He knew he wouldn't.

Especially after Simmy had heard that stick break in the woods. Thankfully, it had just been a small critter, probably a marmot, that had run as soon as it had seen Ranger. Nothing to be worried about.

But that didn't mean there weren't dangers out there. There definitely were.

Though Ranger felt certain his theory was right and that those men would turn around to get a more appropriate vehicle to travel the area, he couldn't know for sure. He couldn't risk letting down his guard.

Besides, he liked the quiet and solitude out here.

He kept himself busy making sure the fire was stoked and there was enough wood to keep Simmy warm.

It felt intrusive for him to stare at her as she slept, yet Ranger couldn't help himself. Just as earlier in the SUV, she looked angelic while she rested. The person after them now—her ex, he assumed—clearly had more resources than Ranger had anticipated. These guys were hired professionals.

Just who was this man? Was he chasing Simmy right now simply because he was obsessed with her?

Either way, Simmy was clearly in danger. She'd said it was only a matter of time until her past caught up with her. She'd even said something once about living on borrowed time. Her words were proving to be true.

That only solidified Ranger's determination to keep Simmy safe. She deserved so much better than how she was living right now.

He waited until the sun rose at five before he began packing. He'd get everything ready before he woke Simmy. Thankfully, there was some extra gas in the back of the vehicle.

When he returned from the side-by-side, Simmy was sitting up. Her sleeping bag draped at her waist, and waves of hair fell in her face as she observed him.

He paused on the other side of the now cold firepit. "Good morning."

"Good morning." She smiled, but her eyes still looked narrow with sleep. "You're already packed?"

"We don't have much time."

"Of course." She unzipped the bag and stood. "Just give me a few minutes, and I'll be ready."

Ranger could admire a low-maintenance woman.

He gave her time to get ready before they walked back to the side-by-side.

"I filled the tank with the rest of the gas," he told her. "I think we can make it thirty more miles. We'll have to take the rest of the way by foot."

"Whatever we need to do."

Of course she wouldn't complain.

This woman deserved all the happiness in the world.

Ranger had to keep her alive long enough to make that happen.

———

JUST AS RANGER HAD PREDICTED, they made it another thirty miles before the side-by-side ran out of gas. Simmy was impressed at the man's abilities. He was clearly experienced at wilderness survival, a fact she'd known but hadn't really seen in action. Not to this extent, at least.

Leaving the side-by-side behind, Ranger and Simmy packed up all the essentials so they could continue on foot.

Ranger had loosened the straps on Simmy's backpack and slid the sleeping bag through the arm loops so she could carry that as well. But he carried most of the extra items himself and didn't ask her to help.

Then they began their trek through the woods. The trail was mostly switchbacks. Thankfully, the altitude was still low enough that trees rose up to offer some cover.

The good part about walking, she supposed, was that she and Ranger could talk, something they hadn't been able to do because of the noise in the side-by-side.

Ranger had said something about an earlier part of the trail being part of the wagon train road at one time. He'd also spouted some facts about this being the largest national park with thirteen million acres and more than a thousand glaciers.

He sounded truly in awe of the area.

"You seem to know exactly where you're going," Simmy murmured as they climbed the switchback.

Ranger continued forward, not even breaking a sweat. "I used to live out here."

Surprise spread through her at the revelation. "I had no idea."

"I don't talk much about my past. It's usually just better if I don't."

"I get that." Simmy looped her fingers through the straps of her backpack and tried to pace herself. Her lungs burned at both the incline and the altitude—and she knew they were only just beginning.

Still, she didn't want to let Ranger down. They needed to make good time.

"I love it out here," Ranger said. "It's isolated but serene."

"I take it you like isolation." He'd never told her that. Simmy simply knew.

"I do. But really, it's born out of necessity more than anything else." Ranger's jaw tightened, and he continued to look ahead.

More questions popped into Simmy's head. There was so much she didn't know about this man.

Maybe this trip would reveal more about him.

However, it was better if the two of them didn't get too close. She didn't want to pull Ranger into her mess . . . but it appeared she was already too late.

That was a fact she wasn't okay with.

If anything happened to Ranger because of her troubled past . . . she'd never forgive herself.

nineteen

I'D HIRED IMBECILES.

That was the only way to describe my situation right now. I didn't care what I'd heard about these people being the best of the best.

They weren't.

If they were the best, they wouldn't have lost Simmy.

They wouldn't have *shot* at her.

Idiots.

I'd told them I wanted her alive. My instructions really weren't that complicated.

Hopefully, I'd gotten through to them during our last conversation.

I climbed off the plane. My original flight had been canceled. That had put me behind. My new flight had meant I'd had to travel overnight.

Unacceptable. But at least I was here now.

In Alaska.

I'd never been here before. Never had a reason to come here.

I wished I wasn't here now, but necessity demanded it.

"Excuse me, sir!" someone called behind me.

I paused and turned toward the feminine voice. When I saw a pretty blonde hurrying toward me, I plastered on a smile. "Can I help you?"

"You dropped this." She handed me my cell phone—one with a clip on the back with my credit card and driver's license.

It must have slipped out of my pocket after I ended the call with my men.

As I took it from the woman, our fingers brushed over each other's a moment too long. I didn't mind.

"Thank you." I flashed another smile. "I really appreciate it."

The woman grinned back. "It's no problem. I know you don't want to be here in America's Last Frontier without this."

"No, I don't. It's nice to know there are still good people out in this world."

"I'd like to think so."

I could tell by the look in her eyes that she was attracted to me.

It wasn't unusual. Women were often drawn to me.

"Enjoy your time here." The woman offered another smile before sashaying away.

As soon as she was out of sight, my smile faded.

Good people didn't exist in this world. But my words had made her feel good, so mission accomplished.

The last thing I needed was for people to get the creeps when they saw me. I didn't want to raise any red flags.

And I didn't. I was good at what I did.

As I walked toward baggage claim, my thoughts again wandered to those men I'd hired.

Their only saving grace was the fact they'd managed to procure motorbikes. This morning, they'd continue their search for Simmy. From what I understood, the path she and that man had taken only led a few places.

I would find Simmy. I wouldn't settle for any other outcome.

I'd researched the man with her.

Thanks to the article recently published with the identities of *The Round Table* podcasters, it wasn't that hard to find his name.

Ranger Garrett.

It was, however, more difficult to find out more about him.

Seemed he was a man with no background.

I knew what that meant.

He had a dark past, one he'd tried to erase. I had men working on that now. They'd find out more information for me, and I'd learn the truth.

I needed any type of leverage I could find.

Vulnerabilities were the key.

Find the right ones, and I could control my enemies like puppets.

I was ready for the show to begin.

twenty

RANGER PACED HIMSELF, purposefully walking slower so Simmy could keep up. But he could see the exhaustion on her features, in her shallow breaths.

The air was thin. The incline steep. The steps many.

"I can't believe I've never asked you this, but where are you from, Simmy?" He wasn't sure if she'd answer—or if she'd answer truthfully.

"Originally? Boston."

"Boston? You don't have an accent."

"We didn't live there long," she told him. "My family moved around a lot. How about you?"

"New Mexico is where I was born," he told her. "My mom was Native American. Strangely enough, she wasn't a Native American with origins in New Mexico. Her ancestry traced back to Alaska."

"Really? That's interesting. Is that why you came here?"

His mind flew back in time. "I actually came to Alaska for a job. I wanted to live here so I could explore my heritage."

"I actually lived in Washington state before coming to Alaska. I worked at a children's home on a Native American reservation."

Now *that* was interesting. He hadn't expected that. There was so little Simmy had told him about her past. Their conversations had been limited to the podcast, the trading post, and living in Alaska.

"How long were you at the children's home?" He stole a glance at her as he asked the question.

"Four years. Then I, uh . . . well, I needed a change." She didn't offer any more details.

But Ranger had a few guesses. Her ex had found her, hadn't he? It was the only thing that made sense. That her ex was chasing her now, trying to claim her as his property.

His stomach churned at the thought.

No woman should be thought of as property.

Ranger sucked in a breath when he saw something ahead. He nodded toward the building. "There it is. John and Shannon's place."

"I guess you didn't call to let them know you were coming?" Simmy asked.

He shook his head. "No, I've never had to. John and Shannon are the type of people who always welcome me with open arms."

At least, they *had*. Ranger had pulled away after what happened with Anastasia.

He probably shouldn't have. John and Shannon had been good friends to him. But seeing them had hurt so much after losing his daughter.

Now, he needed answers.

He and Simmy continued on the path. He couldn't wait to talk to his friends. To find answers.

Plus, it would be nice to take a load off. To give Simmy a chance to rest as well.

Knowing his friends, they probably had some freshly smoked salmon waiting to serve. Maybe even some home-made bagels and cream cheese.

Everything they did out here was off the grid. They only went to the grocery store a couple of times a year. On occasion, they had supplies flown in.

Ranger was all too familiar with this way of living.

Sometimes, he missed it.

A husky ran down the road toward them, barking.

Simmy paused and raised her hands, her eyes widening.

"That's Mr. Knightly," Ranger told her. "He's friendly."

"Mr. Knightly?"

"Shannon is a huge fan of Jane Austin," Ranger explained. "At one point, she had a team of dogs all named after literary characters. Sherlock. Katniss. Atticus."

"I think I'm going to like her," Simmy said.

"I think you will." Ranger cast her a smile.

The husky trotted up to them, stopped, and sniffed.

"Hey, buddy." Ranger gave the canine a nice long

head rub, noticing the dog had lost weight. "Did they put you on a diet, boy?"

Mr. Knightly wagged his tail.

"Where are your mom and dad?" Ranger continued.

Mr. Knightly barked.

Ranger was surprised John and Shannon hadn't heard the dog's excitement and come out. It wasn't as if they had visitors out this way very often—if ever.

Considering where they lived, the only people who ventured here were those who knew John and Shannon. The list was short.

"I think you're going to really like both of them." Ranger rose and nodded farther down the road where he could barely see the house. "I'm glad you have the chance to meet them."

"Me too."

Then they continued the rest of the way to the house, Mr. Knightly prancing at their side.

———

SIMMY COULDN'T WAIT to meet John and Shannon.

For more than one reason.

For starters, she hoped she might get more insight into Ranger.

The man was such a mystery to her. She wanted to know what made him tick. What he liked. What he didn't like.

Curiosity was winning out, she supposed.

She observed the rustic home as they got closer. It was on the larger side and rambling. Whitewashed wood comprised the walls, and the outside appeared peaceful and cheerful. There was even a flowerbed with purple and yellow blooms.

"How does someone even build something like this out here in the middle of nowhere?"

"Cut down the trees. Stack them just right. Frame up the place. Fill in any gaps between the wood. Everything else just kind of falls in line after that."

Ranger sounded as if he'd done it before.

The thought of Ranger doing that made him seem even more manly and intriguing. "It must feel good to live in a house you built by your own hands. To eat food you caught or grew yourself."

"There is a lot of satisfaction in enjoying the fruit of your labor," Ranger said. "I prefer it any day to city life."

Yes, he'd definitely built his own place before, she realized.

Another glimpse into his past.

She wanted to know more, but she was trying to be patient.

They stopped by the front door, and Ranger knocked.

The dog whined beside them as he seemed to anticipate the reunion.

But there was no answer.

Ranger grunted.

"Do you think they went somewhere?" Simmy asked. "Took a walk maybe?"

Ranger narrowed his eyes and shook his head. "I doubt it. It's more likely they went out hunting or fishing. But John and Shannon aren't the types to just take off without Mr. Knightly. Let me check around back."

Simmy followed him to the backyard and paused when she saw the turquoise-colored lake.

It was absolutely stunning, probably fed by glacier waters.

Ranger searched a few outbuildings before rejoining her. "They're not here."

She waited for his next move, fully comfortable letting him call the shots.

"They won't mind if we wait inside," Ranger said. "Besides, we both need some water and to get off our feet."

Simmy didn't argue.

Ranger walked to the back door, twisted the knob, and the door opened. She supposed out here people didn't lock their doors.

But as soon as Ranger stepped in the doorway, Simmy saw his shoulders tense.

She knew something was wrong.

twenty-one

RANGER RAN TOWARD HIS FRIENDS.

They both lay on the floor, blood covering their chests from bullet wounds.

He knelt by John. Shoved his finger to his friend's neck.

Nothing.

His skin was cold. There was no heartbeat. No rising and falling of his chest.

His friend was gone.

Beside him, Mr. Knightly let out a long howl.

Ranger's heart lodged in his throat.

Then a moan sounded behind him.

"She's alive!" Simmy rushed toward Shannon.

Ranger pivoted and leaned over his friend. Her blonde hair was matted with blood. Bruises had formed on her porcelain skin. Her slight frame made her look like a ragdoll as she lay there.

"Shannon, can you hear me?" he murmured. "Talk to me . . ."

"She's barely hanging on." Simmy knelt on the other side of her, pulled off her sweatshirt, and pressed it into her wound.

A rock lodged in Ranger's throat at the sight of Shannon.

How long had she been suffering like this?

Ranger grabbed his friend's hand. "Shannon, you hold on. I'll get you help somehow. I promise."

She moved her lips. But no sounds came out.

"What is it?" He leaned closer, putting his ear near her mouth.

"I'm . . . sorry."

"Sorry?" What sense did that make? Was she delusional? "What are you sorry about? Who did this to you?"

Again, her lips moved. But this time no words escaped.

"Let me get you help," Ranger told her. "You have to hold on for a while longer."

But he knew the truth.

Even if he found a satellite phone to call for medical help, a helicopter was still thirty minutes out, maybe more. They had their own copter, but it would take just as long to get it up and running.

Shannon wouldn't make it.

Her eyes opened, and she stared at him. Desperation lined her gaze, as if she had something she wanted to say.

"I'm . . . sorry," she barely whispered again.

"You don't have anything to be sorry about," Ranger assured her.

She shook her head. Opened her mouth. "I . . ."

Then a wheezing sound filled the air. Followed by a gurgle. One final gasp.

Shannon went still.

"No . . ." Ranger put his finger to her neck.

Patted her cheeks. Shook her shoulders.

But just like that, she was gone.

He doubled over as grief hit him.

His friends had been ambushed.

They'd done nothing wrong. They were good people.

Ranger clenched his fists as he glanced down at his friends' lifeless bodies.

"I'm going to find whoever did this to you," he growled. "I promise you both that."

———

SIMMY'S THROAT tightened with sorrow as she watched everything unfold.

She'd known by the way Ranger talked about John and Shannon that they were special to him.

Now he'd found them like this . . .

She could only imagine how he felt.

Rising, she stepped toward him. She placed her hand on his shoulder, desperately wishing she could offer some type of comfort.

Mr. Knightly let out another low howl.

The poor dog.

Simmy rubbed the canine's head.

Finally, Ranger stood. But the motion seemed heavier than usual. Everything seemed heavier—his actions, his gaze, his words. Everything.

"I'm so sorry," she murmured, remaining close.

Instead of seeing grief in his gaze, anger flashed in the depths of his startling greens.

Ranger wasn't going to let this go, was he? He would track down whoever had done this to his friends. He would make them pay.

Simmy wouldn't expect anything less.

A noise cut into the moment.

The sound of a motor. Maybe two.

Her gaze locked with Ranger's.

Those men were back.

twenty-two

RANGER HAD to make a quick decision.

Hide or run.

Simmy was a major consideration. She was clearly tired from the nightmarish whirlwind of the past couple of days. He didn't want to push her too far. Didn't know how much she could handle.

He grabbed her hand. "Come with me."

He took one last look at his friends.

He would find their killer, he vowed. He would.

But not right now.

He pulled Simmy outside.

Ranger knew this wilderness better than anyone. He needed to use that to his advantage.

Mr. Knightly remained on their heels as he and Simmy ran around the house and into the backyard. They kept their backpacks with them. It was better if these guys didn't know for sure they'd been here.

They reached the woods and kept running.

His friends had built a sauna out here.

Ranger had thought it was silly the structure was so far away from the house. But the building was an original hunting cabin that had been here when the property had transferred owners. John said it was nice because it was close to the lake. Shannon had said it was nice because it preserved the history of the area.

He spotted the sauna just ahead and pulled Simmy faster. "Just a little farther."

Finally, they reached the small wooden building, and Ranger jerked on the door.

It opened.

He led Simmy inside and dropped his bag on the floor.

Then he turned to Mr. Knightly.

"Quiet." He remembered the command John and Shannon had taught the canine.

The dog let out a whine but lay down beside Simmy.

Then Ranger started to step outside.

Panic raced through Simmy's eyes as she stared at him. "What are you doing?"

"I'm going to move higher up the mountain, somewhere I'll have a better vantage point to see what these guys are up to."

"You think they'll track me here?" Her voice trembled.

"I'm not sure. But if they get too close, I have my gun. I can pop them off one by one."

Her eyes widened.

Ranger met her gaze once more. He wished he had

time to comfort her. But he didn't. "Stay here unless I tell you to come out. Okay?"

After a moment of hesitation, Simmy nodded.

Ranger stepped back and closed the door. "Lock this behind me."

He heard a click.

Then he ventured farther up the mountain.

———

SIMMY SLID her backpack from her shoulders and set it on the floor. If anyone showed up here, she didn't want the bag hindering her efforts to get away.

She glanced around. Thankfully, the building had two small windows near the ceiling. The glass panes were too high up to reach but just big enough to scatter some light into the space.

A fire poker shoved beneath one of the benches caught her eye.

She grabbed it and gripped it so tightly her knuckles turned white.

Then she collapsed on the wooden bench running alongside one wall and waited.

Mr. Knightly jumped up beside her and let out a soft whine.

She rubbed the dog's head. "I know how you feel, buddy."

Her thoughts continued to race. What if something happened to Ranger?

A knot lodged in her throat at the thought of losing him.

It would devastate her—in more ways than one.

Ranger might be able to survive out here in this vast wilderness on his own. But not her.

She didn't even know which direction led to civilization.

She stared at Mr. Knightly a moment.

Well, maybe she wouldn't be out here totally alone. She rubbed the dog's head again, and his tail wagged and thumped on the bench.

She'd always wanted a dog, and right now she found immense comfort in having the canine near.

She couldn't focus on anything right now besides survival.

Knave had sent these men, hadn't he? He'd spared no expense in his efforts to find her.

She shouldn't be surprised. Knave had always been extreme. He hadn't minded using his money on frivolous things.

Hiring those men to hunt her down seemed frivolous.

She'd hoped that, with time, he would back off. Leave her alone. Get bored. Move on.

She should have known better.

As silence stretched outside, her thoughts drifted back to John and Shannon.

Knave couldn't have killed them, could he? It didn't make sense.

Simmy was no expert on death, but she'd guess the

couple had been shot at least sixteen hours ago. One of the bullets had hit a clock, and it had stopped at seven. Seven this morning was too early—their blood was too dry. John's body was too stiff.

Which then took her to seven last night, sixteen hours ago.

There was no way that sixteen hours ago Knave had anticipated Simmy and Ranger coming here.

There was more to this story. She and Ranger just might be dealing with not one, but two sets of blood-thirsty killers.

Simmy shivered at the thought.

A bump sounded outside the sauna and snapped her from her thoughts.

Mr. Knightly straightened and let out a soft whine. But he didn't bark.

She patted his head and whispered, "Good boy."

Then she put her finger over her mouth and blew.

Almost as if the dog understood the motion, he quieted.

The windows were too high, so she couldn't see outside.

Couldn't see what was happening. Who was here.

But someone was close. She was certain of it.

Just then, the door rattled.

Her heart thundered in her chest.

A low growl sounded from Mr. Knightly. Quickly, she hugged the dog, hoping to keep him quiet.

If those men knew for sure that Simmy was in here, nothing would stop them from busting through this door.

Terror captured her muscles until she trembled all over.

She held her breath as she waited to see what would happen next.

twenty-three

RANGER REMAINED behind a boulder just up the mountain, gun poised in hand.

He hoped he didn't have to use it. But he would if that was the only way to save Simmy.

Two men wearing all black appeared farther down the mountain.

Several minutes later, they paused outside the sauna.

Ranger's muscles froze. There was no reason for them to think anyone was inside.

But that didn't mean they wouldn't double-check. All they would need to do was shoot the lock, and that door would open.

Ranger centered the men in his sights.

His heart pounded in his ears as he waited.

And waited.

And waited.

The men muttered something to each other, but Ranger couldn't make out the words.

They talked for several minutes right outside the door.

What were those guys going to do?

One of them raised a gun.

Aimed it at the door.

Ranger's finger went over the trigger, and he prepared himself to fire.

————

SIMMY HEARD the men saying something.

Maybe they're not here.

Took a different path.

The boss won't be happy.

Then the door rattled again.

Why hadn't she asked Ranger to leave her a gun?

Not that she'd be any good at using it.

In fact, she was probably more likely to hurt herself than she was to injure someone else.

But she hated feeling helpless.

No, she told herself. Ranger was outside. Keeping an eye on this place. He wouldn't let anything happen to her.

That didn't stop the panic from rampaging through her blood, however.

She could be mere seconds from death.

She refused to even breathe for a moment as she listened.

Then the voices quieted.

Had those men drawn their weapons? Were they about to shoot through the door and burst inside?

If she closed her eyes, she could see it playing out.

But the thought caused even more terror to race through her.

Then the silence continued.

What was going on out there?

She held Mr. Knightly close and pressed her eyes shut.

She would do the best thing she knew to do.

Simmy would pray.

twenty-four

RANGER WATCHED as the men walked away.

They must have decided that Simmy and Ranger weren't here. That it wouldn't be prudent to fire a shot and announce their presence.

Maybe they'd seen John and Shannon's dead bodies inside and didn't want to leave evidence that could lead back to them.

Ranger didn't know.

For now, he was grateful.

However, he knew that even with these guys leaving, that didn't mean the danger was over.

But maybe he and Simmy would have some space to get their thoughts together.

He didn't dare move. Not until he knew these guys were long gone.

His thoughts drifted to Simmy. She was probably

beside herself in the sauna, not knowing what was happening.

He wished he had a way of communicating with her. Of letting her know what was going on.

But he didn't, so they'd have to make the best of things.

He continued to watch.

The men trekked back down the hill. Paced around the outside of John and Shannon's house one more time.

A few minutes later, they climbed back on their dirt bikes and left.

Ranger blinked several times, unable to believe his good fortune.

But he wasn't complaining.

Now he had to get Simmy and let her know everything was okay . . . for now.

———

AS SOON AS SIMMY SAID "AMEN," she opened her eyes.

She continued to grip the fire poker, holding it like a baseball bat as she waited.

If those guys burst in here, she'd fight with everything in her to stay alive.

She'd been a doormat for too long.

Now it was time to fight back.

As the thoughts crossed her mind, a noise sounded outside.

This time from a distance.

Was that . . . another motor?

Had these guys called for backup?

Footsteps came near again.

She sucked in a breath.

Someone was still out there.

Right outside the door.

Had one of the men come back?

She gripped the fire poker tighter.

Then she heard, "Simmy, it's me. Open up."

She released a breath.

Ranger? Was that really him? Was he really okay?

Cautiously, she moved forward. Taking one hand off the poker, she unlocked the door and twisted the knob.

It opened, and Ranger's frame filled the space.

His gaze went to the poker. He carefully took it from her hands and tossed it on the floor.

"It's okay," he murmured as he pulled her into a hug. "It's okay."

Simmy melted into him.

How could one man make her feel so safe?

Maybe it was for the same reason that one man had made her so terrified.

"What happened?" She muttered the words into Ranger's chest.

"Those men must have figured we weren't here. They left."

She sucked in a slow breath and drew back to look him in the eye. "Really?"

He nodded. "Really. But I'm not sure if they're going to come back. For all I know, they may have gone to investigate another path. When they see we're not down there either, there's a chance they'll return here."

"So what do we do?" Another round of panic fluttered through her. "Isn't that road the only way in or out of here?"

"There are some smaller paths we can take. There's one other place we can go to lie low. Neither of us will be worth anything if we don't get a little rest and food."

Simmy didn't argue with his statement.

But she did wonder exactly where he would take her.

Then she realized it didn't even matter.

As long as she was with Ranger, she knew she would be safe.

twenty-five
Then

MONTH SEVEN FELT EASIER than the previous ones, Charlotte mused.

She'd gotten past her morning sickness, but she wasn't yet at the phase where she felt entirely uncomfortable as the baby filled out her abdomen and pressed on her organs.

Charlotte had, however, finally gotten used to her routine here at the house.

She constantly reminded herself not to get too comfortable here. Too attached to Mark and Meredith and the child inside her.

The more the baby moved, the more connection she felt with the child.

Giving her up would be difficult.

Yes, *her*. Mark and Meredith had decided to find out the sex.

In the days leading up to that decision, Meredith had

been crying quite a bit. But finding out they were having a girl seemed to cheer Meredith up.

As Charlotte ate a salad she'd made herself for dinner, Mark stepped into the kitchen.

Charlotte had been hoping she might see him again today. She'd even made extra salad in case Mark or Meredith wanted some.

Any time she had with Mark was the highlight of her day.

That fact scared her and made her want to run.

But in this situation, she couldn't flee. She'd signed a contract to stay here until the baby was born. She had obligations that prevented her from leaving.

She'd feared getting too attached to the child from the start. She'd never dreamed she might become too attached to the child's father.

Charlotte chided herself for the feelings. She vowed not to act on them. Promised herself she'd avert her thoughts instead of dwelling on her attraction.

What else could she do? None of this was healthy. Only nine more weeks.

Nine weeks.

She could get through this with her morals intact.

This evening, Mark didn't look as perky as normal. His eyes were red and his motions heavy and some of the light seemed to have left him.

Charlotte rose from the table, forgetting about her salad as concern pulsed through her. "Mark?"

He grabbed a bottle of water and waved her off. "Don't mind me. It's been a long day."

"Are you sick?"

"It's Meredith . . ." He ran a hand over his face. "I thought this baby would lessen her depression. But sometimes I fear she's getting worse."

"Worse?" Charlotte's heart pounded in her ears. She knew Meredith was moody and unhappy—probably depressed.

But she'd seemed so happy since she found out they were having a girl. Charlotte had even caught her humming once, and her eyes had seemed bright.

"Unfortunately, yes." Mark ran a hand over his face, but his expression remained tight. "I've tried to get her to see a psychologist, but she's not interested. Sometimes, I fear what's going through her mind."

Charlotte shouldn't ask the question, but she did anyway. "What do you mean?"

Mark glanced over his shoulder before turning back to her and lowering his voice. "When Meredith is happy, she's happy. But when she's sad, there's no consoling her. That worries me. It worries me for her. Worries me for our child. Worries me for what kind of life our little girl will have growing up with a mother like that."

Charlotte rubbed her belly, worry rumbling through her. "I thought the baby made her happy. That having a child was the answer she'd been looking for."

"She's very happy about the baby." Mark's voice softened as he stood in front of her and leaned close as if sharing a secret. "But she's still depressed that she can't carry the child on her own."

"I see." Charlotte swallowed hard and nodded.

She looked down and finally noticed the suitcase at his feet. "Wait . . . are you going somewhere?"

He'd taken a few trips since Charlotte moved in. But normally he mentioned them ahead of time.

"I need to go out of town for business. Maybe it will give Meredith some time to cool off. She's upset with me."

"Why is she upset with you?" Mark seemed like the perfect husband. Attentive. Kind. Doting even.

"In this emotional state of distress Meredith has been in, she's misreading everything." He shifted and tilted his head before lowering his voice. "Truthfully, she doesn't like the way I look at you. I keep telling her I only look at you like I do because, when I look at you, I see the baby."

Charlotte swallowed hard. She wasn't sure how his words made her feel. Maybe part of her *had* wanted to think Mark looked at her like she was special.

The other part of her was so glad Mark hadn't said that. She was too weak, too vulnerable right now. She needed to keep her walls up.

She couldn't—wouldn't—follow in her mother's footsteps.

Eventually, she wanted her own family. In fact, for years, all she'd wanted was to be a mom and a wife. While other teens wanted a career or to see the world, all Charlotte had wanted was a family. Maybe even to have the family she'd never experienced growing up.

But not right now. Not like this.

One day, she'd find someone single and unattached. Together, the two of them would start a brand-new life together.

This—she and Mark, a married man—wasn't an option.

"Anyway." Mark shifted, his gaze wandering to Charlotte's belly then back up to her eyes. "She's sleeping right now, so I probably wouldn't bother her. But will you keep an eye on her while I'm gone?"

"Of course."

A soft, grateful grin stretched across his face. "Thank you. I'll only be gone a couple of days. You have my number if you need me."

"I do." She would miss their morning chats.

She expected him to pick up his suitcase. To leave.

That she'd have time to process what he'd just told her.

Instead, Mark dropped to his knees in front of her. His face was eye level with her belly, and he reached for the baby with both hands.

Charlotte sucked in a breath and tensed, feeling unsure of exactly what he was doing.

She should be used to his affection for her belly by now, but she wasn't. His touch still felt like a violation.

Every time, just when Charlotte was determined to say something, she would talk herself out of it. She'd remind herself that *his* baby was inside her, only separated by some skin and muscle and amniotic fluid.

He tugged at her shirt until the skin of her belly appeared.

She sucked in her breath.

He'd never exposed her like this before.

Charlotte reached for the wall behind her, using it to steady herself.

For a reason unbeknownst to her, moisture popped into her eyes.

She felt so . . . violated.

Then Mark pressed his cheek against her skin while still caressing the sides of her belly. "I'm going to miss you, my sweet baby."

Charlotte forced her shoulders to soften.

He really did love his child already, didn't he? That was the only reason he was doing this. It wasn't sexual in any way.

But the feel of his skin against hers was almost more than she could take.

She remained still as he hugged the child in her belly. The moment . . . it was touching, really. Strangely intrusive but touching.

Then he pulled away and planted a long kiss against the side of her stomach.

Heat washed through her.

He should be doing this with Meredith. This baby should be in her belly.

These intimate moments should be between a husband and wife.

The next instant, he tugged her shirt back down and

stood as if nothing uncomfortable had just happened. As if his actions were normal. As if his touch had been welcome.

But the look in his eyes did something strange to her.

There was something different about the way he looked at her.

For a moment, Charlotte wondered if he might lean forward and kiss her also. Wondered if his emotions were fooling him. Were making him forget that Meredith was his wife and this baby's mother.

Not Charlotte.

Even worse, part of Charlotte *wanted* him to kiss her. To bond with her. To see that she was special.

She swallowed hard as he continued to stare.

She needed to squelch her feelings. This was merely a business arrangement.

Finally, he stepped back and grabbed his suitcase. The hunger in his eyes disappeared so quickly that Charlotte questioned if she had just imagined it.

"Don't forget to call me if you need me for anything," he told her. "Otherwise, I'll see you in a few days."

She would never admit it, but she was already looking forward to seeing him again.

Counting down the days, for that matter.

And that was a very, very bad thing.

twenty-six
Now

RANGER CONTINUED to scan everything around them. He didn't want to be taken by surprise. Even though he'd seen those men leave on their motorbikes, there was still the possibility they'd stopped up ahead and would circle back through the woods.

For that reason, he and Simmy needed to be cautious.

Mr. Knightly trailed behind them as they walked back toward the house.

Ranger felt another pang of grief as he remembered finding his friends inside.

If he could stay longer, he would do more. Arrange for John and Shannon's bodies to be taken care of. Make sure they had some dignity when authorities found them.

But John and Shannon were already dead, and there wasn't much Ranger could do to help at this point. The best thing he could do was to concentrate on keeping

Simmy alive. As soon as possible, he'd call the state police to have them come out and investigate.

For now, he walked into a small garage located at the back of the property.

He'd thought about hiding out here but decided it would be too obvious.

He'd made the right choice because he'd seen the men go inside.

"What's in here?" Simmy nodded at the garage.

He pointed to a vehicle in the distance. "Another side-by-side. It's going to be a lot easier to travel with it."

"I can imagine."

He pulled the cover off and checked the gas. The tank was full.

Then he threw their things into the back and motioned for Mr. Knightly to sit in the back seat. The dog jumped right in as if he were used to it.

Ranger opened the garage door and started the vehicle. The engine purred to life.

Perfect.

John and Shannon had always been the type to cover all their bases, so Ranger wasn't surprised the vehicle was full of gas and ready to go.

"Seatbelt," he called.

Simmy snapped hers in place.

Then they were off.

He drove around the side of the house and found another small path.

Just as before, the motor was too loud for him and Simmy to have any type of decent conversation.

The good news was that their destination was only a few miles away.

The bad news was the side-by-side would leave tracks in the mud. If those men *did* come back, there was a chance he and Simmy would be followed. Plus, the loud motor was a dead giveaway.

They'd have to take their chances. This was still their best option.

More landscape blurred by until finally Ranger spotted the place he wanted to reach.

His old home.

He pulled to a stop behind it and cut the engine. Then he climbed out and motioned for Simmy to follow him.

He observed his cabin, one much more rustic than John and Shannon's.

The place had been built out of spruce trees. Ranger had cut them down himself. He'd added the mud between the logs by hand. Had built a root cellar to preserve his food. Had fished for meat and collected berries.

Everything had been done by the sweat of his brow.

He wasn't sure what Simmy would think of it. But he was about to find out.

He turned toward her. "This is my old home. We can take some shelter here . . . for a little while, at least."

SIMMY PAUSED inside the dark house that smelled like dust and stale air. She looked around.

The place was definitely rustic.

A small cot rested against one wall. A kitchen, if you'd call it that, with a counter and a small sink was braced against another wall. There was no refrigerator, and the bathroom was probably located in a separate building she'd seen behind the place.

"Why don't you sit down and rest for a minute?" Ranger found a bottle in the cabinet and poured some water into a bowl for Mr. Knightly.

She perched on the edge of the cot. But curiosity got the best of her, and she scanned the place, looking for any personal effects.

This was her chance to learn more about Ranger.

But nothing here offered any hints about his past. Probably on purpose.

She glanced back at him as he rubbed Mr. Knightly's head. "How long did you live here?"

He straightened. "Eight years on and off."

Eight years? Ranger had said his daughter had died when she was eight years old. A mental timeline came together in her head.

"Here." Ranger reached into the cabinet, grabbed something, and handed it to her. "It's not much, but it's food."

She stared at the MRE in her hands. Chili and macaroni. Not exactly her first choice. But beggars couldn't be choosers.

"Thank you." She tore the top off.

He poured some food from another pack into a bowl for the dog, and then Ranger sat in a wooden chair and opened his own packet. The side of the package read "Shredded beef in barbecue sauce."

Simmy took a bite of her dinner. The taste of it made her stomach turn, but she knew she needed food to keep up her energy. So she continued to eat.

Ranger ate a few minutes in silence before saying, "I was in the CIA."

"What?" Simmy's eyebrows flung up. The CIA? She'd expected some rogue security agency or maybe the military. Not the CIA.

"There's a lot you don't know about me." He offered a half shrug before taking another bite of his food.

"Believe me, I realize that."

He jammed his fork into the foil packet again. "I was a different person back then. I fell in love with a woman, who turned out to be a spy. That was my first mistake."

"Let me guess—in Russia?"

He nodded stoically. "Yes, in Russia. Turns out—part of her mission was to get me to fall in love with her."

"Ouch." She winced.

"Yes, ouch." He glared into the distance. "I'm pretty sure her pregnancy was part of her overall plan. All of it was just a ploy so I'd share classified information."

"That's deplorable. Did you share?"

"No." The word came out quickly. "Sorry. *No.*" He said the word more softly this time. "But she did manage to break into my file and find some information. After that, she basically outed me to the Russian government."

"How could she do that?"

A new edge entered his voice, and he narrowed his eyes. "I found out what she'd done right in the nick of time. I took Anastasia and escaped. If I'd stayed any longer, I would have ended up in a Russian prison—where they would have tortured and killed me."

"I'm glad you got out."

Ranger stabbed his food with a fork again and nodded, though his gaze looked hard—maybe even tortured with memories. "I didn't want to take my daughter away from her mother. I didn't. But Vivian . . . she didn't even know how to be a mom. She hired nannies and essentially neglected Anastasia. Then when she exposed me as a spy . . . I knew taking my daughter away from Vivian and her corrupt family was the right decision."

Simmy licked her lips. "Then what happened?"

She waited for Ranger to continue, anxious to hear the rest of his story.

twenty-seven

RANGER'S STOMACH churned as he thought about his past.

He hadn't shared these details since everything had unfolded. Not to anyone except John and Shannon. Apollo. And Nathaniel, John's brother.

The fewer people who knew, the better.

The people he'd told were his core community. John and Shannon were friends who'd helped him when he'd escaped Russian officials. They'd found him and Anastasia in the wilderness and taken them in. Ranger had told them and Nathaniel the truth about his past.

And Apollo had been his handler. He'd left the CIA also and set up camp in Alaska near Ranger as a matter of security.

They'd all practically become like family.

However, Ranger and Apollo had too many enemies.

So the two of them had set up lives for themselves off the grid in a remote place where they couldn't be found.

"I slipped out of Russia with Anastasia and came to Alaska. I knew I'd need to hide her because Vivian's family would do everything in their power to get her back. I couldn't let that happen."

Ranger swallowed hard. Tumultuous emotions warred in his gaze as he figured out his next words.

"I knew that Anastasia would be safer with John and Shannon. Their own kids were already out of the house, and they were such great people." He shook his head as another wave of grief welled in him.

John and Shannon hadn't deserved to die like that. Ranger would get to the bottom of whatever had happened. Nothing was going to stop him.

"So you left Anastasia with them, and you built this cabin close by?" Simmy squinted as if trying to piece things together.

He nodded. "I eventually got out of the CIA. But it took time. I had unfinished business so it wasn't as if I could just stay out here with her full time. Besides, it was dangerous for her to be with me, and I knew that. She was much better off with John and Shannon than she was with me or Vivian's family. But I still wanted to be close to her. To be her father. I came to see her as often as I could."

"Did she know that you were her dad?"

His throat tightened. "She did. I made sure to make it out here at least once a month. I would have come more if I could have."

"But you said . . ." Simmy cleared her throat like she didn't want to finish. "You said she died?"

His throat tightened until he felt as if he couldn't get any air. "John and Shannon called me. Said that someone had taken Anastasia. I knew right away who'd done it. Vivian. I think . . . I think Anastasia must have tried to escape."

He paused to compose himself. Drew in a shaky breath. Tried to control the pummel of bad memories.

"Anastasia knew the water was too cold. I'd taught her basic survival skills . . . but running into the lake must have seemed like her only option to get away. But then . . ." Ranger's voice caught, and he rubbed his burning throat.

He didn't have to finish. He'd already told Simmy that she'd drowned.

"I'm so sorry, Ranger," Simmy murmured. "How did you find all that out? I can only assume Vivian and her family weren't forthright with the information."

"No, but I was tracking Anastasia. I'd put a device in her favorite stuffed animal just in case something like this happened, knowing she'd never leave that rabbit behind. I arrived . . ." His voice cracked. "I arrived just in time to see them taking her body from the water."

"But if that's true, what about the photo? If it wasn't Anastasia's body you saw, then whose was it?"

"That's what I've been trying to figure out." His jaw hardened. "The body was bloated and impossible to identify. Most likely, it was a cadaver."

Ranger would get some answers if it was the last thing he did.

———

SIMMY LISTENED AS RANGER SPOKE, not wanting to interrupt him, yet wanting to know more at the same time.

With every new reveal, so many puzzle pieces clicked into place.

She knew he was a survivalist.

But the CIA? She'd had no idea.

She'd known there was more to his story.

Finally, she'd been given just a glimpse into his past. The details were a lot to take in.

"I'm really sorry about Anastasia," Simmy said. "And I'm sorry about your friends. I don't understand . . . those men following me . . ."

"They couldn't have been the ones who killed John and Shannon," Ranger finished.

She sucked in a breath. "Wait . . . you think the people or person who killed John and Shannon have something to do with Vivian?"

"I'm wondering if the person who took that picture of Anastasia and sent it to me somehow set something in motion." He crumbled his foil packet and placed it on the table, perhaps with a little too much force.

"I can only imagine that Vivian's family isn't happy with you." She set her empty foil packet on the table also

—much more gently, however—and gave him her full attention.

"When I took Anastasia away from them, it was basically my death sentence." His jaw muscles twitched. "But I would do anything for her."

Simmy squeezed his hand. "I know. I'm so sorry about all of this."

"No need to be sorry," he snapped. "None of it's your fault."

"I know." There was no offense in her voice. "I'm saying I'm sorry as a way of showing my compassion."

He raked a hand through his hair, then shook his head. "I know. Now I'm the one who's sorry. I didn't mean to snap."

"You've been through a lot today."

He looked at her, and their gazes caught again. "So have you."

"I guess we're two peas in a pod."

A grin grazed his lips. "I guess we are."

A moment passed between them.

Then Simmy cleared her throat and took a step back. "So what's our plan now? I know you. I know we're not just going to hide out here."

The tension seemed to leave his shoulders, and he let out a long breath. "I need to find some answers, Simmy."

"But how do you go about doing that?" She observed him carefully.

"There's only one person I can think of who might have some answers, who can tell me if John and Shannon mentioned anything lately. Who can tell me if they saw anything suspicious that might give us a hint as to what happened to them . . . what happened to Anastasia." He paused. "Maybe you could stay at a hotel or somewhere else safe while I do that."

Simmy's heart beat harder as she reached forward and squeezed his arm. "I want to go with you."

Ranger stared at her, still hesitating. "I don't know how everything will play out. But I do know this is going to be dangerous."

"I understand." She squeezed his arm harder. "And I'm okay with that. Some things are worth fighting for."

twenty-eight

RANGER WATCHED as Simmy stepped into a small bathroom near the cabin. He'd left bottles of water there. They would be cold, but she could use those to wash up and then change clothes.

While she did that, he called Apollo on his satellite phone. Confirmed his friend was okay. That those gunmen had gone running.

Then Ranger told Apollo about John and Shannon.

"What?" Apollo's word sounded more like a bark. Then it softened. "You've got to be kidding me."

"I wish I was." Ranger peered out the window, looking for any signs of trouble. "You don't know anything about it?"

"No, nothing. I can't believe it. You want me to call the police?"

"I do. But wait thirty minutes. I need more time before police start investigating out here."

"Will do. Be safe. I don't like any of this."

"Neither do I." Ranger ended the call and strode across the room. He shoved his cot out of the way and pulled up a floorboard beneath it.

He'd stored weapons there. Some passports. Cash.

He shoved several things into his backpack.

Then he spotted something at the bottom of the box.

He sat on the end of his cot and lifted it.

A picture of him with Anastasia when his daughter was only four.

Memories filled him until an ache formed in his chest.

In the photo, Anastasia had lively green eyes. Thick, dark hair cut to her chin. A wide grin. The two of them sat near the lake at John and Shannon's house, fishing poles in hand.

His girl loved fishing and always seemed to get the biggest catch of the day. Nothing delighted her more than showing up everyone else.

She clearly had the competitiveness of her mom.

There were many ways Anastasia reminded him of Vivian—but only the best ways.

Because Vivian wasn't all bad. At least, she hadn't seemed that way at first.

The woman was vivacious and smart. Sassy and fun. The chemistry between her and Ranger had been undeniable.

But lurking beneath all that charm was evil.

A self-serving evil mixed with a dogmatic upbringing.

The combination had created a monster. A beautiful but deadly monster.

Ranger heard the door open and glanced up.

As Simmy stepped back into the cabin, he quickly put the photo in his bag. He felt the moisture at his eyes and pulled his tears back.

This wasn't time to grieve.

It was the time to fight for what he believed in.

———

SIMMY HAD SEEN a brief glimpse of the picture Ranger held.

The picture of his daughter.

Her heart twisted with compassion. It must be so difficult for him. First to lose her. Then to question everything and wonder where she might be.

In her own way, Simmy understood.

"We need to leave before nightfall." Ranger sounded like he had a plan.

"Of course." Simmy snapped from her thoughts and nodded in reassurance. "I'm ready to go whenever you need to."

"Just give me a minute to clean myself up too." He nodded at the front door. "I'll head to the bathroom and be right out, and then we can go."

She watched as he disappeared outside.

Then she glanced around the space, not hiding her curiosity anymore.

She tried to imagine Ranger living here. Tried to imagine him as a dad. Tried to imagine everything in life that had led him to the point where he was now.

He'd allowed her small glimpses into his past. But there was so much more to discover. For example, what did his mom and dad do for a living? Did he have any brothers or sisters? How did he get recruited to the CIA? What kind of missions did he work?

She wanted to learn that information. More than anything. She wanted to unwrap all the layers until she saw Ranger for who he was. Who he'd been. Who he wanted to be in the future.

But this place was barren, absent of any personal effects. If she was going to learn those things, it would be because Ranger told her. She hoped they had that opportunity, that Ranger would open up more one day.

A moment later, Ranger stepped back into the cabin.

Simmy plastered on a soft smile as she turned to him. "Are you ready?"

He nodded, his entire body rigid. "There's no time to waste."

She didn't know what the next few hours would hold, but she prayed for their safety and for answers to come soon.

Ranger needed to find his daughter. Simmy prayed those men after her didn't stop him from doing that.

twenty-nine
Then

CHARLOTTE AWOKE EARLY the next morning as she normally did. She quietly drank her coffee and ate her oatmeal at the breakfast nook.

Part of her wished Mark was home and that he'd come down to chat.

The other part of her was glad he was gone.

What had happened yesterday . . . Mark's actions had thrown her off balance.

Charlotte should have told him no. That it wasn't appropriate for him to tug her shirt up and touch her bare skin. Or that he should at least ask permission before doing so.

The other part reminded herself that the man desperately wanted this baby. That her body was basically on loan to this couple for the duration of the pregnancy. Charlotte should stop being so prudish.

Either way, some space seemed good. The timing of him leaving was for the best.

She sipped on her coffee, finished her cup, then washed her mug and put it away. Before Meredith woke up, Charlotte crept to the freezer where Mark had hidden the ice cream. He'd continued to do so over the past several months.

Standing in the garage, Charlotte took a few bites and let the cool, creamy treat melt on her tongue.

Just a few bites a day. It wouldn't do any harm.

Meredith had been even pickier than usual lately. She'd been watching every little morsel Charlotte ate. She wanted Charlotte to walk more often. To practice her breathing. To up the amount of water she drank.

The cravings had started to come, and they made her so miserable. All Charlotte wanted was a big fat steak. A baked potato loaded with butter, sour cream, and cheese. A salad with croutons and gobs of ranch dressing.

She salivated at the thought of it.

After Charlotte finished her ice cream, she stepped back inside. She wasn't going to walk on the treadmill right now. But she would soon enough.

After Meredith woke up each morning, she liked to find Charlotte and go over instructions with her. *Every day*. Even though her instructions were almost the same day after day.

By eleven, Meredith still hadn't emerged from her room, and Charlotte was getting anxious.

The woman liked to sleep late but not normally this long, and Mark had indicated she was upset.

Was she okay? Charlotte didn't want to wake her unless she had to. She could only imagine how grumpy the woman would be if Charlotte pulled her out of a good dream.

Charlotte decided instead to take a short walk around the property. She'd give it another hour, and then she'd check on Meredith.

She stepped outside the rambling house with its stone-faced gables and walked toward the small pond in the back. It really was beautiful here. They were surrounded by woods, and the nearest neighbor was at least a mile away.

She never thought she would like seclusion like this, but she did.

Her whole life, she'd lived in various apartments with her mother. Her mom's boyfriends had been in and out, a revolving door of new faces—and new challenges.

Out here, it was just her, Mark, and Meredith. Occasionally, Mark's brother came to visit. Dr. Matthews came by.

But otherwise, it was so quiet.

Maybe this was more her speed.

At twelve, Charlotte headed back inside.

She imagined when she walked in that she'd see Meredith sitting at the table with her yogurt parfait and espresso.

But the table was empty.

Tension pulled across Charlotte's chest.

If she knocked on Meredith's door and woke her up, the woman might take out her rage on Charlotte. Not in a way that would hurt the child, of course.

But whenever Meredith got mad at Charlotte, she became even more controlling. She watched Charlotte with a greater intensity. Made snide remarks about everything she did.

Charlotte was sitting too long. She shouldn't take such long, hot showers. Spicy foods were bad for the baby.

Charlotte swallowed hard, shoving aside those negative thoughts, and knocked on Meredith's door.

There was no answer.

Charlotte knocked again.

Still no answer.

After a moment of hesitation, she twisted the handle and opened the door a crack. "Meredith?"

Nothing.

Charlotte pushed the door open more. "Meredith?"

Still nothing.

This time, she pushed the door all the way open, and light from the hallway filled the otherwise black space. The shades were drawn, the darkness as deep as midnight.

But the light from the hallway illuminated someone in the bed.

Meredith.

She wasn't moving, not even beginning to stir.

Was she still sleeping? Charlotte hadn't awakened her with her knocking or calling her name?

Then Charlotte processed the rest of the scene.

The pill bottles on the nightstand and floor. A glass of water spilled on the floor. The way Meredith's hand flopped off the side of the bed.

Charlotte's heart jumped into her throat, and she could hardly breathe.

She forced her feet to move faster.

But as soon as she saw Meredith, the pallor on the woman's face hit her.

No . . . the breath left her lungs.

Charlotte pressed her finger to Meredith's neck.

There wasn't a heartbeat.

Maybe she wasn't feeling the right place.

Charlotte moved her finger to various places along Meredith's neck, just to be sure.

But there was no pulse.

No, no, no . . .

Meredith couldn't be dead.

Charlotte grabbed her cell phone and quickly called 911.

thirty
Now

RANGER STEPPED OUTSIDE with Simmy and Mr. Knightly, and they headed to the side-by-side.

Before he reached it, he paused.

His back stiffened as his senses went on alert.

A sound cut through the air in the distance.

Engines.

"Ranger?" Simmy's soft voice cut into his thoughts.

He held up a finger, signaling for her to remain quiet. He needed to listen. Needed to be sure.

The noise was distinct.

Motorbikes, he realized. Those guys were back and headed toward his cabin.

He grabbed Simmy's hand. "Stay low."

Simmy ducked as they hurried away from the cabin and stooped behind a rocky outcropping.

They didn't have time to go any farther. Instead, they remained hidden only twelve feet from the cabin.

But they got there just in time.

Two guys on motorbikes pulled up.

They climbed from the cycles, took their helmets off, and glanced around.

"They've definitely been here." One of them kneeled on the ground to study some kind of print Ranger or Simmy had left near the door.

The other one made a hand motion to indicate they should circle the cabin.

Ranger's pulse raced. He needed a plan. As much as he'd like to jump on the side-by-side and take off, those guys would hear them. Their motorbikes were faster, and they would catch up too quickly.

However, these guys would find them hiding in the woods in just a matter of time.

Ranger knew what he needed to do. It would risky, but his plan should work.

He waited until the guys burst through the door of his cabin.

Then he whispered to Simmy, "Follow me."

She stayed behind him as he ran toward the motorbikes. Using his knife, he popped one of the tires.

Then he threw his backpack on the rack of the other motorbike. He spotted the keys still in the ignition, climbed on, and motioned for Simmy to get on behind him.

She mounted the bike and wrapped her arms around his waist.

He didn't start the engine right away. He rolled down

the path to buy some more time. Mr. Knightly ran beside them.

Then he heard someone yell behind him. "Hey!"

Ranger cranked the engine, and the bike roared to life. He accelerated down the path. The canine trotted behind them.

Ranger knew there was no way those men would be able to keep up with the pace of the motorbike.

Then a bullet cracked through the air.

His shoulder burned.

He'd been hit, hadn't he?

He didn't feel intense pain. Not yet. Nothing he couldn't handle, at least.

Simmy gasped, and her fingers dug into his chest. "Ranger . . ."

Panic hit him. What if she'd been hit? "Are you okay?"

"I'm . . . I'm fine. But you're bleeding. Your shoulder . . ."

Relief washed through him. Simmy being okay was all that mattered. "I'm fine. Hang on tight and stay low."

He gunned the throttle, desperate to move faster.

Ranger had to get back to John and Shannon's in time to do what he needed before these guys caught up.

———

SIMMY'S HEART pounded out of control.

That had been close.

If Ranger hadn't been with her, there was no way she

would have gotten out of the situation alive. But that bullet . . . it had hit Ranger.

He said he was okay, but was he?

Her grip around Ranger's waist tightened.

His muscles were hard beneath her hands. His breathing steady. His motions confident.

He was her rock right now. If he hadn't been with her . . . she'd be dead.

Knave would have found her. Probably at the airport. Or in Nevada or wherever she ended up.

Now that he'd picked up on her scent, he appeared to have doubled down on his efforts to find her.

She'd imagined the lengths he might go to. But she'd never imagined this.

Hired hands. Guns. Chases.

All of it showed desperation.

A desperation to make her pay.

She swallowed hard at the thought.

Racing down the mountain on the motorbike made her feel sick to her stomach. But she knew she was in good hands.

But where were they headed now? What was his next plan of action?

Simmy had so many questions.

But she didn't ask any of them.

Instead, she pressed her cheek into Ranger's back and held on.

thirty-one

RANGER CONTINUED DOWN THE MOUNTAIN. He knew the guys, while on foot, wouldn't catch up with them anytime soon. But he still needed to move as quickly as possible. Needed to put distance between him and Simmy and those men.

He was all too aware of Simmy's arms around him. Of her face pressed into his back.

He didn't think he'd ever have feelings like this again. Not after Vivian.

But Simmy was so different from Vivian.

At first, Vivian had seemed alive and electric. But Ranger eventually realized that those qualities were really signs of instability.

Simmy, on the other hand, was comfortable. Yet she was also intriguing in her own right. Her eyes held kindness—but also secrets. Pain. Regret.

Life hadn't been easy on her, but she'd clearly bloomed despite her circumstances.

Did she return his feelings? He wasn't sure.

But now wasn't the time to find out. Now was the time to focus on survival.

Twenty minutes later, they reached John and Shannon's place. Ranger took the bike back around to the garage, then stopped and cut the motor. They climbed off and hurried into the garage.

He could think of only one solution right now.

But he was sure Simmy wouldn't like it.

However, they didn't have any other choice if they wanted to get out of here alive.

———

SIMMY RUBBED Mr. Knightly's head as she waited in the dim garage to hear what Ranger was thinking.

She followed his gaze and saw him staring at something beneath an oversized cover in the center of the space. He flipped on a light, illuminating the building.

She blinked with surprise. She'd expected the insides to be rundown or rustic.

But this garage looked state of the art with its metal siding, glossy cement floor, and numerous machines and gadgets she didn't recognize.

Then her gaze went back to the covered object at the center of the space.

It was too big to be a car or a truck. It could be a tank for all she knew.

"Help me take this cover off." Ranger began tugging at it, but he only used one arm.

She would guess his other shoulder hurt from the bullet wound. She didn't think it was deep. But the bullet had still taken a toll, no matter how small.

She helped him pull the canvas off.

Her eyes widened when a helicopter appeared.

She soaked in the details. The aircraft appeared small, made for only two people. It almost reminded her of a dragonfly with its rounded glass front and narrow tail.

"Are you serious right now?" She glanced at Ranger. "We're going to use that?"

He nodded tightly, not taking his eyes off the escape copter. "We are."

"But your shoulder . . ."

"It's just a surface wound. It will be fine." He paused, but only for a second. "Now, we need to move. We don't have much time."

She swallowed back her fear. They were out of options right now. But the thought of going up into the air in that thing . . .

She pushed away the worst-case scenarios that tried to play in her mind. Scenarios where they crashed into the icy lake or mountainside or even into the trees.

Instead, Simmy followed his instructions to get the helicopter ready. A few minutes later, they climbed inside.

Mr. Knightly hopped into the small cargo space

behind them. The canine's tongue hung out gleefully as if he'd done this before.

"Ranger . . ." She hated to point out the obvious. "There's a roof above us."

"Hang on."

He hit a few more buttons in the helicopter. The next instant, the roof spread open above them, almost like a luxurious garage door.

Simmy blinked, certain she was seeing things, even though she knew she wasn't.

What else didn't she know about this man? Was this a skill he'd developed in the CIA? And what about John and Shannon? What had their story been? Most people Simmy met didn't have a helicopter in their garage, just in case.

"Here we go," Ranger muttered as he fired up the copter.

Simmy reached back and rubbed Mr. Knightly's head.

Then she held her breath, praying this little machine was sturdier than it looked.

thirty-two

RANGER IGNORED the pain in his shoulder as they soared into the air.

Just as they rose above the roof, he spotted the men running down the mountain.

The gunmen were still a good half mile away from John and Shannon's. But that didn't mean they weren't a threat. Ranger couldn't afford to let down his guard.

"Ranger . . ." Simmy murmured.

"I see them."

He adjusted the throttle as they cleared the building and then they swooped toward the lake.

He sucked in a breath as he glanced ahead. The sight of these mountains never failed to amaze him.

He'd always loved this area.

The glaciers. The turquoise water. The snowcapped peaks.

It had seemed like the perfect place to raise a family

away from the pressures of the world. It was a place where a person could be at one with nature and with God. Where they could escape the traps of modern-day life.

Another sound split the air.

More gunfire.

These guys didn't give up, did they? Irritation tightened Ranger's spine.

He glanced at Simmy. Saw how pale she looked as she absently stroked Mr. Knightly's head.

Then he shifted the copter again, lifting higher.

The men's bullets shouldn't reach this far. That made him feel better.

Simmy craned her neck to look over her shoulder and gasped. "Ranger . . . I don't know much about guns . . . but the one they're holding looks big."

He followed her gaze, and his throat tightened.

Simmy was right.

That was an AK-47. Where had that come from?

It didn't matter. All that mattered was the fact the gun was aimed at their helicopter.

So much for feeling better.

———

"HOLD ON!" Ranger said.

Simmy's heart pounded in her ears as the helicopter suddenly dipped.

Fear filled her, but she tried to trust Ranger. Tried to remember that he knew what he was doing.

But the same prayer kept repeating in her mind.

Keep us safe. Keep us safe. Keep us safe.

The helicopter swooped toward the lake, taking her stomach with it.

Had they been shot down?

No, she realized.

Ranger had dipped low as the lake wound around a bend—probably so those guys couldn't see them.

Then they flew low above the water, traveling over the lake to the mountains beyond.

The snow-capped mountains.

Uninhabitable. Dangerous.

Those were rugged peaks—all part of a volcano if she remembered correctly. Spaces meant for climbers and explorers.

Not for homesteads.

What if they crashed . . . ? She gripped the seat, the aircraft suddenly feeling flimsy, like not much protection.

She glanced behind her again.

The men looked like small action figures in the background.

It appeared she and Ranger—and Mr. Knightly—were safe.

For now.

But these guys weren't giving up.

That meant this was far from over.

thirty-three

WELL, that explained it. I scowled as I paced the small airport.

I'd had my guys look into that Ranger Garrett guy.

He was former CIA.

No wonder he'd eluded my men so easily.

But I wouldn't let this drop. Not a chance.

I'd landed by bush plane in McCarthy. I was getting close.

I could feel it.

Soon, I would make Simmy pay for everything she'd done.

Pay, and pay dearly.

I would handle this situation myself. Take a hands-on approach. Of course, I'd have my guys as backup. They were close in case I needed them.

I'd become quite good at making people suffer. On the flight here, that was all I'd been able to think about.

Ways to make Simmy regret her actions.

I paused outside on the tarmac and stared at the mountains in the distance.

Such a beautiful place to have to do such horrible things. It was too bad.

Except I didn't really care.

I narrowed my eyes, and I turned away from the scenery that people traveled for days and days to experience.

I had other things on my mind.

More important things.

Simmy came across as pure and innocent, kind and loving.

I'd fallen for it myself.

But none of it was true.

She was vile, selfish, and deadly.

I wanted everyone to know that.

I wanted to strip her naked and parade her around town so everyone could see her for who she really was.

A smile stretched across my face at the thought of humiliating her.

Nothing would bring me more pleasure.

I wasn't going to give up until I got what I wanted.

With that thought, I turned and stepped toward the exit, expecting my vehicle to be there ready and waiting.

It had better be, or there would be someone else paying the price.

thirty-four

RANGER SUCCESSFULLY MADE it over the St. Elias Mountain Range.

He hadn't told Simmy he was worried. But cloud cover could obscure peaks—and that made for dangerous flying conditions. Not to mention the fact he hadn't had time to check the wind speeds.

All those things had to be considered when taking one of these birds up.

Thankfully, they were okay—but only by the grace of God. Ranger couldn't take any of the credit himself.

It had been a long time since he'd flown a copter and since he'd been up in the air in this area.

Now he needed to figure out how to get to Nathaniel's place.

After a few minutes, he found a point of reference. Mount Riggs.

He headed north of the mountain.

Nathaniel had a large field behind his property where Ranger would land.

Several minutes later, he spotted the homestead.

As they drew closer, he saw Nathaniel step out of his home and stare up at them.

The truth hit Ranger.

His friend most likely thought John and Shannon were coming to visit him.

He probably didn't know his brother and sister-in-law had died.

Ranger would need to break the news to him.

He swallowed hard. That was the last thing he wanted to do. But he had no choice. Someone had to do it, so it might as well be him.

He landed and waited several minutes until the chopper blades stopped spinning. Once it was safe, Ranger opened his door. Cool air rushed to meet them.

He glanced at Simmy. "You ready for this?"

She offered a half shrug, half frown. "Have I been ready for anything?"

He understood exactly where she was coming from.

"I think you've been doing great. You've adjusted nicely." He nodded outside. "Let's go."

They climbed out, and Mr. Knightly jumped to the ground behind them.

Nathaniel strode across the grass to meet them. The fifty-something man wore cargo pants, boots, and a moisture-wicking shirt. He was tall and thin, though he was getting a pouch at his belly.

"Ranger?" A knot formed between Nathaniel's eyes. "I thought . . ."

"That I was John?" Ranger swallowed hard.

"That's his copter." His gaze went to Mr. Knightly, and he rubbed the dog's head. "What are you doing here? Your mom and dad have to miss you."

Ranger didn't say anything.

Then realization washed over Nathaniel's features.

He froze. Sucked in a breath. His shoulders slumped. "No . . ."

Ranger placed a hand on his friend's shoulder. "I'm sorry, Nathaniel. I'm really sorry."

———

SIMMY'S THROAT TIGHTENED.

They'd moved inside. Ranger must have sensed his friend needed to sit, needed to be somewhere not so out in the open.

She'd heard Ranger ask about Becca, whom Simmy could only assume was Nathaniel's wife. He'd said something about Becca going to Seattle to take care of her mother, who'd just had surgery.

"What happened?" Nathaniel demanded.

Simmy sat beside Ranger in the cozy living room and listened as he explained what had happened to John and Shannon. As he told his friend how she and Ranger had found the couple.

I'm sorry.

Shannon's words slammed into her mind. With everything that had happened, she'd forgotten about them.

But what had Shannon meant? What was she sorry for? Or had the words simply been said in a state of delirium?

She didn't know, and this didn't seem like the time to bring it up.

Nathaniel slouched, his eyes glazing over with every new detail.

When Ranger finished, Nathaniel turned away from them. Simmy would guess he didn't want them seeing his emotions, his grief. She could respect that.

Finally, he dragged his gaze up to meet Ranger's. His mourning took a back seat to a new emotion—anger. "Who would have done this?"

"I was hoping you could tell me," Ranger said.

Nathaniel swung his head back and forth. "I have no idea why someone would kill them. You and I both know John and Shannon were the kindest, most selfless people . . ."

"They were." Ranger shifted. "Nathaniel, I'm afraid this has something to do with Anastasia."

Nathaniel drew in a sharp breath and met Ranger's gaze. "What do you mean?"

"A couple of days ago, someone sent me a picture of her, indicating she's still alive."

Nathaniel's face grew pale.

He knew something, didn't he?

Simmy considered herself good at reading people. This man was definitely hiding something.

Her throat tightened, and she glanced at Ranger.

He bristled. He knew also, didn't he?

Ranger narrowed his eyes as he stared at his friend. "Nathaniel . . . what aren't you telling me?"

"Nothing," he rushed a little too quickly.

Ranger's hands fisted at his sides as he clearly tried to hold himself together. "Nathaniel . . ."

Nathaniel ran a hand over his face, resignation pulling at his features. "I'm sorry, Ranger. I'm so sorry. None of it was my idea."

Simmy sucked in a breath. What did that mean?

Her heart pounded in her ears as she waited for the man to explain.

thirty-five

EMOTIONS CHURNED INSIDE RANGER.

Not just emotions.

Anger.

Anger that could explode.

He didn't want that to happen, especially not in front of Simmy.

So he needed to keep himself under control.

And he would.

But first, Nathaniel needed to explain himself.

"John told me Anastasia had been abducted." Ranger's voice sounded strained as he started. "By the time I found her she had drowned."

Nathaniel swallowed hard and glanced at the fireplace. Finally, he admitted, "It's . . . complicated."

"I'm barely holding it together right now." Ranger said the words as a warning.

This was his daughter they were talking about. This

wasn't an innocent civilian caught in the crossfire. Those had been bad enough.

But Ranger was talking about the flesh of his flesh.

Nathaniel raised his hands. "I know. I know, man." He leaned back and sucked in a breath, the struggle obvious in his expression. "I guess it doesn't matter now since John and Shannon are dead."

"My patience is wearing thin." Ranger's words came out in a growl.

Simmy placed a hand on his back, her touch bringing him a moment of comfort.

Nathaniel swallowed again. "These men came. Took Anastasia. They told John and Shannon that if they said anything, they'd kill Melanie."

"John and Shannon's oldest daughter?"

Nathaniel nodded. "She has a family of her own in Montana. Melanie had told her parents about a new couple they'd befriended recently. They'd even sent pictures of them all hanging out. That couple . . . they weren't really friends. Melanie and her husband had been set up. John and Shannon knew their daughter would be killed."

Ranger's jaw hardened. "What about Anastasia? Did they think about her?"

"They did. These men didn't want to kill her. She was still safe. Just not with John and Shannon. These men gave them very specific instructions about what to tell you."

Ranger's throat ached at the thought of everything.

The deception. The betrayal.

"You should have come to me with the truth. I went to my daughter's funeral! You're the one who told me not to look in the casket." Anger simmered in his voice.

"I didn't know what else to do. John and Shannon . . . they were torn up about it. But they couldn't risk their own daughter." Nathaniel ran a hand through his hair.

"Who took her?" Ranger demanded.

"I have no idea. I promise. I don't know anything else."

Ranger had trusted John and Shannon. How could they have done this to him? To Anastasia?

"Do you have any idea where Anastasia is now?" Ranger finally asked.

"According to John and Shannon, Vivian had a falling out with her family and fled Russia."

"Where did she go?" Ranger demanded.

"I heard she's somewhere in Alaska." Nathaniel paused and shook his head. "John looked for her. He felt terrible about what happened, and he wanted to do something on his own. But he didn't find her."

Ranger's jaw tightened.

He was going to change that.

He was going to find his daughter.

When he did, he wouldn't trust anyone else to take care of her ever again.

Only him.

———

SIMMY COULDN'T BEGIN to imagine how Ranger might feel as she listened to the conversation.

His daughter was alive.

His friends had lied to him.

Those very friends were now dead. Murdered.

Simmy wanted to reach out to him. To try to offer some type of comfort.

Instead, she kept her hand on his back, hoping her touch would help a little. She watched the emotions wash over his face. Felt the anger the racing through him until his muscles vibrated.

Then there was Nathaniel.

Simmy tried to get a good read on the man. He seemed truly upset over what had happened. But another part of her still didn't trust the guy.

Was he really innocent in all of this? Clueless about everything?

It was hard to say.

She didn't know the man well enough to make a proper assessment. But the stakes here were too high not to be cautious. Not to scrutinize every word and action.

Nathaniel drew weary eyes up to meet Ranger's. "What can I do for you?"

Ranger remained stiff as he said, "We need a place to lie low for the night until we can figure out our next step."

"You're welcome here, of course." He paused and then shifted. "Did you tell anybody about John and Shannon? Do I need to call someone?"

"I had a friend call the state police. Troopers should be there now, and it won't surprise me if you get a call soon."

Nathaniel nodded slowly before pressing his fingers into his eyes as if to stop a leak. "I still can't believe it. Becca is going to be devastated."

"There's a lot that's hard to believe, isn't there?" Ranger's voice cut through the air.

Simmy normally avoided conflict, but she understood the clashing emotions Ranger must feel.

Joy that Anastasia was still alive.

Anger that he'd been lied to.

"I don't have any spare bedrooms here," Nathaniel continued. "So you two will have to sleep on these couches out here. Help yourself to anything in the kitchen."

"What about a first aid kit?" Simmy glanced at the spot on Ranger's arm where the bullet had skimmed.

The blood had coagulated, and the wound was no longer bleeding, but it still needed to be tended to.

"It's in the bathroom." Nathaniel stood. "I'll bring out some blankets and pillows. And, man . . . I'm really sorry. I mean that. This has been hard on all of us."

Ranger didn't say anything, but Simmy felt the rumble in his chest, almost as if he were letting out a silent growl.

Simmy knew he'd probably have more questions in the morning.

It was getting late. The best thing they could do was to get some rest.

Then they could reevaluate the situation and come up with a plan.

But the seriousness of the situation pressed on her.

Men were chasing her and trying to kill her.

But something was obviously going on with Ranger too. Someone had killed his friends—and killed them recently.

His daughter was out there somewhere, and Simmy knew he was determined to find her.

They were swimming in a sea of danger right now, and Simmy wasn't sure how they would ever get out.

thirty-six

RANGER'S ADRENALINE continued to pump.

Nathaniel had brought out blankets and pillows. He'd also found a first aid kit, but Ranger wasn't too concerned about treating his wound. It would be fine.

Nathaniel had told them to help themselves, so Simmy had found some bread and cheese in the kitchen and brought it to the table to eat. Then she made them some tea. While she did that, Ranger cleaned himself up.

Meanwhile, Nathaniel had disappeared into his room. State troopers had called him and told him the news. They'd be coming tomorrow to ask him some questions.

Ranger knew the man was grieving, and he felt bad about that. Losing people you cared about was incredibly hard. But the other part of him couldn't get past the man's deception.

Nathaniel had known Anastasia was still alive and helped cover it up.

How could he do that to a friend?

He understood having to protect others. But still . . . there had to be another way.

John, Shannon, and Nathaniel could have told him the truth. Could have asked for help and protection.

Instead, they'd allowed this to happen. Had allowed Ranger to believe for two years that his daughter was dead.

How was he even supposed to cope with this reality?

Night had fallen outside as he and Simmy munched on their food and drank their tea.

Ranger saw the questions in Simmy's gaze, but she kept quiet, probably giving him space to process everything.

It was one more thing to appreciate about her.

After Simmy took the last bite of her bread, she picked up the first aid kit and sat beside him. "We need to clean your wound."

"It's fine. Just a scrape."

"It still needs to be cleaned. You're lucky it wasn't any deeper." She gave him a knowing look.

Ranger couldn't argue with that.

She reached for his shirt and gently rolled up the sleeve.

His throat tightened at her nearness.

He didn't want to be aware of her touch. But how could he not be? His skin felt alive, and his heart raced out of control.

She opened the kit and pulled out some saline solution. She poured the liquid on some gauze and then began to gently blot his wound.

He ignored the sting. He'd felt worse. Much worse.

"I'm really sorry, Ranger," she said softly. "I can't imagine how you feel."

"I can't believe John and Shannon kept this from me."

"I know it must be difficult. I imagine John and Shannon were in a hard spot also."

Her words made sense, even if Ranger didn't want to accept them. All he felt right now was his own pain.

She dabbed his wound more before placing the gauze on the table and reaching for the antibiotic ointment.

"You're going to find her, Ranger. I know you will."

How did Simmy always manage to soothe him like that? No one else had ever been capable of it. But something about Simmy was different.

She opened a large Band-Aid, pulled off the tabs, and placed it over his wound.

Then she rolled his shirt sleeve down and smoothed it. "All better."

Yes, it was all better. Everything was always all better when Simmy was around.

That thought terrified him. Because he'd told himself he wouldn't let anyone else into his life.

But he feared it was too late.

He already had.

———

SIMMY'S HANDS TREMBLED.

This time, it wasn't from fear.

It was from Ranger.

Because of how close she sat to him.

Because she was all too aware how his skin felt beneath her fingers as she tended to his wound.

It was the fire.

It was everything they'd been through together.

She'd admired Ranger for a long time. But he'd always seemed off-limits. Emotionally closed. Had an edge of danger.

He shifted to face her and paused. Only mere inches lingered between them.

She didn't make an effort to move back, and neither did he.

"Do you remember the first time we met?" he started.

A smile feathered her lips. "How could I forget? You came into the trading post to buy supplies. While you were there, I had to go help someone at the gas pump. Except I slipped on the ice. It was almost like you expected it to happen."

"I just happened to glance outside."

Her smile widened. "You went out there and scooped me up. I'd sprained my ankle. But you bandaged it and told me everything would be okay. Then you'd fixed me some soup and insisted I sit down, that you would take my shift."

"Lloyd wasn't happy about that."

She let out a quick chuckle. Lloyd was her boss, and

the man was both lazy and a jerk. "He wasn't happy. But he didn't question you. He knew better."

Ranger's eyes danced with memories.

"I didn't know that would be the beginning of . . ." She stopped herself as she realized what she was about to say.

"Of what?"

She swallowed hard. Of her falling in love? She couldn't say those words aloud.

What would Ranger think?

She thought he shared her feelings. But . . . she couldn't risk it.

"The beginning of a wonderful friendship," she finally said.

"Yes, it was."

Her throat swelled. "I used to anticipate when you'd come into the trading post. I always looked forward to it. Seeing you was the highlight of my week."

Something shifted in his gaze. "I'm glad to hear that."

Simmy's mind raced. She pictured what it would be like if they kissed. If she opened herself up to love. What it would be like if her future looked bright instead of like a bleak reminder of her mistakes.

"I've never met anyone like you, Simmy," Ranger murmured. "Someone so selfless. Someone who loves people so deeply. Who earns trust so easily."

Her throat continued to swell.

She wanted to let herself go. To enjoy the moment. To relish his words.

But she would be doing both of them a disservice if she did that.

She swallowed hard before saying, "Ranger . . . there's a lot about me you don't know."

"I know enough."

If only Simmy believed that . . . but she knew it wasn't the truth.

There was only one way to prove that to him.

She swallowed hard, nearly choking on the words she was about to say. "What if I told you I'd killed someone?"

thirty-seven

RANGER GAVE himself a moment to process Simmy's words.

He hadn't expected the question to leave her lips. But she clearly needed to get it off her chest. He could see she was still shaken and felt guilty over whatever had happened.

"I'd say if you killed someone then you had a really good reason for it," he finally said.

Her eyes remained orbs of emotion. "What if I didn't?"

That wasn't even a thought he'd consider. "I know you. You did."

Her gaze remained tumultuous, as if she tried to decide if she could believe his words or not. She'd clearly wrestled with something for a long time.

Ranger wished she would open up to him. That she'd share the memories behind the emotions in her gaze.

But he didn't push.

Besides, her past didn't matter to him. He liked Simmy just as she was.

But whatever had happened seemed to matter to her.

His gaze locked on hers. "Simmy . . . I've done some things I'm not proud of also. Everyone has."

Ranger used his thumb to wipe away the tears that washed down her face.

He wished more than anything he could take away her pain.

But there was only One who could do that.

God.

Not Ranger.

He'd all but abandoned God after everything that had happened with Anastasia. Then he'd met Duke McAllister, who'd told him how his life had been changed through God.

Ranger had opened his Bible again after that. He'd been praying more. Searching for answers.

Wanting to believe.

He leaned closer to Simmy, but their lips didn't touch. Not quite.

The energy between them made him feel as if they were connected without ever touching.

"Simmy, I've known from the moment I set eyes on you that you were special," Ranger murmured. "And I've also known that I'm all wrong for you."

Her eyes widened, and she looked as if she was barely breathing. "Why would you be wrong for me?"

"I'm the definition of someone with baggage."

"Honestly, so am I. You don't get to our age and end up in the middle of nowhere, Alaska, without some baggage."

He let out a soft chuckle. "I get that."

She licked her lips. "Maybe . . . maybe we met for a reason."

"I'd like to think so."

He stared at the pools of emotion in her eyes. At her lips that were so full. At her long and inviting neck.

More than anything he wanted to kiss her.

But he also didn't want to scare her away.

He needed to show how much he respected her.

He pressed his lips together as he contemplated how to proceed.

———

SIMMY STARED UP AT RANGER. At those green eyes of his. Those distinguished cheekbones. The messy dark hair.

She'd never felt so at home with someone as she did with him.

In fact, she couldn't imagine her future without him.

At times, that thought terrified her.

Right now, it didn't.

Right now, all she could hear was her heartbeat in her ears.

All she could feel was Ranger's body heat radiating on her skin.

She wasn't sure what she was doing.

Probably making a mistake.

But she reached for him. Her fingers trailed his jaw. Crept closer to his hairline. Toyed with a strand at the base of his neck.

Her other hand rested on his uninjured shoulder. Grasped the strong muscles beneath her fingers.

Her throat was dry. Her mouth felt dry. Her lips even suddenly felt dry.

What was wrong with her? She hadn't thought she'd ever feel this way again.

For that matter, she'd never felt this strongly about someone before.

"Simmy," Ranger whispered.

That was all it had taken to break down her walls.

The next instant, their lips met. She didn't know if she'd initiated it or if Ranger had.

She only knew that, at once, the kiss felt both brand-new and like they'd done this a million times before.

His lips tugged at hers, both hunger and restraint in the action.

She pulled him closer, wanting to disappear into his embrace.

Perhaps it was everything that had happened. Perhaps it was adrenaline. Perhaps it was the danger.

But Simmy's gut told her there was more to what was happening between them than that.

She never wanted this moment to end.

However, she needed to douse some of the fire between them before things got out of control.

Reluctantly, she drew back—though barely.

Their foreheads still touched.

Her arms still clung to his neck.

Ranger's fingers still pressed into her back as he held her close.

Simmy sucked in ragged gulps of air, only then realizing how breathless she felt.

For a moment, hope had returned. Hope that maybe she had a chance at happiness in the future.

Happiness with Ranger.

But she also knew that reality was brutal and apathetic. That the odds were stacked against them.

That they both had their own demons to battle.

"Simmy?" Ranger sounded soft and tender as he said her name.

"Yes?" The lump formed in her throat again.

Then Ranger leaned down. His lips covered hers again.

She let herself get lost in the moment, knowing full well that reality would hit them again soon.

But right now, she'd enjoy this time with the best man she'd ever known.

thirty-eight
Then

AFTER CHARLOTTE HAD CALLED 911, she'd called Mark.

He'd rushed home when he'd heard the news about Meredith.

She was dead, and he was devastated, to say the least.

In the following days, there was little she could do to comfort him. So she'd place her hand on his back when he looked sad. Whenever he needed, she let him talk to the baby.

A suicide note had been found confirming Meredith had taken her own life.

The police hadn't truly opened an investigation. Everyone had been interviewed, of course. But apparently, Meredith's medical records showed how emotionally unstable she'd been.

Her death had been a terrible tragedy.

The days after Meredith died had been a blur of activity.

Mark had taken off work for the first week so he could arrange the funeral. He'd insisted that Charlotte sit with him and his family during the service. For the baby's sake, he'd said. But Charlotte noticed people giving her weird looks. She tried to ignore them.

Charlotte was surprised Meredith had done something like this so close to the arrival of the baby. She'd thought the child would bring Meredith hope.

But maybe the woman's depression and mental health issues were too deeply ingrained for her to see the light. Charlotte hated to think that anyone would feel that lost. But she knew they could.

However, all the changes felt like too much. Meredith was gone. Mark would be a single dad. The baby, Lexi—Mark and Meredith had named her recently—growing inside Charlotte would soon be snatched away, and Charlotte would be forced to resume life as if the child had never been a part of her.

This was what she'd signed up for. Charlotte had just never imagined life would take such a turn.

Six weeks after Meredith died, and three weeks before her due date, Charlotte was sleeping when the sound of her door opening awakened her.

She sat up with a start, her heart stammering out of control. Was it an intruder? Who else would come into her room in the middle of the night?

"Who's there?" she whispered.

The only other person in the house was Mark. But he *never* came into her bedroom.

"Charlotte . . . I'm sorry." Mark's figure came into view. His flannel pants—expensive, no doubt. His bare chest. Ruffled hair.

Grief-stricken eyes.

Charlotte's heart softened, but her guard remained up. What was he doing in here? And why was he sorry? "Sorry about what?"

"Sorry to come in here like this." His voice cracked as if he'd been crying. "It's just that . . . I miss her so much."

Compassion flooded her, and she turned toward him. "I know. I'm so sorry."

"I just want . . . I just need to feel close to the baby."

Charlotte's heart thudded in her ears. What did that even mean?

She waited for him to continue, not daring to jump to any conclusions.

"Can I . . . ?" He stepped closer to the bed and pointed at it. "Can I just lie here with my hand on your stomach? I know it's unconventional. But the baby . . . makes me feel closer to Meredith. Makes my heart not hurt as much."

Say no, an internal voice told her.

Then she saw Mark's face. Saw the anguish there.

How could she say no? How could she turn away someone in pain?

She scooted over in bed, and Mark climbed under the covers. As she turned to face the opposite direction of him, he wrapped his arm around her and placed his hand on her belly.

"Thank you, Charlotte," he murmured. "You are a good woman."

His body seemed to mold into hers, almost as if it belonged.

A few minutes later, he began to breathe softly, evenly.

He was asleep.

Charlotte, however, was not.

She was wide awake.

All too aware of Mark against her. Of his hand on her stomach. Of his baby inside her.

Unconventional? Yes. But this whole surrogacy had been unconventional.

She should have done more research into how these things worked. But she'd walked into the job blindly. She'd been so desperate for a place to live that she agreed too quickly to live here.

Mark breathed softly behind her, not quite a snore.

Was this the first good sleep Mark had gotten since Meredith died?

She couldn't imagine what it must feel like to wrestle with the suicide of a spouse. It would be . . . terrible. So terrible.

Sure, this arrangement right now was weird. But it was okay.

As long as they didn't cross any more lines, Charlotte would be fine.

Then why did she still feel so much unease?

thirty-nine
Now

Ranger had slept on one couch and Simmy on the other while the fireplace warmed them.

The flames matched the warmth in his heart from knowing that Simmy returned his feelings. But feelings were a dangerous thing to have, especially considering his former profession.

He hoped he didn't regret their kiss.

But not because of Simmy. He'd never regret falling for her.

Instead, it had everything to do with the danger that followed him wherever he went.

He'd made a lot of enemies in his line of work. People who wouldn't hesitate to kill him.

That made his future feel murky and uncertain at times.

Nathaniel arose early and started cooking some eggs

and bacon while a pot of coffee brewed. As he prepared breakfast and Simmy got ready for the day, Ranger stepped outside to get some fresh air. He had no desire to make small talk with Nathaniel as he cooked.

Not after learning about the secrets Nathaniel had kept from him. Maybe Ranger would eventually get over it, but right now everything felt too fresh.

Several minutes later, Nathaniel said breakfast was ready, and they all met in the kitchen. Simmy flashed Ranger a smile that made him want to forget everything and just spend the day with her in his arms.

But that wasn't a possibility.

As the three of them sat at the table to eat, Ranger noticed Nathaniel kept his eyes averted and seemed unusually quiet.

Ranger bit into his bacon, chewed, and swallowed before asking, "What aren't you telling me?"

Nathaniel paused, a fork full of egg in the air. "What do you mean?"

"I can read you. I know there's more going on than what you're telling me." Ranger used all his self-control to keep his emotions in check. Anger simmered through him, but he wasn't sure yet if it was righteous.

"I don't know what you mean." Nathaniel let out a chuckle, followed by a shrug to brush off his words.

Ranger's anger grew hotter. "You and I both know that's not true. What else do you know about Anastasia?"

"Nothing, man."

Ranger's hands fisted. "Nathaniel . . . stop lying to me."

Nathaniel lowered his fork and raked a hand through his hair. The ultimate giveaway that, yes, there was something else on his mind.

He blew out a long breath. "I didn't know how to tell you. So I've kept it quiet."

"You need to start talking." Ranger's words came out biting, almost like a growl.

Nathaniel ran a hand over his face. "A week ago, John and Shannon thought they had found some information about Anastasia. I wanted to verify it before I told you."

"What kind of information?" Ranger pushed his plate away, no longer hungry.

Simmy wasn't eating either. She sat there quietly, listening and probably ready to intercede if things got too ugly.

"John and Shannon had been trying to figure out where Vivian took Anastasia," Nathaniel said. "They believed Vivian has been living in Alaska with Anastasia since she took her. Think about it . . . the United States is the safest option compared to the other countries surrounding Russia. Plus, it would be fairly easy for Vivian to catch a boat and come to the shores of Alaska. She probably had someone meet her and take her somewhere to start a new life."

"You think Vivian is living in Anchorage or something?" Simmy eyes widened with surprise.

"Probably not Anchorage," Ranger said. "She'll be

hidden away somewhere no one will find her. Her family has a lot of money, and I'm sure she left with her fair share. She can buy whatever she needs."

Questions glimmered in Simmy's gaze. "Even enough to hire men to kill John and Shannon?"

Ranger's only answer was a grimace.

Simmy let out a soft *hmm*.

Ranger turned back to Nathaniel, more questions pressing on him. "What did John and Shannon find out about Vivian's location?"

Nathaniel hesitated again, something shifting in his gaze. "They believe she ended up outside Tok."

Tok? Ranger's mind raced. That wasn't terribly far away, one of the first towns after people crossed the Canadian border into Alaska.

"Did they say anything else?" Ranger asked.

Nathaniel shook his head, the grief deepening in his gaze. "No, they wanted to find out more. They kept digging, and I'm afraid that's what got them killed."

———

THREE HOURS LATER, they were ready to go.

Nathaniel had helped them charter a bush plane to Tok. Ranger had said the helicopter wouldn't get them there.

Thankfully, the field outside Nathaniel's place was large enough to use as a small runway. Blaze, the pilot, waited for them to board the plane. He was probably in his early thirties, with thick dark hair, intelligent eyes, and an outgoing personality. Something about him screamed "daredevil," though she couldn't pinpoint what.

As they said goodbye to Nathaniel, Simmy's thoughts wandered through possibilities of how this would play out.

Every time Simmy looked up at the mountains in the distance, she felt a tremble of fear. A bush pilot had come into the trading post one time and told her just how dangerous the profession was. Told her about all the crashes in Alaska because of the harsh landscape.

She'd never forgotten those stories. Now the thought of flying over those mountains seemed too scary for her comfort.

"Are you ready for this?" Ranger paused beside the plane and studied her. "I'm sure you could stay here with Nathaniel, and I could come back for you."

She didn't even have to think about her response. "No, I'm going with you."

It didn't matter how scared she was of flying over the mountains in that small plane. She was sticking with Ranger.

He leaned closer, and his hand cupped her neck. His lips brushed her forehead.

Simmy flushed at his affection.

The moment was brief—but his touch was all she needed to reassure her. To fill her with hope.

But hope was a dangerous thing—especially with her past. She reminded herself to be cautious. To be logical.

To protect Ranger while he protected her.

Maybe the best way to do that was by keeping her distance.

She swallowed hard. That was something she would need to figure out later.

"Okay then," he finally said. "We'll have to talk about our next plan of action once we land. For now, we need to go."

She nodded and looked down at Mr. Knightly. The dog had been following her around since they'd met, and being at Nathaniel's hadn't changed that.

"What about you, boy?" she murmured.

"He can stay with me. John and Shannon would want that." Nathaniel's voice faded with wistfulness.

Simmy nodded. She'd halfway hoped to take the dog with them, but she knew it was safer for Mr. Knightly to stay here. Who knew what she and Ranger would face once they landed in Tok.

Ranger extended his hand toward his friend. "Thank you for everything you've done for us. And, again, I'm sorry for your loss."

"Of course." Nathaniel nodded stiffly, still either distant or grief-stricken or both after everything that had happened. "You guys be careful. I'll be in touch."

After one more head rub for Mr. Knightly, Ranger led Simmy to the plane, her backpack slung over one of her shoulders. He helped her into the back seat before climbing into the front with Blaze.

A few minutes later, they were ready to take off.

Ranger seemed to sense her fear and reached back. Took her hand in his.

The action felt natural, as if they'd done it a million times before.

"Squeeze as hard as you need to," Ranger said.

"Thank you."

Then the plane started down the makeshift runway.

This was only part of her worries: getting to Tok in a plane that looked older than the state of Alaska.

But she knew more challenges would be waiting once they landed.

They would need to find Vivian.

Then Ranger would need to get Anastasia.

She couldn't forget about Knave and the way he was pursuing her.

Second Corinthians 4:8–9 filled her mind.

"We are hard pressed on every side, but not crushed; perplexed, but not in despair; persecuted, but not abandoned; struck down, but not destroyed."

Lord, let that be my prayer.

Help us to not be destroyed.

forty

AN HOUR AND A HALF LATER, they landed.

Ranger felt Simmy's relief as they taxied down the runway. For the entire flight, she'd squeezed his hand. He'd watched her. Half the time, she'd looked terrified. The other half, she'd looked fascinated.

The mountains were beautiful, as were the glaciers, lakes, and ice fields.

Beautiful but dangerous.

Like Vivian.

His throat tightened at the thought of her.

He'd heard rumors Vivian might be in Alaska. But he'd suspected she was up north, which was one of the reasons he'd begun to work at Gates of the Arctic. In his spare time, he'd searched for her.

She needed to pay for the trauma she'd put their daughter through. For betraying him.

Ranger didn't know what he'd do when he found

Vivian. He prayed for the Lord's wisdom and that he didn't do something he'd regret.

But Vivian wouldn't get away with what she'd done. Ranger would make sure of that.

He'd borrowed Nathaniel's satellite phone and made a few calls before the flight. He knew in order to successfully complete his mission, he couldn't do it by himself.

He had no doubt Vivian had hired security agents to watch out for her.

Ranger could *not* blow this operation. He had to find Vivian and then, in return, find Anastasia.

He and Simmy stepped off the plane at the tiny airport.

The sun shone down on them as they paused near the steps. The place was simple with several aluminum-sided hangars scattered around the runway.

Blaze motioned for them to follow him into a hangar.

The flight had already been paid for—Nathaniel had covered the cost, although Ranger promised to pay him back once this was over.

The visit in the hangar was for another reason.

Ranger was expecting company. He glanced at his watch.

The others should be here at any time.

The three of them stepped inside the space, which was probably big enough for a couple of planes. There was a desk, a large toolbox, and some other equipment.

"Make yourselves comfortable," Blaze told them. "I'm

meeting a friend for lunch while I'm here in town, but I'll be back in an hour. You need anything?"

Ranger shook his head. "We're good."

"Perfect. Thank you for your business."

As soon as Blaze walked away, Ranger turned to Simmy and pulled her into his arms. "Thank you for being here with me."

A soft smile tugged at her lips as she gazed up at him. "I could say the same for you. At least being here has thrown Knave off my trail."

"Knave?" It was the first time she'd said his name.

She nodded into his chest. "That was what all his guys called him, and it seems more fitting than his given name, which is pretty innocuous."

"It sounds like Knave is a piece of work."

"That may be the understatement of the year." Her voice quivered. "This is what I have feared would happen for many, many years."

Ranger stroked her back. "You don't have to be afraid. I'm here with you."

Simmy's body melted into his. "I know you'll do everything in your power to protect me. But I also know Knave will do everything in his power to hurt me. I don't want to see you get caught in those crosshairs."

"Don't worry about me. I'll keep us both safe."

She nestled her head beneath his chin. "You don't know Knave. You don't know the extent of his evil. How soulless he can be."

"I've dealt with the scum of the earth before," Ranger muttered. "I can do it again."

Before Simmy could respond, a car pulled up.

Ranger froze, caution flaring to life inside him. He couldn't afford to let down his guard or to assume anything.

Who was inside that vehicle? A friend or foe?

———

THE AIR RUSHED from Simmy's lungs when she saw the SUV.

Then she recognized the people inside.

A moment later, Duke McAllister and Andi Slade stepped from the vehicle. Her lungs loosened, and pent-up air rushed out.

Duke with his GI Joe vibes. Andi with her white-blonde hair, blue eyes, and petite build.

Simmy hurried from the hangar toward them and pulled Andi into a hug. "I'm so glad you're here."

Andi returned the hug with equal fervor. "I'm glad to be here."

Then Simmy hugged Duke.

These people were more than friends. They felt like family.

They were fellow members of the Arctic Circle Murder Club. Duke was a former Army investigator, and Andi had been a defense attorney back in Texas.

They were both tough in their own right—Duke as a former cop, and Andi with her determination and smarts.

"We've been worried about you." Andi stepped closer and rested her hand on Simmy's arm.

Simmy placed her hand over Andi's and squeezed. "I didn't mean to make you worry. But there was something I had to do, and it couldn't wait."

"Did it have to do with the fact your identity was leaked?" Andi studied Simmy's face as she waited for an answer.

Simmy nodded, not bothering to hide the truth. "Unfortunately, yes."

Andi frowned.

Simmy wished she could take away some of her guilt. She knew Andi blamed herself.

Andi had been trying to bring down a man named Victor Goodman for years. She feared he was responsible for the leak of their identities and that he'd done it to punish Andi and make her back off.

She turned to Ranger. "And Ranger . . . I hardly recognized you. I like the tidier look."

He rubbed the fresh stubble on his chin. "Thanks."

"He looks amazing," Andi whispered to her.

Simmy couldn't argue. Sometimes, she had to remind herself not to stare.

Before they could talk any longer, Ranger directed them back into the hangar. Just as they stepped inside, another plane landed in the distance.

The group turned to watch as Apollo disembarked.

Seeing how Apollo had fought off those gunmen while Simmy and Ranger had escaped, the man was clearly CIA.

The more Simmy learned, the more everything made sense.

Ranger called them together in the middle of the hangar and made introductions. When he reached Apollo, he said, "He's an old friend from the CIA."

"The CIA?" Duke raised his eyebrows.

"Long story."

"I knew there was more to your past than you let on." Andi nodded, her eyes narrow with thought.

"There's a lot more to all of us, I'd say." Ranger gave them all a pointed look.

No one could argue that.

Ranger snapped back to the mission at hand. "Now that we're all here, I need to go over a game plan."

forty-one

RANGER HAD LEFT Andi and Simmy at the hangar while he went with Duke and Apollo.

He hated to do it. But bringing the women with him would be too risky. The women should be safe for a while. Plus, he felt better having Andi there with Simmy. She operated well under pressure and thought quickly on her feet.

Based on what Nathaniel had told him, Ranger knew the basic area where Vivian might be living. What he didn't know was how many men she'd have guarding her place. That put him at a disadvantage.

His hopes—at the simplest level—were that he could rescue Anastasia, come back, and they could escape. He knew it was more complicated than that. But everything else would fall in place.

During the thirty-minute drive, Ranger filled his friends in on everything, told them what to expect, what his goals were. Duke and Apollo were both on board with him.

A half mile before the location, Ranger motioned for Duke to pull to the side of the road. "We should go the rest of the way on foot."

They hiked the half mile down the lane before pausing near a wrought-iron fence surrounding a massive estate. The Gothic-style gates were decorated with ornamental gargoyles and other mythical creatures, making the property appear as if it were fit for royalty—dark royalty.

Typical Vivian. Even when she was hiding, she had to be extravagant.

As Ranger stared at the stone-faced house nestled in the mountains, he tried to imagine Anastasia here. The place looked so cold and uninviting.

She needed somewhere with animals and a playground. Not somewhere fancy with a massive iron fence enclosing it.

"We need to figure out how many guards are around this place," Ranger told his team. "Let's split up and meet back here in twenty."

"I'll go left," Duke said.

"I'll go right," Apollo said.

Ranger nodded. "I'll stay here and keep an eye on the front of the place."

This was Ranger's chance to get his daughter back.

He prayed he didn't blow it.

————

SIMMY AND ANDI stood in the hangar, biding their time until the men returned.

Simmy prayed their mission went well. That Ranger could find some answers. That everyone stayed safe.

Andi peered at Simmy a moment before saying, "I'm so glad you're okay. I wasn't sure I'd ever see you again."

Simmy pulled her gaze away from the mountains and offered Andi a fragile smile. "It's been . . . rough, to say the least."

Something flashed through Andi's gaze. Concern? Curiosity? Maybe both.

"I'm glad Ranger is with you," Andi finally said.

Simmy rubbed her arms, ignoring her goosebumps. Andi's words clearly had a deeper meaning.

Had other people seen what was brewing between her and Ranger? It was possible. Simmy hadn't exactly tried to hide her feelings.

"Ranger has been a lifesaver," Simmy said. "In more ways than one."

Andi's lips tugged up in a smile. "I'm sure he has been. He's a good man."

"Yes, he is. I'm glad God brought him into my life. I'm glad He brought all of you into my life." Simmy meant the words. She'd thought about the sentiment on many occasions.

The murder club had been a true blessing. Being part of the group had given her purpose again. Made her feel like more than a lost soul on the run.

"God has a way of working things out, doesn't He?" Andi murmured. "I think we all needed each other."

Simmy rubbed her throat. "You think our group is over and done?"

Things had ended poorly between the murder club members last time they were together. Lately, their strong personalities had been clashing. Six people trying to make decisions as a group could be challenging.

If they could figure out how to play off their differences and make them work in their favor, they'd be unstoppable.

But that would take time and effort.

Simmy wasn't sure everyone was willing to give the group that time.

She prayed they could work things out.

"I hope we're not done." Andi headed toward a Keurig in the distance and helped herself to a cup of coffee. "I think God still has things He wants us to do as a group."

"Me too." Simmy smiled. Then she glanced at the open door of the hangar, and a worried frown replaced the grin. "I really hope the guys are okay, Andi."

"They're all very capable men. Well, I don't know Apollo. But if Ranger trusts him, then I do too." The machine gurgled, and Andi grabbed her cup. "What's been going on since you took off?"

Simmy opened her mouth, ready to explain what happened, why she'd left so suddenly.

Before she could, the sound of a motor cut through the air.

Someone was driving up to the hangar. But who?

She peered out a window but didn't recognize the approaching car.

However, the two men inside wore all black . . . and reminded her an awful lot of the men who'd been tracking her and Ranger.

When Andi moved to see who it was, Simmy pulled her back. "We can't let them see us. These guys are trouble."

forty-two
Then

MARK HAD DECIDED THAT, since the nearest medical facility was forty minutes away, a home birth would be better.

Dr. Matthews lived five houses down, and he'd agreed to deliver the baby when the time came. All Mark had to do was call, and the doctor—officially retired—could be to the house in less than ten minutes.

Charlotte wasn't sure how she felt about the plan, but Mark sounded very confident it was the best idea.

Mark was older and wiser than she was, *and* being here seemed more comfortable than going to the hospital. Charlotte had always hated hospitals—especially after she'd had an emergency appendectomy when she was six.

In the meantime, during the last two weeks of her pregnancy, Mark had insisted on working from home. He didn't seem to want to leave her side.

Charlotte should have said no that first night when he'd come into her room to be with the baby.

Because every night afterward, he paid her visits.

He never made any romantic moves. He only cuddled up beside her, his hand on her belly. Charlotte continued to tell herself these were the actions of a grieving man. That there was nothing strange about it. That different people grieved in different ways.

Currently, she stood in the kitchen, drinking a glass of water as Mark downed some freshly pressed juice. He'd just finished working out in the home gym downstairs, something he did on a regular basis.

"Hey, you," Mark murmured. "How's your day going?"

"Not bad." She was bored and achy, but otherwise fine. But he didn't need to know all those details.

Just then an all-consuming pain spread through her abdomen.

She bent forward so quickly that her drink slipped from her hands.

The glass shattered on the tile floor.

She didn't care.

A moan escaped from somewhere deep inside her.

"Charlotte?" Mark rushed to her side, carefully stepping over the glass. "What's wrong?"

"It's . . ." She held her stomach. "The baby . . . I think she's coming."

"Are you sure the contraction is real?"

Was she sure? Absolutely not. She'd never had a baby

before. She wasn't sure what this was supposed to feel like. Death? Agony?

Then, yes. The contraction was real.

"Charlotte?"

She bent forward again as another contraction hit her. It came in a wave, traveling from the top of her abdomen to the bottom. Her muscles squeezed, and the pressure on her back took her breath away.

"I'm calling Dr. Matthews." Mark grabbed the phone from his pocket.

She didn't argue, especially when water gushed between her legs.

A few seconds later, Mark ended the call and turned back to her. "Let's get you back to the delivery room."

Yes, he'd already thought of everything.

The room where Charlotte would deliver Lexi had already been set up. All the equipment was there as well as a hospital bed and bassinet. The space was sterile but functional.

Mark helped her inside. Helped her sit on the bed. Helped her change into a hospital gown.

She tried not to feel self-conscious. She knew Mark wanted to be present for the birth. That had been the plan all along, even back when Meredith was alive. They'd wanted to see their child being born.

So this was no time for modesty.

"Breathe in," Mark instructed her as he gripped her hand. "Hold it. Now exhale. You're doing great. You've got this, Charlotte."

She didn't feel as if she had this at all.

The doorbell rang.

"It must be Dr. Matthews," Mark told her. "I'll be right back."

Dr. Matthews appeared a few minutes later.

Mark turned away as the doctor checked her. He said Charlotte was well on the way to giving birth. That she was already dilated, and things were moving along quickly. So quickly that there wasn't time for an epidural.

"No epidural?" Her words came out as a gasp.

Mark appeared at her side again, instantly reaching for her hand and squeezing. "It's better this way. An epidural will only make the birth take longer."

Charlotte didn't care. She'd rather a long, less-painful birth than a shorter agony-filled one.

But no one seemed to listen to her. She'd hoped Mark might advocate for her. But he seemed intent on doing things his way.

For the first time in a long time, she wanted her mom. But she knew her mom would only make a situation like this more stressful. Besides, they hadn't talked in almost a year now.

Three hours later, the pain nearly made her pass out. Sweat dripped from every pore. She couldn't stop screaming.

"You've got to push," Mark coached her, still beside her and holding her hand.

"I can't," she groaned. "It hurts so bad. I can't do this!"

"Yes, you can," Mark insisted. "You can do this, Charlotte."

"I need something for the pain. Please."

Mark and the doctor exchanged a glance.

Then Dr. Matthews injected something into her IV. "This should help some. But I still need you to push."

"I will. I promise." As another contraction hit, she screamed.

She was never doing this again. Never.

Ten minutes later, the misery gripping her abdomen faded.

Charlotte gave a final push.

Then the pressure left her.

A cry cut the air.

Her baby . . . she was here. Crying. Safe.

Charlotte wanted to feel joy. She should feel joy. Relief.

But . . . something didn't feel right.

"Mark . . ." She thought she said his name aloud, but she wasn't sure.

"Dr. Matthews . . . I think she's crashing." Mark rushed to her side.

The doctor handed Lexi to Mark and peered at Charlotte.

He muttered something, but his words garbled in her mind.

Her vision blurred.

Her head swam.

"The baby . . ." she murmured.

She blinked. Saw Mark holding Lexi, rocking her back and forth in his arms. Heard another cry.

But everything felt fuzzy and unclear.

Then the room began to spin.

Before Charlotte could say anything else, everything went dark.

———

WHEN CHARLOTTE CAME TO AGAIN, Mark was sitting on the bed beside her.

She blinked as she tried to remember what had happened.

She reached for her stomach so she could stroke it, so she could comfort the baby.

But it felt deflated. Empty.

Then reality rushed back to her.

Her baby had been born.

The breath left her lungs at the thought.

No, *her* baby hadn't been born.

Lexi was Mark and Meredith's baby.

Charlotte glanced around the room, searching for Lexi. Waiting to hear her cry. She wanted so badly to see the baby's face. To feel the baby's soft skin. To smell the fresh scent.

But everything felt strangely silent.

Mark peered at her, uncertainty in his gaze. His lips were pressed together in a tight line, and wrinkles appeared on his forehead.

"I'm sorry, Charlotte." His words seemed to come from a distance, almost as if they hadn't left his lips, though Charlotte knew they had.

She pushed herself upright, and pain stabbed at her abdomen. Her lungs felt stiff and unmoving as she stared at Mark. "What do you mean?"

"Lexi . . . she didn't make it." His voice cracked.

A lump lodged in her throat. "W-what? But . . . she has to be okay. I saw her, heard her crying."

"I'm sorry." Mark shook his head and gripped her hand more tightly. "You must have been hallucinating. You were in a bad place. I thought we were going to lose both of you."

"She's . . . dead?" She couldn't have heard correctly.

But Mark nodded. "I'm so sorry."

"No!" A wail escaped from Charlotte.

She curled into a ball. Her body ached, still sore from childbirth. But she ignored the pain.

The discomfort was a stark reminder that she'd given birth.

But there was no baby to prove that.

"I know . . ." Mark pressed a kiss into her forehead. "I'm so sorry. So, so sorry."

He held her as she sobbed. Lexi may not have been her flesh and blood, but Charlotte felt as if the child had been.

When her sobs subsided, Charlotte looked at Mark through blurry, tear-laden eyes. Questions pummeled her. Doubts. A fresh round of hurt.

"What happened?" Her voice sounded raw.

"The umbilical cord . . . it was wrapped around her neck, and . . ." He rubbed his throat and looked away, moisture filling his gaze.

Mark's pain hit her. He'd lost his wife and now his child. And here Charlotte was thinking about herself.

She'd failed him—in more ways than one.

She couldn't find the words to say.

When Mark pulled her into his arms, she held him. He held her.

Then they both cried together.

forty-three
Now

FOUR MEN GUARDED the exterior of Vivian's place.

But not for long.

Duke and his guys had already taken them down and tied them up. The hired hands wouldn't be a threat—for now.

With that taken care of, Ranger, Apollo, and Duke headed toward the house.

Ranger knew Vivian could have another guard—or two or three—inside with her.

If she was there.

His team would have to cross that bridge when they got there.

They walked around back, climbed onto a massive stone patio, and skirted around some outdoor furniture to the sliding glass door. Duke carefully peered inside. He didn't see anyone.

When he tugged at the door, it opened.

Ranger motioned to Duke and Apollo, and they slipped inside one by one. Quietly, they spread out, each moving through a different section of the house.

Ranger paused in the kitchen and glanced around. The house was devoid of any signs of a child living here. There were no toys. No books. No junk food sitting on the counter. No art on the fridge.

No family pictures. No warmth. No homey scents even.

The place was practically a blank canvas. A cold, blank canvas.

It might as well have been a mausoleum.

His gut tightened.

What if Nathaniel had gotten this wrong? What if Vivian didn't live here at all?

Ranger's heart pounded harder in his chest at the thought.

But then why have the guards outside? She had to be here. It was the only thing that made sense.

With gun in hand, he moved through the house.

He hadn't seen any more guards so far. Could there have only been four?

Carefully, he walked up a staircase in search of the master bedroom.

He opened door after door.

He found nothing but empty rooms.

Finally, he reached the last door at the end of the hallway.

Twisted the knob.

Slowly pushed it open.

As his eyes adjusted to the dark room, he braced himself for whatever he'd find on the other side.

———

"ANDI . . ." Simmy whispered as she grabbed her friend's hand. "This way."

She pulled Andi behind a large, rolling toolbox in the corner and motioned for her to hide behind it.

"What's going on?" Andi whispered as she crouched on the concrete floor, her coffee sloshing in her hand.

"I'm pretty sure those men are the ones who've been tracking me." She started to peer out but quickly ducked again, afraid she'd be seen.

Andi's eyes widened. "They followed you here?"

"I think so, but I don't know how. Our flight to this area should have thrown them off our trail." Simmy kept her eyes fixated on the hangar door.

She didn't have much time to figure this out. She and Andi were trapped here in this corner. If those men found them . . .

She swallowed hard.

The men stepped inside the space and paused.

"Where'd they go?" One of the men scowled, gun in hand, as he stood in the middle of the hangar and glanced around.

"Your guess is as good as mine," the other one said. "We heard this is where they came."

"We need to find them. Our client is losing patience with us. We'll wait. Keep looking around."

Simmy and Andi exchanged a look. The longer those men were here, the more likely the two of them would be found.

If they were, things would turn ugly.

She peered around the toolbox at the men again. Knave had hired them, hadn't he?

They were talking about him. He was coming, wasn't he?

It was the only thing that made sense.

Her nerves stretched taut inside her.

The men began to pace the perimeter of the hangar, guns in hand. Thankfully, they started on the other side. That would buy her and Andi some time.

Andi carefully picked up a large wrench from the cart beside them and gripped it.

Simmy looked around for something she could use as a weapon also. She settled for a screwdriver. It might not be much, but it was better than nothing.

Then she braced herself.

forty-four

"**WHY DON'T** you come on in?" someone purred from the shadows. "I've been waiting for you."

Vivian.

Ranger would recognize her voice with its distinguished accent and sultry undertones anywhere.

Tension rippled across his muscles.

She'd been expecting him.

Anticipating his arrival.

Was this a trap?

Ranger gripped his gun as he stepped inside the room and glanced around.

Candles flickered around the perimeter, and an oversized bathtub rose in front of a massive window overlooking the mountains.

Vivian lounged inside.

Vivian with her black hair, cut sharply at her chin. Her expressive eyes. Full lips. Flawless skin.

Bubbles covered her body, a glass of wine sat beside her, and classical music—Rachmaninoff—played from a speaker somewhere. The cigarette at her lips created a plume of smoke around her head.

She'd been sitting here the whole time, watching everything happening outside, hadn't she?

She'd known Ranger would come, and she'd been waiting. But how? How had she known?

He would figure that out later.

"I'm surprised it took you so long." Her thick, Russian accent cut into every word. "I thought you'd be here sooner."

He stepped closer and paused. "Where is Anastasia?"

Vivian acted as if she didn't hear him. "Ranger . . . you're looking good. I like you without that big beard and bushy hair. You've always been handsome. My guards liked to call you Rambo. But I always thought you were more handsome than him. I prefer The Rock."

A growl rumbled inside him. "Where is my daughter?"

Vivian glanced out the window, still ignoring him. "I've always wondered what it would be like to live here with you. I thought you might like it. There's lots of quiet and solitude. Those things seem to fit you."

"I will *never* live anywhere with you." He barely contained the anger in his voice. "You were a mistake."

"Are you calling our daughter a mistake also?" She glanced at him, mischief dancing in her eyes as if she wanted to catch him revealing an ugly truth about himself.

"You and I both know the answer to that question." Ranger raised his gun, tired of playing Vivian's game. He pointed it at her as they locked gazes. "Now, don't make this harder than it has to be. Where is Anastasia? I know she's alive, and I know you took her. So where is she?"

———

SIMMY GRIPPED the screwdriver as the men paced closer.

Please, God . . . please.

God knew exactly what she was asking, even if the words didn't formulate in her mind.

The men paced closer. Closer. Closer.

They were headed directly to the toolbox.

Breathe, Simmy. Breathe.

In and out. In and out.

Don't pass out.

Then the footsteps stopped.

Alarm straightened her spine. Had Simmy and Andi been spotted?

"Can I help you?" a deep voice asked from the distance.

Simmy sucked in a breath.

"Who's that?" Andi whispered.

"It sounds like our pilot. His name is Blaze."

What would these men do? Would they hurt him?

She pressed her eyes closed.

The footsteps hurried away from Simmy and Andi.

Blaze may have bought them some time. But she didn't want him to pay the price either.

For now, she'd sit tight and see what happened.

"I'm Chubby—Chuck really, but Chubby is the unfortunate nickname—and this is Eric," one of the men started. "We're hoping you can help us. We're looking for the people you flew in an hour or two ago."

"The people I flew in?" Surprise cut through Blaze's voice. "What about them?"

"Where did they go?" the other man demanded.

"I don't know," Blaze said.

"We think you do."

Silence passed. Probably only a few seconds, but each one felt like eternity.

"I don't know what you want from me, but my passengers didn't tell me where they were heading," Blaze said. "It wasn't any of my business."

"Did you overhear any of their conversation?"

"Wasn't paying attention."

"You might want to rethink that," one of the men growled.

"There's nothing to rethink."

A thump sounded followed by a groan.

These guys were beating Blaze, weren't they?

Simmy couldn't just sit back and let that happen.

But how could she stop two men with guns? She would literally be bringing a screwdriver to a gunfight.

forty-five

"ANASTASIA RAN AWAY," Vivian announced before taking a long drag of her cigarette. "You just missed her."

The gun trembled in Ranger's hand as he stared at Vivian. Was she serious?

He knew she was.

Anastasia wasn't here.

Contempt coursed through him at the shallowness of her words.

The woman was unfit to be a mother. He'd known that. He'd tried to protect Anastasia.

What if he was too late?

One little slip of his finger, and he could pull the trigger. But he needed more information first before he did anything rash.

Ranger swallowed hard, his throat swollen with emotion. "What are you talking about?"

"There's no 'what are you talking about?' No language breakdown or misunderstanding." Vivian's voice sounded smooth, velvety, and smug. "Anastasia left."

"When did she leave?" His voice sounded eerily calm, especially considering the thoughts running through his head.

"This morning." Vivian answered the question with ease, as if they were talking about a sports game or catching up on old friends.

"This morning?" His voice cracked.

"I may have told her she'd be stuck here for the rest of her life and that her dad was never coming for her. That she should get used to it." She shrugged. "I didn't want to get the girl's hopes up."

"You just happened to tell her that this morning?" he snapped.

"I couldn't let you get here and take her from me."

Lava flowed through his veins. "So if you can't have her, no one can? You knew those words would make her leave. How can you even call yourself a mother?"

Vivian smashed her cigarette in the ashtray beside her. "If she wants to leave, it's her right. She's so demanding anyway. Kind of like her father. I thought this might teach her a lesson."

"She's a child! Those mountains are dangerous."

"I guess she'll learn what she's made of very quickly." She said the words nonchalantly, as if she didn't have a care in the world.

Anger tried to burst from him.

It was so easy to imagine his finger slipping. Tugging on the trigger.

A bullet flying and giving Vivian what she deserved.

But he didn't have it in him to kill the mother of his child, even if she was vile.

Just then, Duke and Apollo flooded into the room.

"Ranger . . ." Duke stared at him, suddenly turning into a negotiator. "Don't do anything rash."

"She let Anastasia leave." He said the words through gritted teeth. "My daughter is out there in this wilderness somewhere. Alone." The last word caught in his throat and nearly choked him.

His little girl . . . it was his job to protect her.

He'd failed.

Ranger hadn't come this far only to lose her again.

If she really was out there, then Ranger would find her.

———

"WE HAVE TO DO SOMETHING," Simmy whispered to Andi. "We can't just let them beat Blaze."

Andi peered around the toolbox, her gaze on the scene in front of them as she continued to grip the wrench. "Yes, we do."

They remained in place, both realizing their limitations. Rushing out would only get them hurt or killed.

But they couldn't watch an innocent man be beaten either.

Blaze let out a moan as the men punched him again.

"Vivian, all right?" Blaze muttered. "All I heard them say was something about a woman named Vivian they were going to visit."

"Smart man," Chubby muttered. "What else?"

"Nothing. I promise. There's nothing."

Simmy closed her eyes. She couldn't handle the sound of someone suffering. She wanted more than anything to help.

Another punch sounded, and Blaze moaned.

"I'm telling you—I don't know where they were going," Blaze said.

"They had to have said something!"

Simmy glanced at Andi again. Saw Andi's gaze was fixated on something above them. She lifted her head to see what she was looking at.

A fire alarm.

Was she thinking . . . ?

The next moment, Andi crept toward the wall. She nodded at Simmy before rising and quickly pulling the switch. Then she ducked again.

A siren filled the air.

The men froze.

"What's going on?" Chubby yelled.

"We gotta get out of here before too many people see us."

Simmy peered around the toolbox in time to see the men shove Blaze to the floor and then take off in a run toward their car.

She and Andi waited until the men had driven away before they turned off the alarm and rushed toward Blaze.

Simmy knelt on the floor beside him and quickly observed him. Blood dripped from his temple, and he held his side. Those men had done a number on him.

"Are you okay?" she murmured.

He sat up with a groan and rubbed his jaw, which was already swelling. "I've been better."

"I'm sorry—I wanted to come out," Simmy rushed. "I wanted to help."

Blaze swung his head back and forth before wincing with pain. "They would have done worse things to you. You were right staying where you were. I don't know what's going on, but it looks like you're in trouble."

"I am." Simmy knew better than to deny it. Then she glanced at Andi. "Actually, I'm afraid both of us are now."

Blaze's gaze met hers. "What can I do to help?"

forty-six

I **HATED** it when people underestimated me.

Which was exactly what Simmy had done.

Things had worked out quite fortuitously really. Before I'd left the small airport, I'd overheard a conversation between two men. They'd been saying someone deep in the heart of the mountains was looking for an emergency flight to Tok.

My gut had told me to linger and listen. So I'd faked a phone call while eavesdropping.

The charter had been for two people, a man and a woman. They were willing to pay a large amount to get there quickly.

Tok . . . I'd never heard of the place. So I'd looked it up. Saw it was to the north.

Then I called some of my men. Told them to go check it out. Thankfully, they were only an hour away.

I needed to cover every base.

Now I would go to Tok myself. By the time I arrive, my men should have already found her.

I couldn't wait to look Simmy in the eye and let her know just how disgusted I was with her.

So I'd secured my own charter. Told the pilot I needed to go to Tok, that my plans had changed. No one batted an eyelash.

The pilot was preparing his plane for flight right now, so I waited outside.

I glanced around, taking a better look at this place.

Really, how could people live out here? Alaska might be pretty, but it was the most boring place on earth. Mountains and glaciers had to get old after a while. I'd take the lights of the city any day—along with fine dining, shows, clubs.

Endless networks. Clients. Business opportunities.

Money and power. That was all I needed.

And . . . her.

Then my men called. "You better have something good."

"We're in Tok," Chubby said.

"Find anything?"

"The other plane landed, and we 'questioned' the pilot." He paused dramatically.

"And?" I tapped my foot impatiently.

Idiot.

"All the guy could tell us was that they'd mentioned something about Vivian."

"Vivian? Who is Vivian?"

"We were hoping you knew."

"Well, I don't!"

My jaw tightened.

Had I been tracking the wrong couple?

No. It had to be Simmy and her new friend who'd chartered that flight.

I was so close to finding her.

She was so close I could practically smell the sweet scent of her hair. Feel the softness of her skin. See the fear in her eyes.

A grin curled across my lips.

I couldn't wait to see that fear in person.

Fear had always filled her gaze when I put her in her place.

It had all been for the best. Good people weren't born. They were made. And sometimes, in order to be made, they had to learn their lessons the hard way.

Simmy was one of those people. When I'd first met her, she'd been so obedient. But she'd slowly changed over time.

That wasn't okay.

I'd been forced to make her see things my way, and she hadn't liked it.

My hands fisted as I remembered how those moments had unfolded.

She'd grown obstinate.

She'd ruined everything.

Sure, in the years since then, I had built my business back up. I had pivoted and gone in a different direction.

I was still successful, but I didn't forgive those who betrayed me.

And Simmy had betrayed me.

I wanted to teach her a lesson.

Up close and personal.

I could hardly wait.

My pilot called me over, motioning that it was time to go.

I slipped on my sunglasses and glanced around.

I needed to figure out who this Vivian was and what her association was with Simmy.

Then I needed to discover where Simmy had gone. I'd track her down once and for all and make her regret everything she'd done to me.

forty-seven

AS SIMMY, Andi, and Blaze stood in the hangar, Simmy's phone rang. Not her phone, really, but the one Ranger had left with her.

Simmy quickly answered, praying he had good news to share.

"Simmy," Ranger started. "If I drop a pin, can you and Andi find a car and meet us? I can't leave this area, not until I do something. And I'm not sure how long it will take."

Simmy glance at Andi. She could clearly hear Ranger's booming voice through the phone line.

Andi nodded.

"We can do that," Simmy rushed. "What's happening? Did you find Anastasia?"

"We found Vivian. But Anastasia isn't with her."

Simmy's throat tightened as possible scenarios went through her mind. Was the girl still alive? Had something happened to her? What if Vivian had done something awful?

"What . . . ?" The question came out as a croak. "What do you mean?"

"She ran away. My daughter's out there in this wilderness somewhere. Alone. I need to find her."

Her breath caught. How horrible. That poor girl . . . poor Ranger.

Simmy's thoughts shifted as another realization hit her. "But . . . how do you know Vivian is telling you the truth?"

"Because I know how she operates." Ranger's voice hardened at the mention of Vivian. "She doesn't care about anyone except herself. That's true even when it comes to her daughter."

"I'm so sorry, Ranger."

"I don't want you guys to be at the airport any longer than necessary. I'd rather have you both with us. Come as soon as you can. It's about a forty-five-minute drive."

"Send us the pin," Simmy said. "Andi and I will be there as soon as possible."

She needed to tell him about Blaze. About the fact he'd been beaten. About the fact Knave's guys were here.

But it seemed like bad timing to share right now after what Ranger had just told her about his daughter.

Anastasia was more important.

She ended the call and looked at Andi. "How are we going to find a car?"

Blaze raised a hand. "I have one a friend of mine will

let me use. I'll take you wherever you need to go."

"Are you sure?" Simmy hated to drag him into this any more than he already had been.

"I'm positive." His voice left no room for doubt. "You're not safe here. Those men might decide to come back."

She released the breath she'd been holding and nodded. "Thank you."

It appeared Blaze was an answer to prayer.

———

APOLLO HAD VOLUNTEERED to stay with Vivian—someone had to. He'd called a contact with the CIA, and they were sending someone here to pick her up. It would take a while for them to arrive, however.

All of it seemed too simple, Ranger mused.

Why was Vivian giving herself up so easily?

Ranger wasn't sure about her end game. But he'd worry about that later.

Right now, all he could think about was finding Anastasia.

Every time he thought about his little girl being lost alone in the wilderness, an ache filled his chest. Anastasia deserved a better childhood than this. He'd tried to protect her from any trauma, but he'd failed.

He would have a hard time forgiving himself for that.

He and Duke had searched the perimeter of the property for any indications as to where Anastasia might have gone. Unfortunately, all they'd found so far were some bear tracks.

Not what Ranger wanted to see.

They needed to be smart. Ranger didn't have a large team, and time wasn't on their side. Spreading out to search random places wouldn't work.

Ranger needed direction and to figure out a plan.

He paused near a stream and crouched low. He gently moved a leaf away.

Beneath it was a footprint.

A footprint approximately the size of Anastasia's feet.

"This is where we need to look." Ranger rose and pointed across the gurgling stream.

"Let's get ready then." Duke gave him a firm nod.

Thankfully, Duke had some supplies in his SUV. He and Ranger headed there and loaded their backpacks with water, food, emergency blankets, and flashlights. Going into the wilderness unprepared was never a good idea.

Just as they finished, a vehicle rumbled down the gravel road.

Ranger held his breath, hoping it was Simmy and Andi.

They could come help in the search. He'd rather have them within sight until this was over.

A moment later, he saw a truck with a man behind the wheel and Andi and Simmy in the seat beside him.

His muscles tightened. Was that one of Knave's guys? Had he captured them and then brought them out here? He wasn't sure that made any sense.

Besides, Simmy and Andi didn't seem to be under duress. In fact, their motions appeared easy and relaxed.

As they got closer, the man's face became clear.

The pilot.

Ranger released a breath.

Blaze parked the truck, and the three of them climbed out.

Ranger tensed again when he saw Blaze's swollen and bruised face.

Simmy paused in front of him and lowered her voice. "Knave's men found Blaze and beat him, demanding he tell them where we were."

Ranger sucked in a breath. "What? They're here?"

Simmy nodded. "They were. Blaze mentioned Vivian's name to them. Long story short, they left. But it probably won't be long before they find us."

Ranger's jaw tightened, and he nodded toward the woods. "We should get moving. There's no time to waste."

"Blaze said he knows this area," Simmy continued, louder this time. "He offered to help."

Blaze stepped closer. "I can take my plane up and search."

"That would be great." A huge help actually.

Blaze nodded toward his SUV. "I'll go then. If I see anything, I'll let you know."

"Please, do that." Ranger's voice cracked. "We can use all the help we can get."

forty-eight

WITH RANGER TRACKING Anastasia's steps, Simmy followed him through the wilderness with Duke and Andi.

Simmy's heart ached every time she imagined the girl being out here. Was she scared? Frightened about being alone in such a vast place?

Part of Simmy couldn't wait to meet the girl. She wanted to know more about her. Wanted to see her personality.

Was she quiet and serious? Fun and lively? Adventurous or withdrawn? Was she fearless like her father?

She wanted to know what the girl looked like. If she bore a resemblance to her dad. If she looked like her mother—who Simmy imagined to be boldly beautiful.

She wanted to see Ranger as a father. To see how he softened around his daughter. To see him as someone other than the mysterious, gruff man who'd wandered into the trading post that day.

Sure, he'd warmed up around her. She'd seen beyond his rough edges. But there was something about seeing a father with a daughter that touched her heart. The bond was undeniable.

Simmy truly hoped she had the chance to witness that.

As the group hiked, it was almost as if no one wanted to speak. As if they feared talking might make them miss a clue. So everyone remained mostly quiet, making only occasional comments.

Simmy had to admit that part of her loved seeing Ranger in action. In his element. So confident and determined.

That was probably why she was drawn to him. He was everything she wasn't.

Yet he wasn't like her ex. Her ex had been confident but in an arrogant way. In a controlling way. In a way where he manipulated others.

Not Ranger.

Yet as much as Simmy was attracted to him, she also knew there were things that kept them apart.

So many things.

So many reasons she should spare him a relationship with her.

The smartest thing to do would be to keep her distance—especially if Ranger found Anastasia. Simmy didn't want to put the girl in danger.

Knave would always be trouble for her—and anyone with her.

Ranger paused ahead of her and offered his hand to help her up a rocky section of the trail.

His kindness and concern weren't lost on her.

She cared about Ranger—cared about him so much that maybe she should let him go.

The thought caused her throat to burn.

Then again, maybe it was time to stop living in fear. To stop hiding.

What would that be like?

She held a branch out of the way as they climbed higher up the mountain. The air was getting thinner and cooler.

She was the only one who seemed bothered by that fact. Everyone else was a more natural athlete.

Not Simmy. Her mom hadn't had time for her to play sports when she'd been growing up. Instead, Simmy had played with dolls. When she'd outgrown dolls, she'd played with her own hair and makeup. Then she'd begun to enjoy the attention she got from the guys in her class.

But she hadn't been ready to date back then, though she'd thought she'd been. She'd simply been searching for a sense of belonging—something she'd never gotten from her mom.

Life certainly hadn't turned out like she'd expected.

Ranger paused near the edge of a small cliff and glanced around.

Simmy instinctively knew something was wrong. But she didn't ask. She waited instead.

Finally, he turned to the rest of the group. "Her trail stops here."

How could Anastasia's trail go cold? What did that even mean? The girl hadn't been beamed up into space.

"There has to be something." Simmy prayed the girl would be okay as she scanned the wilderness surrounding them. "She didn't just disappear."

———

RANGER DIDN'T LIKE the bad feeling growing in his gut.

Why had Anastasia's trail ended like this? It didn't make sense.

There weren't any animal prints.

No evidence of a struggle.

But still . . .

He glanced at the sky, which was suddenly pregnant with moisture. At any minute, rain would start falling. Then he'd really lose her trail.

The tension pulled tighter across his back.

Duke turned toward him, waiting with his hands on his hips. "It's your call. What do you want to do?"

Ranger glanced around. He pictured his little girl. Pictured what she might do.

What could have happened here.

Ranger raised a finger, indicating for everyone to give

him a minute. He'd learned to trust his instincts. But he needed more information first.

He glanced at the boulder beside him. A smudge of dirt streaked across the side of it.

From a foot, he realized.

Anastasia had climbed this rock, hadn't she?

Then where had she gone?

Silently, Ranger moved to the other side. A footprint appeared there.

He pictured his little girl climbing the rock to survey her surroundings.

Where had she been trying to go?

Then the truth hit him.

Anastasia was headed back toward John and Shannon's place.

She must have seen the mountain ranges. They would have indicated which direction she should head.

However, there was no way Anastasia could make that trek. In her ten-year-old mind, maybe it seemed possible. But even the most skilled climbers would have trouble scaling those mountains. Crossing those rivers.

In between here and John and Shannon's place were glaciers and ice fields and other unimaginable dangers.

These mountains were no place for a ten-year-old girl to wander alone.

No place for anyone to wander alone.

Ranger needed to find her. Now.

Just as the thought went through his mind, a raindrop hit his face.

Then another.

And another.

His gut tightened.

This trail would quickly disappear.

Along with any hope he had of finding his little girl alive.

forty-nine
Then

AFTER THE BABY DIED, Mark insisted Charlotte stay at his house while she recovered from her pregnancy and childbirth.

She had nowhere else to go so she'd agreed. Plus, Mark hadn't paid her yet.

It seemed like poor timing to ask for that money, especially while he was grieving the loss of his child.

So Charlotte had stayed in her room, craving time by herself. She'd slowly regained her strength and had begun to feel halfway normal again.

Mark had made her comfort foods like grilled cheese sandwiches and chicken noodle soup and turkey with mashed potatoes. He'd bought lots of cookie dough ice cream. He'd been attentive, doing whatever she'd asked as she healed.

Tonight, four weeks after she'd lost Lexi, Charlotte finally ventured out of her room. She escaped to the den and sat with a cozy blanket around her and the lights out. She hadn't even turned the TV on.

She simply needed a change of scenery. The bleak white walls of her bedroom were growing tiresome.

She stared out the window at the darkness outside. She really had to figure out a plan for when she left this place. She couldn't stay here at Mark's forever. Besides, there were a lot of bad memories. So much lost hope.

Tomorrow, she decided. Tomorrow she would ask Mark for her pay and begin to figure out her future. She needed to look for an apartment. A job.

Maybe she'd go back to the daycare. She hadn't minded it there. Or maybe she'd try for one of those telemarketing jobs. She'd heard they paid well, and she might even be able to work from home.

If nothing else, Charlotte could apply at Walmart. The company always seemed to be hiring, and she could handle retail work. Maybe she'd make enough working there to pay her bills, especially if she found a roommate.

Leaving this house would be good.

Meredith's ghost seemed to haunt this place. Not literally. Charlotte didn't believe in ghosts.

But touches of the woman were everywhere. In the frilly decorations. In the scent of the cleaners and air fresheners and candles. In the pictures of her and Mark together.

The woman in the photos seemed to watch Charlotte's every movement. Seemed to condemn her. To remind her that this place wasn't hers and she was no longer welcome.

This was where Mark and Meredith were supposed to build their future. Their family. All of that had been destroyed.

Mark needed to move on, and Charlotte was certain that would be difficult to do with her being here. They both needed to move on.

"Charlotte?" A deep voice cut into her thoughts.

She glanced up and saw Mark standing in the doorway. Even in the darkness, the tears rimming his eyes were apparent.

The ache in her chest grew more intense. He'd been grieving but taking care of her. He just needed some time to grieve on his own. To not worry about her.

Instinctually, she opened her blanket, silently inviting him to share the comfort she'd found in the warmth.

He didn't hesitate to cross the space and sit beside her.

He wrapped himself into the folds of the fleece, and Charlotte held him tight. She let him grieve. Let him mourn everything he'd lost.

Picking up the pieces could be so hard.

"I've lost so much," he murmured into her neck. "I don't even know what to do."

"I know," Charlotte murmured as she stroked his hair. "I'm so sorry."

"You've been my rock throughout this all. You know that, don't you?"

"I don't know if I'd say that." Charlotte's words sounded soft and unobtrusive.

"I don't know what I would have done without you." Mark pulled away from her embrace just far enough to look at her. "You've been a real lifesaver, Charlotte."

Her cheeks heated at his closeness, his attention, his compliments. Each made her feel complete. Made her feel like she had purpose.

They made her feel seen. She didn't usually feel that way. If she were honest with herself, she usually felt . . . used.

"I'm glad I could help," she told him. "But I should have been able to deliver a healthy baby for you. I'm the one who's sorry."

Now tears poured down her cheeks. She couldn't shake the guilt. Shame haunted her day and night. Dr. Matthews had even put her on some medicine that made her feel tired. Said it would help her depression.

Was she depressed? Maybe. Maybe that was why she hadn't wanted to leave her room.

How could she have lost the baby? What could she have done differently? Should she have sensed something was wrong?

Using his index finger, Mark tilted her chin up. "Listen to me, Charlotte. You have nothing to apologize for. You understand that?"

He stared at her, his gaze unwavering, until she finally nodded. Despite her affirmation, Charlotte wasn't sure she believed the words.

"You are an amazing woman, Charlotte," Mark murmured. "A truly amazing woman. I want you to know that."

Warmth oozed through her blood. It had been a long time since anyone had said she was amazing. If ever.

Her mom hadn't exactly been encouraging. Nothing Charlotte had done was ever right for her. Her mother—a former beauty queen whose self-worth had faded with her looks—only felt happy when basking in the attention of a new man.

So that was what her mom had done. She'd found a new man to give her affirmation as soon as she got bored with the old one.

She'd done whatever it took to keep the men—even at Charlotte's expense. A couple of those "boyfriends" had dared to come into Charlotte's bedroom at night.

Her mom had blamed her. Said Charlotte had seduced them.

Charlotte hadn't, but her mom didn't believe her.

Those men . . . they were nothing like Mark. Mark was a gentleman. Respectful. He'd had the opportunity to cross lines, but he hadn't.

Charlotte's gaze locked with Mark's. Meredith had been such a lucky woman.

The next instant, Mark's lips covered hers. Slowly and tentatively at first. Then with passion and urgency.

Charlotte didn't fight the kiss.

Mark was no longer a married man. The two of them

were no longer bound together through the legal obliga-
tion of the surrogacy.

Right now, they were simply two grieving adults.
They both needed each other after everything they'd gone
through. They both craved comfort and understanding
and . . . connection.

Their lips tangled and tugged at each other's until
Mark finally pulled away from the kiss.

Instantly, Charlotte missed his touch, his nearness.

"I know I shouldn't say this, but I've wanted to do
that for so long," he whispered, his thumb absently
stroking her cheek.

Joy burst inside her. He'd felt the same things she had?
She thought she'd imagined it.

"Me too," she murmured.

He smiled. "You have?"

Charlotte nodded, still leaning into his touch. "I tried
not to want it. I told myself I didn't. But I did."

"That makes me happy to hear." Mark pushed a hair
behind her ear as he stared into her eyes. "I think God
brought you to me at just the right time, Charlotte. It's
like you were sent from heaven."

"You really think that?"

"I do." Then, as if to prove his point, he went in for
another kiss.

———

A MONTH after their first kiss, Charlotte and Mark had married.

She was sure some people thought their relationship was scandalous. But it wasn't. The two of them hadn't acted inappropriately while Meredith was alive. They'd both had feelings, but neither had acted on them.

The first six months after their nuptials were complete bliss, despite their loss and pain. They kissed often. Ate dinner together every night. Took long walks around the property. Went on several vacations. Even went camping a few times.

Mark had given her an allowance, and she'd bought new clothes. Expensive clothes. Her hair had been high-lighted. She'd gotten new makeup, along with a session with a beautician on how to properly apply it.

She now looked like someone fit to be married to a man like Mark. She looked high-class. If that made Mark happy, then it made Charlotte happy also.

Charlotte wanted to have children with Mark right away, and she thought he'd be on board—especially after his loss. But he insisted they both needed more time to heal. She understood his hesitation, especially after losing Lexi.

Then eight months after they got married, she noticed Mark seemed preoccupied. He'd had some rather tense phone calls lately, and she didn't know what they were about—only something to do with work. His brother had shown up often, trying to help him work through some details.

Then Mark sat her down for dinner one night with a proposal.

He reached across the table over their filet mignon and squeezed her hand. "I have something I need to tell you."

His tone indicated bad news, and dread pooled in her stomach. "Of course. What's on your mind?"

He swallowed hard before starting. "Charlotte . . . when Meredith died, I spent a lot of time grieving her death. I felt lost and uncertain."

"I remember. That's normal, I'm sure."

"You're probably right. Unfortunately, as a result, my work suffered."

Charlotte tried to hold back her surprise. Mark always seemed to have everything so together. She'd never suspected he was struggling to that extent.

"I didn't want to burden you with the information, especially since it didn't concern you. Besides, I thought everything would work out." He paused and swallowed hard again. "But now I've found myself in some debt that I'm trying to get out of. I've been trying to figure out a way to do that."

Her thoughts raced as she tried to come up with a solution, a way to fix this and ease his worry. Her dinner was now growing cold and forgotten.

"Maybe you could sell one of the cars," she suggested. He had four, after all. "Would that help pay for it?"

"I'm afraid not." He drew his gaze up to hers, and Charlotte saw a flicker of anxiety. "I was wondering . . . how would you feel about being a surrogate again?"

Charlotte blinked, unsure if she'd heard him correctly. Those were the last words she'd expected. "What?"

His expression softened, and he reached for her, resting his hand against the side of her face. "I know everything with Lexi was traumatic. I want to be sensitive to that. I really do. But selling cars or cashing out savings isn't the solution we need. We need a way to bring in more money. Business is down. Like really down. I should have done better. Should have stayed on top of things more. Besides, you were so wonderful as a surrogate. You glowed."

Fear clutched her lungs until she couldn't breathe. "But the umbilical cord . . . it was wrapped around her neck. My body . . . it could be broken or ill equipped for pregnancy. I don't really know. I don't think I'm a good candidate for a surrogate anymore."

The excuses tumbled from her lips. Sure, she'd just earlier been thinking about having her own baby. But the thought of being a surrogate . . . it just seemed like a bad idea. Not anything that was in her plans for the future.

"I talked to Dr. Matthews, and he feels like what happened was simply a terrible tragedy. He doesn't believe you're at risk for it happening again."

Charlotte's eyes widened. "You've already talked to Dr. Matthews about this? Without coming to me first?"

"Sweetie, I didn't talk to him about you being a surrogate, of course. But I talked to him about what it would be like if you and I had kids together one day. I was concerned." Mark paused and shook his head, his gaze suddenly burdened. "I know I'm going about this the wrong way, and I apologize. I didn't know the best way to bring the subject up, and now I'm making a mess of things."

In one sense, it was sweet that her normally overconfident husband seemed so flustered. Charlotte felt better knowing he wasn't so gung-ho about this proposition that he was insensitive to Charlotte's feelings. At least he'd been considering the idea that Charlotte wanted to have children of her own when he first talked to Dr. Matthews.

It showed he was listening.

However, this new proposition also showed he was desperate. Desperation made people do things they wouldn't normally do.

Charlotte was a case in point. Desperation had led her to Mark and Meredith in the first place. In normal circumstances, she would have never agreed to their terms.

"I see." Charlotte nodded slowly as she thought it through. "You really think another surrogacy could be the solution?"

She *would* like to make some type of financial contribution to their family. She never liked to freeload, so maybe this could be the answer they were looking for.

"I think being a surrogate again could help you heal also." Mark stroked her cheek with his thumb. "I know what you went through was incredibly hard. I don't want to downplay that."

As the months had passed by since Lexi was born, the memories had stayed with her.

More liked haunted her.

Charlotte thought for sure she'd heard Lexi crying after she was born.

But she'd asked Mark, and he'd said she was wrong. That when Lexi entered the world, the child had made no noise whatsoever.

That was when Dr. Matthews had known something was wrong. Charlotte had been so out of it when everything happened that her recollection of the event was inaccurate.

Yet the moment seemed so vivid in her mind.

"So what do you think?" Mark peered at her, hope in his gaze.

How could she tell him no after everything he'd done for her? He could have kicked her out. Could have blamed her for the baby's death.

Instead, he'd cared for her, and they'd fallen in love. He'd freely given her everything that was his, and now she had a beautiful home, beautiful clothes, and even a luxury car.

However, getting pregnant again would mean going off her anxiety medicine. That would be a challenge. She'd grown dependent on those pills. They helped her get through each day.

But she could handle this. She could be strong.

She licked her lips before saying, "I . . . I can think about it."

Mark smiled softly and squeezed her hand again. "I think that would be great. Just consider it, okay? It could be a good solution all around, one that might make both of us feel better."

———

CHARLOTTE SUCCESSFULLY CARRIED out her surrogacy and gave birth to a baby boy eleven months later.

Everything had gone so smoothly that Mark had convinced her to do it again. So she carried another baby, only three months after her last delivery.

Apparently, Mark's debt was more than he'd wanted to admit. Because of his connections in the business world, he knew people who'd pay a hearty six figures for the surrogacy.

Her contribution to their family's income seemed to appease Mark, and Charlotte wanted more than anything to make him happy. She didn't want to simply have to depend on someone else for her every need. She wanted to feel like she was doing something to help meet the needs of this household.

Besides, his brother liked to make comments about how she looked. About her relationship with Mark. About her "contributions." And the way he looked at Charlotte . . . it reminded her a lot of her mother's boyfriends. The ones who'd sneaked into her room at night.

She couldn't stand the man, but she didn't dare tell Mark that.

He seemed to think the world of his older brother.

Her thoughts shifted back to the subject at hand.

The problem with being a surrogate was that Charlotte *really* wanted a baby of her own. If she kept having babies for other people, when would she ever have time for her own child?

These two surrogacies had been different than her first one. She met with the couples and stayed in touch with them weekly throughout the pregnancy. They went with her to ultrasounds. Talked to the doctor about her health.

These were nothing like her surrogacy with Mark and Meredith.

As she remembered those days, her cheeks often warmed.

There was *nothing* normal about that surrogacy, although Charlotte had been too naive to realize it at the time.

She'd rationalized so much, and now she realized how inappropriate things had been. How boundaries had been crossed.

Back then, she'd tried to deny the fact she had feelings for Mark. But, in truth, they were there. They were part of the reason she'd acted as she did. She'd put him on a pedestal.

The longer the two of them were married, the more challenging it became. Not because Mark wasn't great. But because he had to work more. Be out of town more. The stress of the job got to him. The demands made him crankier than normal.

But Charlotte was thankful to be so well taken care of. Growing up, there had been times she and her mother had been homeless for brief stretches. That insecurity still played with Charlotte's emotions to this day. More than anything, she craved stability.

This surrogacy was going to be it, she'd decided. In a few months, she'd deliver a baby girl to a family in New York City. Then she was done with this line of work.

She needed to move on and plan for her own future.

She desperately hoped Mark saw it the same way.

———

MARK HADN'T SEEN things the same way Charlotte had.

Apparently, they were on the verge of losing the house.

Charlotte didn't think losing the house was a big deal. The place was too large for her and Mark anyway. There was more than enough space for a couple with two or three kids to live here.

That was when she realized that Mark saw the house as more of a status symbol. Not just the house—his cars and his lifestyle also.

Did he see Charlotte as a status symbol? Was that why he'd talked her into buying expensive clothes? Learning to apply expensive makeup? To getting highlights at the best salon in the area? All so she could help him maintain a certain image?

She knew she was attractive in a very conventional manner. There was nothing special looking about her, she supposed. But she had a toothy smile, nice hair and skin, and classic features. When she wasn't pregnant, her build was slim and willowy, like a dancer.

Her personality was pleasant. She'd learned to be a peacemaker, and nurturing others came naturally to her. It was what she'd grown up doing—taking care of her mom. Trying to soothe disagreements. Trying to be the adult in the relationship.

Basically, Charlotte was a prime target for being walked on.

Her mom had taken advantage of that fact every chance she could.

Was that what Mark was doing now?

Charlotte asked herself that often.

She didn't want to believe it. Then she realized the blame really rested on her. *She* was the one who let others get away with taking advantage of her. She had to learn to be stronger, to stand up for herself more.

Then why did she dream about getting away from this perfect life sometimes? Why did she dream about what the future would be like if she had a normal family? If she had a husband who didn't want her to carry other people's babies?

She didn't care about money. She never had.

She just wanted security. Happiness. Belonging.

Real security. Real happiness. Real belonging.

What she had here . . . none of it felt real.

Maybe she would have been better off working at Walmart, living with a roommate, and struggling to make ends meet.

She hated to think that way, but it was true.

Every so often, she saw a different side of Mark. She blamed it on the stress. But he was short with her. Snappy. Impatient.

He wanted her to keep the house a certain way. Dress a certain way. Always wear makeup. When she didn't lose her baby weight quickly enough, he made snide comments.

Basically, he liked things his way. All the time.

Was this simply what marriage was like? Charlotte had never seen an example of a healthy marriage, so she wasn't sure. But after time, perhaps manners and politeness faded. Perhaps it was normal that couples became more honest with each other.

But she didn't like it. Didn't like the way she felt when Mark talked to her like that.

It was just a phase, she told herself. Once his stress at work was over, things would get better.

So why did doubt linger in the back of her mind?

———

MARK HAD LEFT for another business trip this morning.

While he was gone, Charlotte had ventured up into the attic. She was getting bored and restless. She had no social life beyond Mark and the people he brought in and out of the house.

So when Mark was out of town, she'd begun to explore.

She'd just started in the attic two weeks ago, and it was by far the most interesting space in this house. The previous owner had left antiques and books. An old wedding dress. Some porcelain plates.

She'd gone through those first.

Meanwhile, things hadn't gotten better with Mark. In fact, they'd gotten worse.

His condescending tone had morphed into a short temper and aggression. One time she'd been curled up in a chair reading, and he'd grabbed her to get her attention. While gripping her arm, his fingers had pinched her a little too tightly, leaving bruises.

His worry over her weight had turned into constant snide remarks.

She'd carried six babies now—six babies for other people. How did he think her stomach would look? Her skin had stretched and didn't have time to bounce back. Her body hadn't had time to fully recover.

The pregnancies—transactions, really—had come with a cost.

As did everything in life.

Trying to get her mind off her marriage troubles, Charlotte walked around the dark space on the third floor, amongst some old furniture and uncountable boxes of books and photo albums. Nothing that truly interested her.

She stopped at a set of boxes with "Meredith" written on the side.

Charlotte's throat tightened.

Then she sat down and opened one.

Inside were pictures of Meredith and Mark from when they'd first gotten married.

They looked so happy, so happy that the pictures were hard to stomach.

The couple Charlotte remembered had been anything but happy.

Her fingers paused on a leather journal. Was this a . . . diary? Meredith's diary?

Charlotte swallowed hard.

She shouldn't open this. She shouldn't read Meredith's words.

Yet she couldn't seem to stop herself.

The woman was dead now. What did her privacy matter?

She opened the book and saw the handwritten words there, the script neat and tidy.

She began reading.

At first, the journal entries sounded happy. Meredith talked about how lucky she felt. How perfect Mark was.

But as the months went on, the tone had changed.

One journal entry in particular made Charlotte stop.

When I first met Mark, I would never have guessed how our love story would unfold. I'd come to him as a surrogate for him and his wife, Anna. Then Anna had died in that terrible car accident. So I'd had his baby, only to lose the child during childbirth.

The air left Charlotte's lungs. What?

Meredith had been a surrogate also? And she'd lost her baby?

Why hadn't Mark or Meredith mentioned that to her?

There could only be one reason: because someone had something to hide.

fifty

Now

SIMMY SAW the worry in Ranger's eyes.

The rain couldn't have come at a worse time.

At least he'd figured out which direction Anastasia had headed before the downpour started.

As sheets of water fell from the sky, Simmy pushed wet strands of hair from her face. Her clothes were drenched. Her shoes and socks also.

Not only that, but they were climbing higher up the mountain. She'd even seen clumps of snow nestled in shadows unreached by the sunlight. Had heard Ranger mention something about a glacier not far from here.

She'd prefer that they head into the valley.

Somewhere safer. Less exposed.

But that option wasn't on the table right now.

Finally, they reached a clearing. As they did, a noise rumbled overhead.

A plane.

Simmy paused and looked at the sky.

"It's Blaze!" she murmured.

He was flying low overhead. Looking for Anastasia.

"He came through, just like he said," Andi added.

Gratefulness filled Simmy.

The man didn't really know them. He hadn't needed to help.

But she was incredibly thankful he'd kept his word and done so.

As they watched the plane pass over, Ranger's phone rang.

"It's Blaze," Ranger muttered, his expression tightening. "Maybe he has an update for us."

Simmy held her breath as she waited to hear what Blaze said.

———

RANGER PUT the phone to his ear, anticipating what the pilot might say.

"This is my second pass over," Blaze said. "And you're not going to like this."

"Not going to like what?" Ranger's back pinched with tension.

"I think I see someone." Blaze's voice sounded tinny as he spoke over the hum of the plane's engine. "It looks like a little girl."

"That's good news."

"Yes, but the bad news is . . . she's on a mudflat."

Ranger's heart pounded harder. "What?"

"She's not moving. I think . . . I think she may be stuck."

His adrenaline pounded harder.

Mudflats were nothing to be messed with. They were made of glacier silt. When disturbed, the debris resettled more tightly and packed together, almost like cement. From a distance, the mud looked almost solid, but it wasn't.

The most famous and dangerous were the mudflats at Turnagain Arm near Anchorage. Several people had died there through the years after getting stuck and having the tide come in.

Thankfully, this wasn't a tidal area. But it was still dangerous.

He had to get to her. Now.

"How far away are we?" Ranger asked.

"You need to go probably a half mile to the north. That's where you'll find her. Do you want me to call backup?"

Ranger's mind raced. "How long do you think it will take help to get here?"

"I'm guessing Alaska Search and Rescue would be able to get someone out there tomorrow morning at the earliest. This rain certainly isn't helping." His voice cut in and out through the bad connection.

"In other words, it's not looking promising." Ranger could read between the lines. Tomorrow would be too late. But it was better to put the call in now anyway. "Call the situation in. But I can't wait for them to get here."

"I figured you'd say that. I'd do the same if I had a child. Best of luck, man. I'm going to have to land after this. It's getting too windy up here to fly. Visibility isn't good."

Ranger thanked him, ended the call, and put his phone away. Then he turned to the rest of the group and gave them the update.

He knew by looking at their faces they were thinking the same thing he was.

The situation was dire.

He had to believe there was a way to help his daughter.

"What can we do to help?" Duke stared at him as he waited for an answer.

He glanced at each person in the group. "This will be dangerous. None of you have to go with me. I totally and completely understand if you all want to stay here. Or if you want to turn around and go back. Most likely, I'm not going to get back to the car before dark. It's too dangerous to walk through these mountains at night. You need to know what you're getting yourself into if you decide to stay out here with me."

"I'm staying with you." Duke's voice left no room for argument.

"Me too." Andi raised her chin in affirmation.

Then Ranger's gaze fell on Simmy.

Part of him wanted her to say she would turn around. Go back. Stay away from danger.

But he knew Simmy better than that.

Her voice was unwavering as she said, "I'm in this with you. Until the end."

Ranger knew that she meant those words. Her support—all their support—meant the world to him. He'd learned not to trust, not to rely on others, through his time with the CIA.

But the people surrounding him right now were different. He knew that without a doubt.

"All right." Ranger offered a stiff nod. "Let's keep moving. But just to warn you, it's only going to get more treacherous from here."

———

QUEASINESS GREW inside Simmy with every step.

She didn't know what exactly they would encounter up ahead. But the sky was growing darker, and the rain felt frigid, especially as the temperatures dropped.

But she wouldn't let Ranger face this alone.

If his daughter was out here and in trouble, then Simmy would help. She couldn't turn her back on someone in need—especially not someone so young and innocent.

They continued hiking. The distance may have only

been half a mile, but in this terrain, it might as well be twenty.

Sometimes they scrambled over rocks and up the side of the mountain. Sometimes they grabbed onto tree limbs to pull themselves upward. Sometimes the ground gave away beneath them, and they slid down, their legs and chests covered in mud.

But they moved forward.

Finally, they reached the crest of the mountain and began to descend toward the river.

The ground leveled, and the trees cleared.

Simmy paused and glanced around, suddenly chilled. But why?

She saw nothing.

It was probably just the situation. Everything was messing with her head. So much had happened. That mixed with the strenuous hike and weather would be a lot for anyone. That had to be the reason she felt so unsettled right now.

She shivered and turned back toward the rest of the group, following them down the trail and toward a river in the distance.

As Simmy glanced toward the water, she spotted someone in the mud.

A girl with long, curly dark hair, wearing a red stocking hat and gloves.

Mud covered her up to her waist.

The girl turned toward them and waved her hands in the air. "Someone . . . help me. Please."

Based on the weary sound of her voice, she'd been out there a while. Scared and alone.

The poor girl . . .

But Simmy had no idea how they would get her out of the situation.

fifty-one

I GLANCED AT THE SKY. I was in Tok now. My guys had met me.

Had tracked down Vivian's location.

Then they'd followed some tracks into the woods.

This was where Simmy had gone.

So now I was tracking her.

Since I'd ventured out into the forest, a plane had flown overhead twice. Each time, I'd ducked behind a tree, not wanting to be seen.

That had to be the pilot my men had talked to. They'd told me what his plane looked like. This was an exact match.

He seemed to be searching for something below. I couldn't be sure what.

Simmy? That would be too easy, wouldn't it?

But if she'd gotten herself into trouble while out on

this hike . . . then maybe this pilot had been called in to find her and her friend.

It made sense to me.

When the wind kicked up, the plane turned and headed back toward town.

That meant the pilot must have seen whatever he'd been looking for.

A grin spread across my face.

Without realizing it, that pilot had given away her location.

Maybe I would thank him later.

Or maybe not.

Once the plane had passed by, I stepped from beneath the tree.

If I had to guess, that pilot was helping Simmy and her friend right now. When I made it back to the airport, I would find the pilot and demand answers. I'd do what my men should have done.

However, I couldn't imagine why in the world Simmy and her friend would be trekking through this wilderness.

At this point, Simmy had to know I was following her. How could she not?

But it made no sense for her to take off with her friend into the mountains. She'd never been much of an outside girl. Was she running from me?

I had to admit that I was never much of an outside guy, though I'd given it a shot a few times—mostly when I'd been trying to impress people. I preferred to have my adventures in dark back rooms or on the computer.

But I could make this work. In fact, it was perfect.

Even though Simmy was probably with other people, I couldn't imagine she would be with *that* many. At least one. Perhaps a few more.

That would make it easier for me to catch her alone.

I just had to wait. To be patient.

When I saw the right moment, I would seize it. I'd grab her. The rest of the group would probably think she'd wandered off. Fallen from a cliff. That a bear had found her.

So many things could go wrong out here.

I needed to use those facts to my advantage.

It wouldn't be an easy hike up the rest of this mountain. I did work out every day. Not on a mountain but in a home gym. I could do this.

I was so close that I could taste victory.

And the flavors were wonderful.

fifty-two

RANGER STARED AT HIS DAUGHTER.

He couldn't believe his eyes.

It was her. Anastasia.

She really was alive.

Tears rushed to his eyes in a flood of gratitude.

Gratitude that quickly turned to worry.

He hadn't found her just to lose her again.

But this situation . . . it was treacherous, at best. Impossible at worst.

He wished he could run to her. Could pull her from her muddy prison.

But he'd only sink also, and then they'd both be stuck.

He had to think of another plan.

Just then, Anastasia's eyes widened, and she waved her hands. "Daddy! Daddy! I knew you would come for me."

His heart beat harder.

He wouldn't let his little girl down.

He threw his backpack on the ground and reached for a rope he'd brought. "We're going to help you, honey. Try to stay still, okay? Can you do that for me?"

"I can, Daddy. I will." She paused before saying, "I'm scared, Daddy."

The catch in her voice made an ache pulse through his heart.

His job was to protect her.

He'd failed once. He wouldn't do it again.

"I know you're scared." He tried to soothe her as he made a slip knot in the rope. "We're going to get you out of there."

He realized how dire the situation was.

Anastasia had probably thought she was simply walking out toward the river.

Then the earth must have enveloped her until she could no longer move.

If Ranger hadn't found her . . .

His throat tightened until he could hardly breathe. He didn't want to think about it.

The important thing was that he'd found her. That was what he needed to focus on.

He formed a lasso with the rope, much like a cowboy might do when rescuing an animal.

Duke stepped closer, his hands on his hips and muscles bristled and ready for action. "You let us know what you need us to do, and we're there."

Ranger nodded, glad that his friends were with him. "Right now, you can pray."

"We've been doing that," Simmy muttered. "And we won't stop."

Ranger surveyed the area around him again as his thoughts raced. He had to figure out a plan using the resources they had—which weren't many.

"Okay, sweetie," he started. "Listen carefully. I'm going to throw this rope to you. When I tell you to, I want you to grab it, pull it over your head, and tuck it under your arms."

"But you said not to move, Daddy."

"It's important that you don't move until I tell you to," he said. "You can do that, right?"

"Yes, Daddy." Fear trembled in her voice.

The sound both infuriated Ranger and made him more determined to rescue her.

The truth was, Anastasia should never be in this situation to begin with.

But that was something he could deal with later.

He twirled the lasso above him before tossing it.

The loop missed Anastasia.

He bit back a choice word.

Then tried again.

But this time as it came near, Anastasia tried to grab it.

The movement caused her to sink deeper into the mud.

She let out a cry as the earth reached to her chest.

Ranger's heart seemed to lodge in his throat. "Anastasia, don't move. Remember, not until I tell you to."

More than anything, he wanted to run out there and rescue her. But he knew that wasn't an option.

Next time he threw the rope, he had to make sure it landed over her body.

He didn't have any other options.

———

SIMMY COULDN'T BELIEVE the scene unfolding in front of her eyes.

The fragileness of the situation hit her.

That poor girl.

Poor Ranger.

She knew they didn't have much time. The girl was sinking deeper, and the rain wasn't helping the situation. They needed to secure her before it was too late.

Andi stepped toward Ranger. "I think I can help."

He didn't hide the confusion in his eyes. "What do you mean?"

"I mean, I grew up in Texas. On a ranch. We roped things for fun."

He continued to stare. "You're serious?"

Andi nodded. "I am. I was a rodeo queen. But don't you dare tell anyone else outside this group."

Any other time, Simmy might have giggled. But there was nothing to laugh about in their current circumstances.

Ranger hesitated a moment before finally handing the rope to Andi.

With a pensive expression, Andi began to twirl the lasso over her head.

"You can do it," Duke encouraged.

The next instant, Andi tossed it.

Almost as if in slow motion, the rope flew through the air.

It flew. Flew. Flew.

Then it began to descend.

Simmy could hardly breathe as she watched.

The lasso landed . . . right on top of Anastasia.

Simmy let out a soft squeal of victory. "You did it!"

"Thank God." Andi released a quick breath, the action betraying the confidence she portrayed.

Carefully, she handed the rope to Ranger so he could take over.

"I need you to listen to me, Anastasia," Ranger started. "When I tell you, I want you to slowly put your arms through that rope and then hold on. Do you understand?"

"What if I can't get my hands out of this mud? What will I do then?" The girl's voice cracked with fear.

"You should be able to lift them from the mud. Go ahead and try."

Simmy appreciated the patience and kindness in Ranger's voice right now. He was trying to soothe his daughter, trying to stop her from panicking.

He was fatherly in a way that Simmy hadn't even known was possible. Tender and gentle. Gone were all his rough edges.

"All right, on the count of three, that's what I want you to do," Ranger continued. "As soon as your arms get through that rope and you're holding on, you're going to feel a tug. It's going to be me. I'm going to pull you toward me."

Simmy paused at his words. *You're going to feel a tug. It's going to be me. I'm going to pull you toward me.*

She couldn't help but think that his words were a lot like the words she often read in the Bible.

Words from Matthew 18 came back to her again.

"What do you think? If a man owns a hundred sheep, and one of them wanders away, will he not leave the ninety-nine on the hills and go to look for the one that wandered off? And if he finds it, truly I tell you, he is happier about that one sheep than about the ninety-nine that did not wander off. In the same way your Father in heaven is not willing that any of these little ones should perish."

Just as Ranger would do anything to rescue his child, so would Jesus pursue those far from Him. People like Simmy.

The picture of that—the analogy of Ranger and Jesus—pulled on her heartstrings.

She held her breath as Ranger began counting.

"One. Two." He paused but only for a second before saying, "Three."

As soon as Anastasia moved, she seemed to slip farther into the mud.

fifty-three

AS RANGER SAW Anastasia slipping deeper into the mud, his adrenaline surged. "No!"

He began to pull the rope.

The tension was stronger than he'd anticipated.

The earth didn't want to let her go.

Neither did Ranger.

But he had to be careful. He didn't want to injure her further by pulling too hard. Ideally, he'd have a hose to spray water or air beneath the mud to loosen it. But those things weren't an option right now. He had to make do with what he had—and it wasn't much.

Moving his hands on top of each other in slow, steady motions, he tugged.

With every movement, he prayed.

He didn't think he'd ever prayed for anything so fervently before.

But he'd do anything to save his daughter. Even sacrifice himself.

His muscles burned. Even though the rope was moving, nothing seemed to be happening.

Anastasia was still mired in the mud. Was she buried? Or simply covered and blending in to the extent they couldn't see her?

He wasn't sure.

Everyone around him watched in trepidation. There was nothing they could do either except pray. He knew they were.

"Anastasia!" he yelled.

Hopelessness captured him, and his pulse roared in his ears. *Please, God . . . help her. Please!*

Suddenly, Anastasia's head popped up.

Her mud-covered face appeared.

Relief washed through him. She hadn't been totally buried.

Somehow, in the mess of things, she'd managed to grab onto the rope after all.

Yet Ranger knew they weren't out of danger yet.

He had to get her back to solid ground. Things could still go wrong.

With one hand over the other, he continued to pull and pull and pull. His muscles burned, but he didn't let that slow him down.

He could ask his friends to help. But pulling too fast, too hard could harm Anastasia. He couldn't risk that.

Slow and steady wins the race, he reminded himself.

He pulled. And pulled.

Finally, Anastasia's small body slid onto the rocky shore.

He darted toward her and lifted his daughter into his arms.

She was okay.

She was here.

Alive.

He'd never felt so grateful for answered prayers.

———

TEARS FILLED Simmy's eyes as she watched the reunion.

She was so happy for Ranger. So glad his daughter was okay.

That she was alive.

With Duke standing close, Andi looped her arm through Simmy's. They watched Ranger and Anastasia embrace.

After several moments passed, Ranger pulled away ever-so-slightly from his daughter. He still held the girl in his arms, looking as if he never wanted to let go.

As to be expected.

He turned back to the team. "Everyone, this is Anastasia. Anastasia, this is everyone."

Despite the ordeal the girl had just gone through, she smiled, the motion cracking the mud covering her face. "Lovely to meet you all."

Simmy returned the smile, already sensing a spunk about the girl. She wasn't surprised.

"I'd love to stay here and rest a bit, but it's not smart," Ranger said. "The rain is only going to come down harder, and we're going to get colder as night falls. We don't have time to make it back to Duke's SUV tonight either. I suggest we head to the other side of the mountain to find some shelter, and we stay there for the night. Then we can make our way back to the car in the morning. How does that sound?"

Simmy glanced around, her unease still present, though she had no evidence to justify it. In truth, she'd prefer not to spend the night out here. But she understood Ranger's reasoning.

So she nodded. "If that's what you think is best, then that's fine."

Andi and Duke also agreed.

"Perfect," Ranger said. "Then we should probably start back so we can make sure we have some shelter sooner rather than later."

The happy moment was interrupted as Simmy felt the skin on her neck rise.

Reluctantly, she glanced at the vast landscape behind her.

Was someone out there watching this?

So far out in the wilderness?

That couldn't be.

Or could it? Had one of Vivian's men come out here and found them?

Certainly, it wasn't Knave. How would he have found her out here? It didn't seem possible.

Or maybe it was a wild animal.

There were so many—too many—possibilities for danger right now.

She didn't want to be the girl who cried wolf. But she didn't want to stick her head in the sand either.

Before they even took a step, the hair on Simmy's neck rose again. That familiar feeling of being watched filled her.

But she saw nothing and no one.

She glanced at the others in her group.

No one else seemed to sense it but her.

Ranger and Duke's instincts were much more refined than hers. If there really was someone out there, wouldn't they feel it too?

Or could it just be her imagination?

She wasn't sure.

But she'd keep her eyes wide open, looking for any signs of danger.

fifty-four

Then

THE FACT that Meredith had been a surrogate seemed like something that would have come up in one of her conversations with Mark.

Nausea churned in Charlotte's gut at the thought.

She continued reading the journal.

Vast chunks of time had been skipped. Then the journal started back up again after Charlotte had moved in as their surrogate.

Meredith wrote:

I remember those days well, the days when I came to live here at the house.

At first, after the loss of the baby, I found immense comfort in Mark. Then slowly, our feelings began to grow. I'd had feelings all along, but I told myself I didn't. Told myself that they weren't appropriate.

Then things just happened.

I thought what we had was real.

But now the same thing is happening with Charlotte, isn't it? My story is being lived out again except through a different person. Part of me hates her. The other part pities her.

All because I was her.

Should I tell her my story? Tell her how I'd given birth to other children? Tell her about how by the time Mark and I were ready for our own child that my body was too worn down to make it through another pregnancy?

I don't want to tell her these things. It would raise too many concerns. She might ask too many questions. Questions I don't want to answer.

Things will be different with her.

But truthfully, I don't know what to do.

Should I warn her that her future will be the same as mine if she stays here? Or should I let her figure that out herself?

Even more . . . what if I end up dead like Anna?

Charlotte slammed the journal closed.

No.

No, no, no, no!

No wonder Meredith had given Charlotte the looks she had.

The whole time Charlotte was here, Meredith had feared a replay of what had happened between her, Mark, and Anna.

Then the woman's fears had come true. Mark had fallen for Charlotte.

Another thought slammed into her mind. What if . . . what if the same thing happened to Charlotte?

Would she mysteriously die of either an accident or supposed suicide? Would Mark find a replacement for her? What if he already had one?

How many times had he done this? What if there had been other women before Anna and Meredith? What if he'd killed them all and made it look accidental or like suicide?

The breath left her lungs.

She shouldn't have to ask herself those questions.

But she was.

She'd need time to sort through all this.

And Mark couldn't find out she knew anything.

He'd make up lies. He'd tell her she was crazy.

He'd get rid of her sooner rather than later.

She needed an escape plan, Charlotte realized. A way to get away if Mark proved to be the man—not of her dreams but of her nightmares.

Then she heard a door slam downstairs, and she realized Mark was home.

She stood quickly and wiped the dust from her jeans.

She needed to greet him and pretend like nothing was wrong.

And whatever she did, she couldn't let him know she'd read the journal.

Not until she had a plan first.

fifty-five
Now

RANGER HAD CLEANED Anastasia up the best he could. Simmy had some wipes with her, and she'd gotten some of the mud off the girl's face. Then Duke had pulled a granola bar and some water from his pack for her.

That taken care of, the team set out, knowing they had no time to waste.

Maybe Ranger should have let Anastasia walk. But he sensed she was still shaken and weak. Besides, he didn't mind carrying her. In fact, he preferred it.

If he had his way, he'd never let her go.

"I've been thinking about what we can do when I saw you again, Daddy," she murmured.

Warmth filled him. Anastasia had known he would find her. At least he'd instilled that knowledge in her.

"And what do you want to do?" He held her more tightly as he climbed down a rocky outcropping.

"Can we go dogsledding again?" she asked. "I really

want to do that. And maybe fishing. I loved when we caught salmon. And that game you taught me with the beans?"

"Mancala?"

"That's the one. I really want to play that with you. While we eat popcorn and drink hot cocoa. In the winter, I want to wait outside for the northern lights. There's so much I've missed doing with you, Daddy."

His heart ached.

He'd been given a second chance. Everything in his life had changed when he thought his daughter was dead.

But here she was. Alive and well.

As well as she could be after being on the run in the wilderness and nearly swallowed by the mud.

But she had a fighting spirit, and Ranger knew she would be okay.

Soon, he'd have lots of decisions to make. Decisions for her future and what would be best for her.

Each of those decisions ended with Ranger and Anastasia together.

His throat burned with emotion at the thought.

He'd never trust anyone else with her care again. He hadn't realized how much of a mistake that had been to leave her with John and Shannon.

As they hiked, Ranger remembered a place they'd passed earlier that would be good to set up camp. The area was flatter than most of the surrounding terrain, but it was enclosed by trees. It was also far enough away from the water that not too many animals would walk that way in search of hydration.

Even though it was still raining, maybe they could find enough dry wood to start a fire. Ranger would need to try everything he could to keep everyone warm. It would be cold tonight, and they were all wet.

Finally, they reached the area, and he called for everyone to stop.

Reluctantly, he set Anastasia down. But he kept his hand on hers as the group turned toward each other.

"Let's leave our things here," Ranger said. "Then we need to grab anything dry we can to start a fire with. It's going to get cold tonight. Look underneath logs and in places where you might find some moss or leaves—anything we might be able to burn. But don't go too far away either. We need to stay close. These mountains are dangerous, especially at night."

He glanced at Simmy, and she nodded.

His heart lodged in his throat at the sight of her. She'd been pushed beyond her comfort zone but was handling it like a pro.

He'd love a moment alone with her. A moment to see how she was doing.

But this wasn't the time.

Right now, they simply needed to survive.

———

THIRTY MINUTES LATER, the team brought their findings back to the area where they'd left their bags. Simmy had managed to find a couple of branches she thought would work.

Ranger made a small firepit using some stones. They added their kindling, and Ranger pulled a lighter from his pocket. It took several tries but finally a flame blazed to life.

If anyone was looking for them, the smoke would be a dead giveaway. But they needed warmth. This fire was essential. The emergency blankets from Duke's and Ranger's backpacks would help, but they needed more.

Simmy had been keeping her eyes open as she searched the forest, looking for signs that someone was out there. But she hadn't seen or heard anyone outside their group.

The feeling was probably just her paranoia, and she knew that.

She was grateful they were all back here safe and could get warm.

Ranger sat at the fire—Anastasia beside him—with his arm wrapped around her shoulders as he held her close.

Considering the trauma the girl must have been through, she seemed to be doing remarkably well. Her face still had some mud on it, though most of it had been removed with the wipes. There were no other visible injuries or cuts or bruises. Only mud.

Simmy hoped the fire would keep her warm.

"I need to make a phone call," Ranger told her. "Could you keep an eye on Anastasia?"

Simmy nodded. "Of course."

Andi and Duke were in a conversation by themselves, several feet away so it gave Simmy some time to talk to the girl alone.

But before she could start a conversation, Anastasia did. She studied Simmy a moment before saying, "You're pretty. Are you friends with my dad?"

Simmy smiled at the girl's inquisitiveness. "I am. He's so glad he found you."

"I knew he would." Confidence rang through the girl's words.

"Is that why you left? Because you knew he'd come after you?"

Anastasia frowned before shrugging. "I left because my mother is a terrible person. She told me Daddy wasn't ever coming for me. Then I overheard her talking to the security guards. Heard her say Daddy was at John and Shannon's and probably coming this way. I was afraid she'd try to hide me before he got here. So I knew I had to leave. To hide out. Then I thought, maybe I could head toward their place."

She said the words as if she were a world-weary adult.

Growing up too fast could do that to a person.

"That was very brave of you." Simmy hated to think about the girl fearing her mother, yet she also understood what that was like. "Not too many kids would want to venture out into these mountains alone."

"I never wanted to stay here with my mom. I started exploring the woods when we first got here. Explored them a little more every day—just in case I had to get away. Daddy always told me it's important to be aware of your surroundings." Her face fell. "But I didn't know about the mud. I'd never made it that far before."

"I'm sure that was scary. But you handled yourself really well."

The girl shivered. "I'm glad you guys found me and not my mom. She would've only yelled at me."

"Does she yell at you a lot?" Maybe Simmy shouldn't ask the question, but she was curious. What had the past couple of years been like for Anastasia?

"Not really. Mostly she ignores me. Sometimes she leaves for days for fancy shopping trips, and I'm left alone. Well, not totally alone. Karen is usually there with me."

"Karen?"

"She's my nanny."

"Your nanny? Oh, that sounds fun."

"I like her."

Simmy's thoughts continued to race. "Where is Karen now?"

"She left about a week ago. I don't know where she went. Mother said she went to visit family. But I don't believe anything she says."

Simmy tried not to show her thoughts, tried not to show how little she thought of Vivian. Remaining neutral was the best option now.

"What about school?" she asked instead. "Who did schoolwork with you?"

"My nanny gave me some books to read, and I've been doing schoolwork on my own. I fixed my own food and washed my own clothes. I learned to take care of myself."

Again, Simmy was reminded of her own childhood. Anastasia's story sounded awfully similar to what Simmy had gone through.

She felt another moment of connection with the child.

A moment later, Ranger joined them again. "Is anyone hungry?"

He gave no indications what the call had been about. Instead, he put on a pleasant demeanor. Simmy knew him well enough to know that something was up.

But she didn't dare ask him about it in front of Anastasia.

"I packed some granola bars and beef jerky." He reached into his bag.

He kept searching.

Simmy's concern grew as she sensed something was wrong. "What's going on?"

"I know I put food in here." Ranger's eyes narrowed. "But . . . it's gone."

"What do you mean gone?" Simmy's thoughts raced. "Did it fall out of your bag?"

Ranger's gaze met hers. "That's what I would like to know also."

fifty-six

RANGER KNEW it didn't make sense. He knew he'd packed that food.

Only one conclusion came to mind, but he didn't want to go there.

Duke heard the conversation and checked his own bag. After ruffling around inside a moment, he straightened and frowned.

"I gave Anastasia my granola bar earlier, but I brought some peanut butter crackers too. But they're not here." Then he reached into another compartment, and his face tightened. "Neither are my car keys."

"What? Who would take your things?" Then Andi softened her face as if not wanting to freak out Anastasia.

Wordlessly, all four of them exchanged a glance.

Ranger didn't say the words out loud. But he knew what had happened.

When they'd left their bags here to go gather wood, someone had grabbed their food and keys, leaving them stranded in the wilderness without any viable means of getting back to the airport.

That also meant someone was out here.

Watching them.

Vivian's men?

Knave?

Ranger had no idea.

He slowly glanced around, looking for any signs of danger.

But the darkness concealed any faces.

"Is everything okay, Daddy?" Anastasia stared up at him.

He forced a smile and put his arm around her again. "Everything's fine. None of us are going to starve if we don't eat until morning, right?"

They all nodded in agreement, clearly putting on an act for Anastasia.

Ranger wished he felt as lighthearted as he sounded.

Because he knew they were still in danger.

In fact, danger might be within a stone's throw away.

———

THAT FEELING Simmy had felt earlier hadn't been her imagination.

Someone else was out here with them.

Watching.

Trying to sabotage them.

Panic tried to claim her muscles. Caused her to shiver. Caused her thoughts to race.

It had been a thirty-mile drive to even get to the place where they'd started their search. Hiking from here back to Duke's car and then trying to find help would be challenging.

They could go to Vivian's place, but Ranger had said he didn't want to trigger anything in Anastasia. They would figure it out one way or another.

Blaze had said he'd call for backup. So at least there was that.

Unless someone sabotaged that plan as well.

Simmy repressed a shudder, trying to hold herself together.

"The best thing we can do right now is to get some sleep." Ranger's voice cracked with tension as he said the words. "But we should take shifts. We'll need to keep a lookout. Two at a time, and we can rotate so the others can get rest."

"For what?" Anastasia stared up at her father, the firelight dancing across her face.

Ranger turned toward her with tenderness in his voice. "There are all kinds of dangerous things in these mountains. Bear. Moose. It can't hurt to have someone on guard."

She snuggled into him. "No animal is dumb enough to mess with you, Daddy. Nothing can take you down."

Simmy's heart squeezed. The girl obviously thought her father was a superhero—as most girls did.

Simmy only wished those words were true.

But no one was invincible.

Not even Ranger.

fifty-seven
Then

CHARLOTTE KNEW what her husband had done.

Meredith's death hadn't been suicide. He'd simply made it look that way.

When he got tired of Charlotte, he'd figure out an inconspicuous way to get rid of her also.

It had been three months since she'd found Meredith's journal. She hadn't mentioned it to Mark. But she hadn't forgotten about it either. In fact, she thought about Meredith's words daily. Multiple times.

Mark wanted her to do another surrogacy. He said this was the last one, and then they could have their own children.

They'd been married for eight years now. She'd been pregnant six times.

How many more pregnancies could her body take? She didn't know, but everything didn't feel the same in her body. Dr. Matthews didn't say anything, but she saw the look on his face. She saw him talking to Mark in hushed tones.

When she asked, they'd both insisted it was nothing.

But Charlotte was certain her body couldn't handle many more pregnancies.

Every time she told Mark she didn't think another surrogacy was a good idea, he got angry. Sometimes he threw things. Sometimes he shook her in an effort to make her see things his way.

She had the bruises to prove it. Thankfully, those injuries always healed. But she also had some scars, mostly on her back. They were from the time Mark had broken a vase by throwing it on the floor. Then he'd pushed Charlotte down.

The glass had cut her back. Mark had tried to treat her wounds, but she'd needed stitches. She hadn't, however, gone to the hospital.

Afterward, he'd been the perfect gentleman. He apologized. Said it would never happen again.

She almost believed him.

But she knew about Meredith.

In the days since she'd found the journal, Charlotte's eyes had been wide open.

She'd paid more attention to Mark. Especially when his brother came over. She was pretty sure the two of them were up to something, though she wasn't sure what. She hoped to figure it out soon.

She had begun to stash money away. Begun to plan how she would escape when she was finally able to.

Not only that, but she'd found an old Bible in the house. Had begun to read it. Had begun to feel something changing inside her.

She hadn't given much thought to Bible reading or prayer in the past several years.

But now she realized she missed it. She found comfort in the words on the pages.

For so long she had been searching for something to give her hope. She hadn't found it.

She'd felt like a battered, beat-up mess because of her past. Felt like someone who wasn't worthy. Especially when her mom's boyfriends had taken advantage of her. It had altered her view of men and relationships. Her self-esteem had suffered. But that needed to change.

The words she'd read in the Bible made it sound as if she were chosen. Loved. Created with purpose.

Romans 5:8: "But God shows his love for us in that while we were still sinners, Christ died for us."

John 3:16: "For God so loved the world, that he gave his only Son, that whoever believes in him should not perish but have eternal life."

Romans 8:37–39: "No, in all these things we are more than conquerors through him who loved us. For I am sure that neither death nor life, nor angels nor rulers, nor things present nor things to come, nor powers, nor height nor depth, nor anything else in all creation, will be able to separate us from the love of God in Christ Jesus our Lord."

Charlotte had clung to those words. They had given her the courage to do what she knew she needed to do.

To leave.

She would do that tonight.

Mark was headed out of town with his brother, and she knew this would be the perfect opportunity to flee.

She'd wait until after he pulled away in his car.

She'd take her own car to the airport and would leave it there. She knew Mark would eventually find it.

From the airport, she'd take a cab to the bus station. She hoped the move would throw him off her trail.

Mark would definitely come for her.

Charlotte hefted the backpack onto her shoulders and took one last glance at this house, a place she'd once thought was flawless. Now it had become a place of nightmares.

But no more.

Just as she turned to leave through the door, a footstep sounded behind her.

Her stomach sank, and her heart fluttered with nerves.

Before she even saw his face, she knew who it was.

Mark.

Had he sensed she was going to do this? After all, he was supposed to be out of town.

She slowly turned. Saw him there. Saw the gun in his hands.

She sucked in a breath.

She knew exactly what was about to happen. Would

he stage this as a home invasion gone wrong? Most likely, yes.

The one thing that was certain was that Mark wouldn't let her walk away. She knew too much.

Charlotte could ruin him, and he would never let that happen.

"What do you think you're doing?" He hulked over her.

"Just running an errand." She'd considered telling the truth, but she thought he might buy her excuse. That he might let her go on her errand—only she wouldn't return.

"Don't lie to me. I know what you're trying to do." His eyes narrowed. "You can't leave me. You're mine."

She trembled at the anger in his voice. Mark really believed those words.

That was the scariest part of it all.

"I don't want to stay anymore," she told him. "You can't keep me here."

He stepped closer. "Sure, I can. I've made you the person you are. All that you have is because of me. Without me, you're nothing. Just like you were when you came here."

She flushed. His words felt like a slap—no doubt what he intended.

That was why Mark had chosen her. He'd seen that insecurity in her. Had known she didn't have a strong family background.

Those facts had made Charlotte the perfect victim.

Plus, she'd fit the profile of what he wanted in a wife.

He'd been able to mold her right into the person he wanted. Someone stylish. Poised. Quiet.

But no more.

She was created for a purpose. That purpose wasn't to be this man's slave. It wasn't to be manipulated. It wasn't to be a doormat.

She could be gentle and kind without being walked on.

She wasn't even thirty years old, so she had plenty of years left to figure things out.

But first, she had to get away from this man.

"I'm going to leave," she told Mark.

His nostrils flared. "You leave here, and I'll tell everyone you murdered Meredith."

Her blood turned icy cold until her entire body felt frosted over. "What?"

"I heard your fights. The way you resented her, and she resented you. You wanted the baby for yourself. For yourself and for me so we could be a family."

"You wouldn't tell people that . . ." Her pulse raced in her ears.

"Sure, I would. And who do you think they'll believe? Me or you?"

Him. Charlotte had no doubt about that.

But she couldn't stay here a moment longer. "I'm still leaving."

"No, you're not." Mark grabbed her hair.

He jerked it back so hard that she yelped. Then, with her chin in the air, Mark placed the gun beneath her head.

"You're not walking away," he growled.

She could hardly breathe. She anticipated the pain of the bullet going through her skull.

She prayed her death would be quick.

But she wouldn't beg this man for anything, not even her life.

"I will lock you in your room until you become obedient. Do you understand that?" he asked through clenched teeth.

Charlotte didn't answer. She had no doubt he meant those words.

"Why aren't you talking?" he demanded.

She still didn't say anything. There was nothing she could say that would appease Mark. Not unless she lied. She didn't plan on doing that.

"Talk!" He jammed the gun harder.

Then before she realized what she was doing, she grabbed his hands.

Wrestled with him for the gun.

Mark struggled against her, clearly surprised by her actions.

The next moment, a blast filled the air.

The gun had fired.

But Charlotte wasn't sure who had been hit.

fifty-eight
Now

RANGER HAD VOLUNTEERED to take the first shift, and Simmy had offered to sit with him.

The two of them were perched on a rock probably ten feet away from the rest of the group as they stood guard.

Anastasia had fallen asleep near the fire. Ranger's backpack lay beneath her head, and a blanket covered her body. Duke and Andi slept on the other side of the crackling flames in the same positions using their backpacks and blankets.

The arrangement was perfect. Because Ranger would love some time to talk to Simmy. To hash things out. Simmy was a great sounding board, and he'd come to lean on her more than he'd anticipated.

But they'd need to be careful not to wake anyone, and they'd need to be careful to remain alert to any sounds around them.

Ranger knew someone was out there.

Watching them right now.

Part of him wanted to search the woods himself.

But he didn't. His best bet was to stay put and wait for this person to make the next move.

Simmy turned to him, her blanket wrapped around her shoulders. "Do you mind if I ask what that phone call earlier was about? You seem concerned."

His gaze darkened at the memory. "I tried to call Apollo to get an update. He didn't answer."

Her brow wrinkled. "Why wouldn't he answer?"

"That's what I'm wondering also. I'm hoping it was because of a bad connection or something."

She frowned but nodded.

A few moments of silence passed until Simmy said, "I'm so glad you found Anastasia, Ranger. She's a lovely girl."

His throat tightened when he realized how close he'd come to losing his daughter again. "Do you think she's going to be okay?"

"She seems tough," Simmy said. "I do think she'll be okay, especially if she has her dad."

"Thank you for being here with me through it all." He grabbed her hand and squeezed it.

He wished there was another way to show her his thankfulness. But maybe there would be time for that later. Time for him to take her for a nice dinner. Buy her flowers.

He hoped their futures would contain some type of normalcy. That he could somehow show Simmy that, despite everything they'd both been through, there was a chance for happiness.

He wanted to spend every day of his life proving to her that there were decent men out there. Men who would love and appreciate her. Men who didn't give her attention with false motives. Men who didn't want to take advantage of her kindness.

"I'll always be there for you, Ranger," Simmy murmured.

Gratitude filled him at Simmy's reassurance. She always had a way of making everything feel better.

"Thank you, Simmy." He kept his voice low as he said the words. "You seem like you'd be the perfect mom. Was that ever on your radar?"

As soon as he said the words, he realized he shouldn't have. Simmy's gaze clouded. But it was too late to take his question back.

Now he was even more curious, however. There was a story there. A piece of her past. An explanation for the quiet pain in her gaze.

"That's something that I've wanted to talk to you about." She swallowed hard and pushed a hair behind her ear. "Because the truth is, I've had six children."

Ranger's eyes widened as he processed what she'd said. But what sense did it make? If she had kids, then surely she'd talk about them.

It didn't fit her personality to be a mother yet to remain quiet about her children.

So what was he missing?

———

SIMMY SAW the confusion in Ranger's gaze.

Maybe this wasn't the right way to share this information. Yet she wasn't sure how else to go about it.

She knew she had to tell Ranger the truth about her past sometime. So why not now? They had time to kill as they kept watch anyway.

Besides, once he knew the truth about her, things would change. He'd see her in a different light. Maybe that light wouldn't be positive.

She sucked in a deep breath. Knowing that once she started, there was no turning back.

"I was a surrogate," she told him. "My real name is Charlotte, but I changed my name when I moved to Washington. I changed it again when I moved to Alaska. I couldn't let anyone find me."

Then she told him about how she took her first surrogate job out of desperation to make ends meet. About how the wife died. How she fell in love with the husband, and they later married. How her new husband had convinced her to continue being a surrogate.

How she'd suspected there was more to her husband's story than he'd let on.

Ranger's jaw flexed with each new detail. "So what happened?"

"I figured out what he was doing. He was using me almost like an incubator. When I began to ask questions is when he began to hurt me." She tugged up her shirt and pointed at the scars there.

Ranger's gaze darkened when he saw them, and he let out a soft growl.

"I learned Meredith, his wife before me, had also been a surrogate," Simmy finished, tugging her shirt down. "Maybe even Anna too—she was his wife before Meredith. I suspect he killed both of them."

"What?" Surprise—and outrage—filled Ranger's voice.

Simmy nodded somberly. "I knew I had to leave. Otherwise, he would keep using me until I 'accidentally' died. All the dreams I'd had about having a family of my own and a happy ever after disappeared. I realized I'd been tricked, and it felt like a sucker punch, to be honest."

"What happened then?"

"Mark caught me trying to leave and pulled a gun on me. I reached for his gun. We wrestled, and it fired. Hit him in the chest, and he fell to the floor, dead."

"That's what you meant when you said you killed someone?" Realization spread through his voice.

She nodded, though the action felt heavy and forced. "Maybe I should have gotten help. But I didn't. I ran instead. I left New York. But Knave found me."

"Knave?"

"Mark's brother and business partner," she explained. "I thought he was going to kill me. But I managed to escape. I took a bus to Washington state where I found a job at a children's home. I worked there for four years, and I loved it. Then I began to get the feeling he'd found me again. I don't know that he did. I never saw him. But I knew I had to leave."

Ranger nodded slowly. "Why Alaska?"

She fiddled with the edges of the blanket around her, her nervous energy needing a release. "One day, out of the blue, I called my mom. Maybe that was the mistake that led Knave to me. I'm not sure. But she was drunk. That's when she told me my father's name. I began to research him, and I realized he was a podcaster in Alaska. I decided I needed to find him."

"Makes sense. So then you found Craig."

Ranger knew a lot of that story already.

The problem was that by the time Simmy had found out Craig was really her dad, he'd been murdered.

"I decided I could continue to hide out in Alaska until I figured out my next plan," she continued. "At least Knave hadn't followed me here . . . until now."

Ranger reached for her hand and squeezed it. "I'm sorry, Simmy. I can't imagine everything you've been through."

She appreciated his compassion. But she also reminded herself to be cautious. There was a lot at stake here—for both Ranger and for herself. This was no time to jump into anything. Ranger's first priority should be to his daughter.

Before she could say anything else, a stick cracked in the woods.

Her spine stiffened.

Who was out there?

Only one image came to Simmy's mind: Knave.

fifty-nine

RANGER HEARD the noise and grabbed his gun.

Then he waited for someone to appear.

A moment later, a moose stepped out.

A moose?

Not what he was expecting but still dangerous.

He braced himself for whatever the animal would do.

He wanted to wake the rest of the gang. But he also knew the sudden movements could set the animal off.

People didn't realize how dangerous moose could be, but they were strong and aggressive.

The moose paused. Stared at them a moment.

Ranger pushed himself in front of Simmy and waited.

A moment later, the moose put his head back down and sauntered away.

He released the breath he'd been holding.

The animal didn't care about them. He'd just been curious.

As soon as the moose wandered away, he and Simmy exchanged a look and let out a little chuckle.

Thank goodness, it had just been a bored moose. It could have been much worse.

He and Simmy sat on the rock silently for another moment. Their conversation returned to his mind.

Anger surged through him as he remembered what Simmy had told him.

Not only that, but he sensed a wall had gone up around her with every new detail she revealed.

Did she think he would judge her? Was that why?

Ranger didn't know. He wanted to reassure her. Tell her that her background changed nothing about his feelings.

But would she even believe him?

It was hard to say.

They would talk more about this later. Sometime when they had privacy. When people weren't chasing them. When they weren't camped out in the middle of the woods with a potential madman watching their every move.

But the two of them definitely needed to talk . . . and he needed to tell her how he really felt.

THEY'D SURVIVED THE NIGHT, and Simmy was ever so grateful for the fact.

But she'd hardly gotten any rest. She had too much on

her mind. At any moment, she'd expected Knave to appear.

But he hadn't.

But if the man was out there—if he was the one who'd taken their food and keys—then why wasn't he making any more moves?

Only one answer made sense to her.

Because he was meticulously planning something else.

He'd wanted Simmy to feel fear. Wanted to show he had the upper hand.

She shoved those thoughts aside as everyone began to stir.

Everyone was hungry, though Anastasia was the only one vocal about it. Ranger had foraged the woods and come back with some berries for them to eat. Cloudberries, salmonberries, lingonberries.

After they'd all gotten their fill, they packed up and began the rest of the journey back to the SUV.

They probably had a good three miles to hike, but the hardest part of the hike was behind them.

Everyone made small talk as they walked. But were they all just thinking the same thing? Were they all just waiting for the next shoe to drop?

Finally, Simmy noticed a clearing ahead. Not long after, they stepped onto a road, close to where Duke's SUV had been left.

The SUV they didn't have keys to.

Ranger had called Blaze to see if he could pick them up. Right now, he was their only contact in the area.

Other than Apollo.

But Ranger hadn't mentioned much about his friend, which she found curious.

Ranger put away his phone and turned to them. "Thankfully, Blaze was still in town. He and a search and rescue team were getting geared up to come out for a rescue. But now he knows that Anastasia has been found . . . he told the rest of the team they could leave. He's going to come pick us up. We can figure out your SUV later, Duke, if that's okay."

"Whatever we need," Duke said.

As they stood there a moment, Simmy's gaze traveled to a house in the distance.

Was that where Anastasia had lived? What a cold, dark-looking place.

The poor girl . . .

She glanced at Ranger and saw he was looking at the house also. She could see the thoughts percolating in his mind.

He wanted to go back inside, didn't he?

Was that even a good idea? Was Vivian still in there?

She didn't know. But she prayed for the best.

sixty

RANGER DIDN'T WANT to go back into Vivian's place. Not by any stretch of the imagination. Yet something in his gut told him he should.

Apollo still hadn't answered his phone, and Ranger was worried. He knew what Vivian was like. Knew how cunning she could be. Knew there was a possibility she'd had something else up her sleeve.

After all, why had she come this far only to practically wait for Ranger to show up?

Something didn't fit.

What if Apollo had been caught in that crossfire?

"I need you guys to stay here." Ranger's gaze met Duke's. "Can you keep an eye on everyone for a bit?"

"Of course," Duke said.

"What are you going to do?" Worry tinged Simmy's voice as she stared at him.

He knew better than to hold back the truth. "I need to

go check out the house, see what's happening. But I also need to know that you guys are safe."

She stared at him a moment, concern filling her gaze, before she finally nodded.

Ranger turned to the group. "Stay out of sight. I don't know what's going on, but I don't want anything to take you by surprise."

Everyone nodded in agreement.

Then he leaned toward Anastasia, wanting to speak a special reassurance to her. "I'll be right back, okay? My friends will stay with you."

"Okay, Daddy. Be careful." She blinked up at him, an innocent expression on her face.

He grinned, her sweet voice filling him with warmth. "I will, darling. I love you."

"I love you too."

His heart twisted at her words. Anastasia had always loved him. Unconditionally.

It was something he hadn't known before becoming a dad. His parents did their best to raise him. But his dad worked construction jobs—often out of town for long stretches of time, and his mom had been an alcoholic.

Ranger had never felt complete at home.

He'd never felt complete until he met Simmy.

With one last glance at everyone, he slipped toward the house. He kept his gun in hand, just in case.

As before, he went around to the back patio. He figured it was a better bet—and that the door was still unlocked.

Cautiously, he crossed the patio and headed to the sliding glass door.

He carefully opened it and then turned to look inside.

His breath caught.

The place had been ransacked.

What had happened here in the time since he'd been gone? There had obviously been a struggle.

Was Apollo okay? A bad feeling brewed in his gut.

Carefully, Ranger made his way around the house, looking for any signs of his friend or Vivian.

But there was nothing.

Until he reached the bathroom.

The place he'd last seen Vivian.

Ranger knelt on the floor for a better look.

Six drops of blood formed a trail toward the open window.

Each had started to dry, indicating that some time had passed.

Did the blood belong to Apollo? Or Vivian?

Ranger wasn't sure. But something was going on here.

He needed to get Anastasia somewhere safe.

The question was, was there anywhere truly safe?

———

SIMMY SAW the scowl on Ranger's face when he returned.

Something was wrong.

He paused in front of them, his gaze even more troubled than she'd imagined it would be. Before he could start, Anastasia ran up to him and hugged him. He rested his hand on her back as he addressed the rest of them.

"Apollo and Vivian are missing, there are signs of a struggle inside, and the guards we left tied up have been shot," he explained. "I checked the garage to see if she had any vehicles we could borrow. All the tires have been slashed. I'm not sure what happened or what's going on. But I don't like any of this."

Duke's gaze darkened with concern. "How much longer before Blaze arrives?"

Ranger glanced at his watch. "At least twenty minutes. And I'm not sure we're safe out here in the meantime. I think we should go inside and wait until he gets here, just to be certain. Out here . . . we're exposed."

"Agreed," Duke said.

"Can I get something to eat inside, Daddy? I'm kind of hungry."

"Of course, sweetheart."

Ranger took Anastasia's hand, and they led the way. Anastasia chattered as they walked, sounding clueless about the real danger they were in.

Was Simmy once that innocent? She'd had to grow up fast. Then again, so had Anastasia.

A few minutes later, they stepped inside, and Simmy glanced around the ornate place.

Vivian and Knave would have gotten along well, she mused. This looked like the kind of place he would like with these cold but fancy decorations. Except it was too far out in the middle of nowhere for Knave's taste. He was different from his brother in that he preferred to live in the city.

Duke remained near one door and Ranger by the other. Andi, Simmy, and Anastasia grabbed some crackers from the kitchen and then moved to an interior room, out of sight from any windows. They munched on the crackers as they waited.

"This is where I used to live." Anastasia glanced around with an exaggerated swoop of her head and frowned. "Isn't it terrible?"

"The house itself looks quite enchanting." Simmy chose her words carefully.

"You're being nice," Anastasia said. "I think it's creepy. I miss John and Shannon's place."

Simmy's heart panged again. Ranger hadn't told the girl yet what had happened to John and Shannon. She'd most likely be devastated. Yet this didn't seem like the ideal time to tell her either. Then again, when was a good time when it came to these things?

Simmy wandered the perimeter of the room before coming to a stop at a photo sitting on a shelf near the fireplace.

Her eyes widened.

Simmy pointed at the photo before looking back at Anastasia. "Is that your mom?"

Anastasia nodded. "It is. Why?"

Tremors overtook Simmy. "Because I've met her before."

sixty-one

SIMMY ESCAPED to the bathroom to clean herself up. She felt gross and muddy, and she'd give anything for a toothbrush right now.

She closed the door, grateful for a moment of privacy. She had so many thoughts going through her head.

Vivian . . . she'd come into the trading post before.

The thought still seemed unbelievable. But it was true.

Probably four times within the past couple of years, she'd come in. She hadn't had an accent, and she'd told Simmy she was visiting Prudhoe Bay about a business deal.

Simmy hadn't thought anything about it. That reasoning wasn't unusual for the trading post. Many travelers had connections up in Prudhoe Bay. Simmy had figured she must have been married to one of the CEOs or something. She didn't seem like a CEO herself. She was too prissy, too out of place with her furs and fancy jewelry.

The way she turned her nose up at the simple offerings at the trading post made her seem shallow.

But there had been one time . . .

Simmy hadn't even thought about it until today.

There was one time the woman had mentioned something about looking for a man she'd met on the road once. A man who was an outdoorsman. She said she had some business with him she wanted to take care of.

What had Simmy told her? Had she mentioned Ranger?

The thought made her sick to her stomach.

Had Vivian used her to find information about Ranger?

She turned on the water, let it warm for a minute, and then splashed her face. She washed off all the grime before finding a fresh towel and drying her skin.

When she looked into the mirror, she hardly recognized herself. Hardly recognized the woman she was or the woman she used to be.

Sure, she was older now. Wiser. Not quite as much of a doormat, and definitely not as naive.

She was also a woman who'd been through some hard times. Who'd experienced a lot.

The freshness was gone from her skin. But she was still thin. Her teeth still white. Her hair still naturally light brown with only a few strands of gray.

She stared at her reflection. Was she doomed to be a product of her mother's past?

For years, she'd thought she was. But now, looking at

Anastasia, she would unequivocally tell the girl she could choose her own destiny. That her past didn't have to chain her down. That the heartache she'd been through would make her stronger.

So she could tell herself the same thing.

Simmy felt a rush of determination.

She would heed the words her father had left her. She'd found a letter after he died that read:

> I see so much potential in your eyes. Although I love the fact you're working at the trading post, I know you were created to do so much more.
>
> Don't make the mistakes I did. Don't wallow in grief over the things that have gone wrong in your life. But keep pressing forward, and remember you only live once—at least here on this earth.

Was Simmy strong enough to take control of her future?

She knew the answer.

Yes, she was.

But that didn't mean it would be easy.

She finished cleaning herself up and rinsed her mouth with some water. This would have to do for now. But what was taking Blaze so long to arrive? She was anxious to get away from this place.

She stepped out of the bathroom and into the small hallway.

As she did, the hair on her neck rose.

She jerked her head around.

A man stood there.

Gun in hand and a smile on his face.

Then he said, "Hello, Charlotte. Long time no see."

Nausea rose in Simmy so quickly that she thought she might vomit.

———

WHERE WAS BLAZE? He should be here by now.

Ranger had tried calling him again, but he hadn't answered.

Why weren't people answering their phones? First, Apollo, now Blaze.

Ranger's muscles felt ready to snap as he mentally prepared himself for whatever would happen next. He could feel trouble brewing in the air, and he didn't like it.

But there was more going on here than met the eye.

He stepped away from the back door and glanced into the living room.

Andi looked at some photos with Anastasia. Duke lingered near the front door, peering outside every so often.

Where was Simmy?

Andi looked up at him and seemed to read his thoughts. "She ran to the bathroom."

He nodded, a touch of relief softening his muscles. That made sense.

Ranger stepped toward the back door and began pacing again.

Still no Blaze. Still no answer. When he glanced back into the living room, Simmy still wasn't back.

"You mind checking on her?" he called to Andi.

She was probably fine, and he knew that. But he needed to be on the safe side.

Andi disappeared down the hallway. Knocked on the door.

Ranger waited, fully expecting to see the two women step back into the room at any minute.

But only Andi returned.

As soon as Ranger saw her pinched expression, he knew something was wrong.

"Simmy's not in there." Andi rushed toward Anastasia, reaching for the girl's arm.

"What do you mean?" Ranger's breath caught, and he took a step toward the hallway. "Where is she?"

Andi's uneasy gaze met Ranger's. "I don't know where she went. But she's not in the bathroom."

He heard the subtext of her words. She didn't want to say too much and upset Anastasia.

But something was wrong. Simmy wasn't the type to wander away without telling anyone.

Ranger darted down the hallway.

He hoped this was a misunderstanding. That Simmy

had gone off to explore the house. That she'd sought out a different bathroom.

But in his gut, he already knew none of those things were true.

Something had happened.

sixty-two
Then

BEFORE MARK HAD DIED, he'd gone on another business trip. He was traveling more and more frequently in the days before his death. Charlotte didn't mind. In fact, she wanted him to go.

Charlotte had already finished exploring the attic. Had read all of Meredith's journal.

And her sense of desperation had only grown.

She paused outside of Mark's office. He always kept it locked. But what inside was so important that he needed to keep this room locked? That he wanted to keep his own wife away?

Last night, Charlotte had asked him again, casually during dinner, about what he did for a living.

He'd told her he brokered business deals with high-paying clients overseas.

She'd asked what kind of business deals they were. Did he sell a product?

He'd looked at her, something flashing in his gaze. Then he'd told her that he helped set up businesses in other countries.

Charlotte didn't believe him. Mark thought she was so ignorant that she'd believe anything he said.

It had taken her a long time to wise up. But finally, she did. It was as if the scales had fallen off her eyes.

There was something wrong with this whole scenario.

It was time she discovered what.

Even though Charlotte knew his office was locked, she twisted the door knob.

No luck.

But she'd planned for that. Over the past couple of weeks, she'd been searching the house for any keys that might fit this door.

She'd found one in a secret compartment at the bottom of his dresser.

Her throat went dry as she held the key now and stared at the door. Once she went inside this room, there would be no going back. She would be aware of whatever it was she discovered.

And if the truth was as nefarious as she thought it was, she could either confront him or go to the police.

Or if it was entirely too scary, she supposed she could simply run.

She wasn't sure yet. She needed to see what was locked inside this room first.

She slipped the key into the lock.

It fit.

All the moisture left her mouth as she twisted it and the door opened.

Even though she knew Mark was gone, she still felt the need to shut the door behind her, just in case. Plus, she'd purchased some small alarms at the store and had set them up by each exterior door. They were so small no one would know they were there. She would get an alert on her phone if anyone came inside.

Urgency pressed on her, the reminder that she didn't have any time to waste.

Charlotte went to Mark's desk. Sat in the leather seat. Made note of how nice and neat everything was.

She began searching through his drawers, but all she found were office supplies. Notepads and pens and paper clips. Nothing that gave her any information, except a few random photos of some of the surrogate parents.

Why did he have these pictures here in his drawer? They were candid shots, taken unaware.

Weird.

She stopped at one photo. An older one of Mark with another woman. A blonde bombshell.

Charlotte touched her hair. The woman looked a little like her, for that matter. She looked like Charlotte ever since Mark had given her the makeover. The highlights. The makeup. The fancy clothes.

Was this . . . Anna?

Charlotte's throat tightened. It had to be.

Why had he kept a photo of her? Somehow, Charlotte

had the feeling this woman meant more to Mark than she'd assumed.

She knew that his calendar was on his phone as were all his contacts. So she wouldn't find that here.

No, the best place to find out anything was on his computer.

She tapped one of the keys there, and the screen lit. She would need a password.

But she'd already thought this through.

She tried Mark's name and birthday first.

It was boring and predictable, but Mark could be boring and predictable, even though Charlotte hadn't seen it at first.

The screen gave a little jerk to let her know that wasn't correct.

She'd need to try her second choice.

She typed in Merrybear. It was what he'd liked to call Meredith.

Before hitting Enter, Charlotte held her breath.

But the screen made that same jostling motion.

Only one more try or she would be locked out.

She nibbled on her bottom lip, suddenly second-guessing herself.

She might as well just try this. She had no other options.

So she had typed in CharlotteofHearts.

It sounded cheesy, but that was what he called her as a corny nickname. She wasn't even sure where it had come from. She'd thought it was adorable at first.

But no more.

Swallowing hard, she hit Enter again.

This time, the screen didn't do its little dance.

Instead, it changed to a desktop loaded with files.

One victory down, many more to go . . .

She quickly scanned all the titles, none of which meant anything to her.

They seemed like random numbers and letters placed together by the file folders.

She nibbled on her bottom lip and frowned.

Where did she even start?

———

CHARLOTTE GLANCED AT HER WATCH.

She'd been in Mark's office for three hours.

So much for not losing track of time.

But she'd gotten so caught up in everything she was learning.

The results left her sick to her stomach.

She couldn't be sure, but she was fairly certain Mark was a baby broker.

He'd made a career out of selling babies to couples who were desperate, who couldn't have children of their own.

From what she'd seen, she wasn't the only surrogate. He had a long list of women he used. An even longer list of clients.

She'd even found a waitlist for the innocent newborns.

From what she could gather, Mark had been doing this for more than a decade. He'd made millions doing so, while paying the women working for him a pittance.

Including her.

Something about her must have been different, however. Because Mark had married her and not the others.

Why? Why marry her instead of just keeping her on the payroll like these other women?

Why marry Anna? Why Meredith? Was it some kind of cover for him? To make him look normal?

Charlotte wasn't sure, but it didn't make sense.

She stared at the names. Both of the surrogates and of the parents.

Mark must have the doctors on his payroll—including Dr. Matthews.

Disgust roiled inside her.

Then, making a split-second decision, she printed the list. She didn't know what she would do with this information. But something told her she needed it as evidence.

Should she go to the police? If Mark caught her trying to do so, he'd hurt her. She had no doubt about that.

Would the cops even take her seriously? Besides, one of Mark's friends was a judge in the area. Others were doctors. A couple were lawyers.

Why would anyone believe her over Mark?

Just as the final paper printed, her phone dinged.

Her heart raced into overtime as she glanced at the screen.

Someone was at the house.

She glanced at the video showing the person coming into the home.

Her stomach dropped.

It was Knave.

If he caught her in this room, she was certain she'd also face a sudden, tragic death.

sixty-three

Now

EQUAL PARTS of tension and shock thrummed through Simmy's body as she stared at the man standing in the hallway with a gun in his hand.

But it wasn't Knave.

It was . . . Mark.

He was alive.

And he'd found her.

But . . . Simmy shook her head. Nothing made sense.

She blinked as she continued to stare, her body frozen in place.

It was definitely Mark. He'd aged some. His dark hair had streaks of gray now. His face bore a few fine lines. His muscles didn't seem quite as taut.

But it was him. Ten years later.

Ten years after she thought she'd killed him.

"Make a sound, and I'll kill your friends," he growled.

"I have men outside the house. At my signal, they'll shoot."

Simmy believed him. She would never put her friends at risk.

"What do you want from me?" Her voice trembled.

"I want you to come with me." He grabbed her arm. "Quietly."

She let him lead her away. Was doing so the right thing? She wasn't sure. But obedience felt like the only option at the moment.

With his gun to her back, Mark led her down the hallway. Near a transition strip on the floor, Simmy pretended to stumble. Her shoe scraped the wall, leaving a small mark behind.

A mark Ranger could find. That he could trace.

They went out a window on the side of the house, to an area out of sight from the front and back doors.

Mark didn't speak again as they walked. He probably didn't want to chance it.

They headed across the yard. Over the fence. Through the woods.

Finally, they reached an SUV stashed on the side of the road.

"Inside," Mark grumbled.

Simmy did as he directed.

Once in the back seat with Mark beside her, the driver took off down the mountain road.

She felt hyperaware of everything around her. Of Mark's intense gaze. Of his gun. The rough roads.

Chubby sat in the driver's seat, with another man beside him.

This had to be a nightmare.

But Simmy knew it wasn't.

What did Mark have planned for her next? She had so many questions for him. She still couldn't believe he was alive.

But she didn't dare speak.

"I thought I'd never find you," Mark finally said. "I've missed you."

She swallowed hard before saying, "I thought you were dead."

"Thankfully, Knave was close by after you shot me, and he got Dr. Matthews to the house in time. The doc saved me." His gaze darkened. "He did what my wife should have done. Instead, you left me there, dying and alone. What kind of person does that? You aren't the woman I thought you were."

"You put the gun under my chin. You weren't exactly the husband I thought you were either." Her voice trembled at the memories.

"You really think I would have pulled the trigger?"

"The gun was loaded, wasn't it?"

He shook his head, a mocking look in his gaze. "You're so precious. So, so precious."

She hated it when he spoke to her in patronizing tones like that.

"You tricked me," she said through gritted teeth. "Used me. I wasn't a surrogate for nice couples who couldn't have babies. You were selling those children to the highest bidder."

How could she have been so dumb? Why hadn't she seen it earlier?

She thought of those children she'd carried . . . wondered where they were now. How they were doing.

If anything had happened to them, Simmy would blame herself.

She should have asked more questions. She shouldn't have trusted Mark so easily. Shouldn't have thought he was one of the good guys.

She shouldn't have fallen for his good looks and easy charm.

She'd been so, so wrong.

She stared at him, at a face she'd once thought was so handsome.

Now he just looked like darkness and evil.

"What are you going to do with me now?" she asked.

"Now we get to ride away into our happily ever after." He grinned, though the action didn't reach his eyes. He was still mocking her. His words lacked sincerity. "Isn't that what you always wanted?"

Simmy had said that was what she wanted on more than one occasion.

But this wasn't her happy ever after.

What she had with Ranger was the real deal.

She knew without a doubt Ranger would never hurt her. Would never do the things Mark had done.

But it might be too late.

She was paying for her sins.

As she should.

Every exchange is a transaction. For everything given, something is taken.

People attract what they reflect.

Concepts Simmy had read about in the books she'd found at Mark's place.

Even the Bible said something about an eye for an eye.

So maybe right now Simmy was simply getting what she deserved.

This was the price she had to pay for her actions.

A price she should have paid years ago.

She'd known she was living on borrowed time.

Nausea churned in her stomach at the confirmation.

———

RANGER SEARCHED the house for Simmy, trying to keep his panic under control.

But she was nowhere to be found.

He leaned toward the wall and saw a scuff mark, along with some dirt.

Simmy had left that, hadn't she? On purpose so he could find her.

He darted out the front door in time to see an SUV pull down the lane.

He sprinted after it, knowing he wouldn't catch up. But he tried anyway. Tried to see the license plate.

Because he instinctively knew Simmy was inside.

He didn't stop until he reached the gate. He gripped the ornate iron there, his knuckles white as he watched the vehicle disappear down the road.

Knave had been waiting here, hadn't he? He'd followed them.

Then the man had seized the opportunity.

Ranger should have seen it coming. But he'd been too focused on Vivian.

He kicked the fence, his hands fisted at his sides.

He couldn't let things end this way. He couldn't.

"What's going on?" Duke jogged to a stop beside him.

Ranger scowled at the now-empty road. "A man named Knave grabbed Simmy. It's . . . well, it's a long story. But this isn't good."

"What? No . . ." Duke glanced down the road and determination spread through his gaze. With more urgency to his tone, he asked, "How long until Blaze is here?"

Ranger glanced at the time on his watch. "I thought he'd be here by now."

Duke shifted as if uneasy with the situation. "How well do you know this Blaze guy?"

"Not well. But he took a beating for us. Seems trustworthy. I hope I wasn't wrong."

"Is there any other backup we can call?" Duke continued.

Ranger's mind raced through the possibilities. "There's Apollo, but he isn't answering his phone."

"I can try to hotwire my SUV," Duke offered. "We may not have any other choice."

Ranger didn't have to think about it long. "Let's give it a shot."

He prayed this plan worked.

He needed to find Simmy before she got too far away.

sixty-four

SIMMY FELT the tension growing inside her as she, Mark, and his henchmen raced down the road. She needed more information—especially if she had any hope of escaping.

Maybe the thought was crazy. Impossible.

But she had to fight, at least.

She swallowed hard before murmuring, "I don't understand why you're doing this. Why don't you just let me go?"

Her question was sincere. Mark clearly didn't care about her anymore—if he'd ever cared about her in the first place. Why go through all this trouble? When she'd thought it was Knave after her, she'd assumed it was out of revenge.

But Mark? What was his reason?

Mark grinned. "I have many reasons I've been hunting you."

Her mind continued to race, but nothing made sense still. "I'm too old to be a surrogate."

"I don't need you to be a surrogate anymore. I have others."

Nausea pooled in Simmy's stomach as his words hit her. "Then why come after me?"

"I assure you, there's been no one like you." He flashed a devious grin. "You were so beautiful and gentle and . . . moldable."

"I reminded you of Anna, didn't I?" she murmured. "That's why you're obsessed with me. I remind you of your one true love."

His gaze darkened. "She was a wonderful woman. Unable to have children. We tried and tried for years. Even did IVF."

More thoughts clicked together in her mind. "Wait . . . those embryos used for the surrogacies . . . ." She couldn't finish the statement.

Mark grinned. "They were all mine. Mine and Anna's. We had quite the army stored up, thanks to Dr. Matthews."

Her lips parted in horror . . .

How could he be this vile?

Anna's death must truly have been an accident.

She licked her lips, determined to keep a level head. "What happened to the other surrogates? Did they end up like Meredith?"

His gaze darkened for a moment. "Unfortunately, two died in childbirth. But the others are alive and well."

"That still doesn't explain why you want me right now."

"You remind me of my Anna." Mark reached for her, resting his hand on her knee.

Vomit churned inside her at his touch.

"You were profiting off these babies I gave birth to," she told him, wanting him to know that she knew the truth. "Couples paid good money for your little 'business deals.' You're telling me there's more to it than that?"

Mark chuckled before shaking his head. "One thing that I've always loved about you—you've always been so innocent and trusting."

Simmy's thoughts raced. What could she possibly be missing? It seemed pretty cut and dried to her.

"You see, Simmy, only wealthy couples come through my agency. This is, of course, on purpose. Then after the baby is older and the parents have grown attached, I move in for the real money. I've made millions and millions." He flashed a grin to show how proud he was.

The sick feeling in her stomach only grew stronger. Did that explain the photos she'd found in his office?

"What kind of real money are we talking about?" Simmy shook her head, waiting for something to make sense. But it didn't. She was missing some pieces still.

"Once these couples have their babies, they'll do anything to keep them," Mark continued. "So when I tell them that their surrogate was underage and that the police might be looking into them, of course they panic. They're afraid they'll be arrested because of their involvement."

Realization smacked her in the face. "Then you make them pay or you'll 'turn them in' and their baby will be taken away."

"Very good. You're finally catching on."

Simmy ran a hand through her hair, appalled at the audacity of his scheme. "But I wasn't underage."

"You looked young, so they believed it. Then I dig up all kinds of dirt on these couples. There are many ways to get money. Knave and I became pretty good at what we do, to say the least."

"That's despicable." Disgust roiled inside her.

Mark shrugged. "It's a way to make a living. And babies make people happy."

Another thought hit her, and emotion clogged her throat. "What about Lexi? Did she really die?"

He snorted. "Of course not. I had a nice family lined up to adopt her. I thought things would get too sticky if you knew that."

"So the baby was never yours and Meredith's?" The words left a bitter taste in her mouth.

"No, she wasn't. She was mine and Anna's. Anna's death devastated me, and I knew I wanted her legacy to continue."

Simmy squeezed her eyes shut. She really *had* been young and naive. And Mark had pounced on her weaknesses like a wolf smelling blood. He'd even gone as far as using the baby as an excuse to sleep next to her.

She forced herself back into the present. "I still don't

know why you need me. It's been ten years. Why not just let me go?"

"Because you have the power to bring my empire down. If the police find you and question you, then my whole scheme will be ruined."

She didn't tell him she'd sent copies of those lists she'd found to the police, along with a note.

She'd expected to hear something. To get a response. To see a story on the news.

There had been nothing.

That was because Mark had those people in his pockets, wasn't it? It was the only thing that made sense. Either that, or Mark had dirt on them as well.

Simmy stared outside at the trees as they passed by. "So why not just kill me then? That makes the most sense."

"I have other plans. There's no one else who's reminded me of Anna as much as you. I have a special place in the house prepared just for you." He grabbed her hand, squeezed it, then brought it to his lips. He pressed a soft kiss there. "Like I said, I've missed you."

Bile rose in her throat.

He'd lost his mind, hadn't he? And he wanted to drag her down with him.

————

RANGER WAITED while Duke hotwired the SUV.

Thankfully, it took less than five minutes.

As soon as the engine roared to life, they all piled inside. They didn't have much time, so they needed to move.

Ranger sat in the back seat with Anastasia beside him. She asked questions—as to be expected.

He answered them to the best of his ability, being careful not to frighten her too much.

The girl was remarkably strong. Other kids in this situation would be terrified. Every once in a while, he saw a touch of that in her gaze. But mostly, she looked determined.

He wasn't the least bit surprised. When she was just four or five, she'd come face-to-face with a snake. Instead of being scared, she picked the snake up and moved it somewhere "safe." She hadn't thought twice about it.

Ranger's thoughts continued to bounce back and forth. He needed to find Simmy. Had Knave tracked her down here? Waited for just the right moment to grab her?

Or was Vivian responsible? Had she somehow managed to kill Apollo? Had she then hidden his body and waited for Ranger to return? Maybe she'd taken Simmy as a way to punish him.

Ranger didn't know the answers to any of those questions. But he needed to figure those things out.

"I see something up ahead," Duke said.

A moment later, they pulled to a stop beside a truck that had hit a tree.

Ranger's heart beat harder when he recognized the vehicle.

Blaze. That was Blaze's truck.

"Stay here," he told Anastasia before climbing out of Duke's SUV. He rushed toward the other vehicle, Duke on his heels.

He opened the door, expecting the worst.

But to his surprise, he saw Blaze lying across the front seat of the vehicle. Blood trickled from his forehead, and his hands and feet were bound with zip ties.

"I thought you'd never come," Blaze said, his voice strained but his eyes alert. "Untie me."

Ranger went to work on the ties. "What's going on? What happened?"

"I was coming to get you when this man ran out in the road. I swerved to miss him, and that's when I hit the tree. Before I could climb out to see if everything was okay, the man reappeared again, this time with a gun. He tied me up and left me here."

"Are you okay?" Ranger tried to determine the man's injuries.

"Bruised ego, but otherwise fine." The ties fell from his wrists, and Blaze shook his hands before flexing his fingers, which had probably gone to sleep.

"How long ago did this happen?" Ranger asked.

"I'm guessing fifteen minutes."

Ranger's gaze locked on his. "Blaze, did you recognize the person who did this?"

"No. He was wearing a hat and a dark coat. But he didn't look familiar."

"We'll have to come back for your truck later," Ranger

said. "Why don't you climb in with us right now? Someone took Simmy. I'm trying to find her."

"I've been listening to the CB radio. I heard someone call for a helicopter."

Ranger stilled. "You think it's the person who took Simmy?"

"I think there's a really good possibility that's the case," Blaze said. "That's the easiest way to get out of this area. That or heading into Canada."

Canada? Ranger hadn't thought of that. But he hoped that Simmy wasn't crossing the border. That would only make things more complicated. Given the fact she didn't have a passport, he didn't think they'd risk trying to get past the border patrol agents there.

But everything was a possibility right now.

An unnerving possibility.

sixty-five

SIMMY WATCHED as they pulled into a metal building, possibly a hangar.

The driver cut the engine and waited for Mark's next command.

Mark turned toward her, his gaze hardening. "Get out. But don't make any sudden moves. You understand?"

She nodded, still aware of the gun he held.

Sometimes, she thought it would be easier if he just pulled the trigger and got this over with.

Because if he succeeded with his plan, she would end up in his basement never to be seen again. She had no idea what kind of things would be happening in the meantime. She didn't want to imagine them.

But another part of her held onto hope.

Maybe Ranger would find her. Maybe she'd walk away from the situation. Maybe she'd get her happy ever after.

But at what cost?

Every exchange is a transaction. For everything given, something is taken.

Mark scooted out behind her, staying close.

Simmy had tried to pay attention on the drive. Had tried to figure out where they were.

A hangar on the outskirts of the airport? Or somewhere else?

She wasn't sure.

"It's just a matter of time." Mark gazed at her, something devious in his eyes. "Then you'll be away from this barren wasteland."

"Alaska is the best place I've ever been."

"Well, extreme people live in extreme places. Maybe that's why you're here. Because you're extreme." The pointed look he gave her drove home the fact that his words weren't a compliment.

What did he mean by that? Simmy stared at him, waiting for him to explain.

"You were never like everyone else," he explained. "You were naive, yet you had a fighting spirit. You reminded me so much of my Anna. That's one of the reasons I know I can't let you go. You make me feel young and alive again."

Simmy repressed a shiver. She wanted to shout at him. Tell him she wasn't his.

But that would only get him more riled up. She couldn't afford that right now.

Instead, she remained quiet. Then she heard a footstep.

Was it Ranger? Had he found her?

Or was it someone sinister?

———

DUKE PULLED up at the airport.

Before the car even stopped moving, Ranger opened the door, and he was out. If Simmy was here, he needed to find her.

There weren't that many buildings at the small airport. But Ranger planned on checking all of them.

He darted into the first building he came to.

The inside was empty.

He checked two other buildings, but it was the same.

Simmy wasn't here.

His jaw tightened along with the muscles in his entire body.

If Simmy wasn't here, then where could she be? Where would Knave have taken her?

Duke and Blaze caught up with him, waiting to hear what he had to say.

"I don't know where to look next," he admitted. "I don't think they would've gone to Canada, especially if they have to get past border agents."

"I can take my plane up and see if I can spot a vehicle, even though we don't know what they're driving." Blaze shrugged. "So that seems like a long shot. But I'm willing to give anything a try."

"You're right, though," Ranger said. "We don't know

what they're driving. That could just be a wild goose chase."

"Maybe we need to call Gibson," Duke suggested. "See if we can get some of the state troopers involved."

Logan Gibson was not only a state trooper but a friend. He was normally stationed up north, but sometimes he worked in Fairbanks. However, Fairbanks was a good three hours—if not more—from here.

"I think you're right," Ranger said. "We should let Gibson know. I'm sure he knows of guys stationed in this area. We'll need backup. Maybe the police will put out an APB for Simmy and Knave. Maybe they can let the border guards know."

"I'm on it." Duke stepped away and put his phone to his ear to make the call.

Ranger prayed that would help. But there was no way he would just stand here and wait for the police to do this job. Not when he was the best bet for finding Simmy right now.

His thoughts continued to race through the possibilities until he finally turned back to Blaze. "You said that someone called for a helicopter."

"That's right." He glanced at his watch. "Should be here in about ten or fifteen minutes according to what I heard. Why?"

"Because if the person who requested the helicopter is the same person who took Simmy, then they should be here. Where else would the helicopter land?"

"Smart thinking. Some people have homesteads where

copters could land." Blaze paused as if another thought hit him. "But . . ."

Ranger stared at him, waiting for him to finish. "But what?"

"There *is* a place about five miles from here that some of the locals use when the airport is busy. There's a runway and hangar there."

Ranger's breath caught. "You said it's about five miles from here?"

Blaze nodded. "That's correct."

"Then let's not waste any more time. Let's go." Ranger motioned for them to head back to the SUV and get moving.

SIMMY'S EYES widened when she saw the person who emerged from the shadows with a gun.

It wasn't Ranger.

Instead, Vivian stood there.

The woman was even more stunning—and deadly looking—than Simmy remembered. She could see why Ranger would have fallen for the woman.

She was slender with pale skin, dark hair, and icy blue eyes. Her cheekbones were high and her nose pert.

"I don't know why you had to come and mess up all my plans." Her Russian accent sounded thick but elegant.

"Who are you?" Mark raised his own gun as the two stared at each other.

Simmy started to edge away, but Mark grabbed her arm. Brought her closer.

"Who are you?" Vivian countered.

They continued their stare off.

Simmy wondered who would be the first one to break.

It was Vivian.

"Sorry about your men," she muttered. "They were really quite incompetent. I had them taken out."

Simmy's gaze flew to a window. How many men had Vivian brought with her?

"I need information from Ranger," Vivian continued, a purr to her voice. "Simmy here is the best way to get it. I know Ranger-Poo will be coming for her. I figured I'd wait."

"I don't know who you are or what kind of game you're playing, but you need to leave." Anger laced Mark's words.

Simmy heard the tremble in his voice. Saw the sheen on his forehead.

He hadn't planned for Vivian, and her appearance was throwing him off-kilter.

Good. He needed to be knocked from his throne of cockiness for a minute. It would do him good.

However, having Mark and Vivian here, both with guns, could prove deadly.

"Where is Apollo?" Simmy remembered Ranger's friend. Remembered how he'd held those gunmen back so she and Ranger could escape.

She prayed Vivian hadn't hurt the man—or worse. But anything was possible right now.

Vivian smiled with her eyes. "It's not important. The only thing that's important is that Ranger knows if he doesn't give me what I want, then I'll kill you."

"You'll kill me?" Simmy stared at her in disbelief. "Why would you do that? I don't understand."

Her eyes narrowed, and she let out an annoyed sigh. "I saw the way he looked at you. I've never seen him look at someone like that before. I think he truly loves you."

Simmy's throat swelled. Could he love her?

She already knew that answer.

She licked her lips and kept her words even as she asked, "So you're going to kill me because you're jealous?"

Vivian let out a harsh laugh. "Not quite. Ranger has some information I need, a fact that has only recently come to light. I had to figure out a way to lure him back here. Anastasia did the trick. I just didn't expect him to bring others with him. He's usually such a Lone Ranger."

"You had the chance to find out information from him when he showed up at your house," Simmy reminded her. "Why did you wait until now?"

"Can't these questions wait?" Mark growled.

Neither woman acknowledged him.

Vivian raised her thin eyebrows. "I almost did question Ranger then. But I thought I could toy with him a bit first. I wondered if I might be able to seduce him into giving me the information. It worked before."

"But?" Simmy asked.

"*But* . . . when I saw him, I knew that everything had changed. So I let him go look for Anastasia. I truly didn't want anything to happen to the girl. She *is* my daughter, and I do love her in my own way, I suppose. But she's so much like her father. She drove me crazy. Pregnancy was never on my radar, but I hoped to use it to my advantage."

What was it with people using babies to their advantage?

Disgust roiled in Simmy's stomach.

"Enough talking!" Mark turned to them with his nostrils flaring. "Both of you, be quiet."

But Vivian raised her gun higher. "I'm afraid you're not the one calling the shots here."

Simmy sucked in a breath and held it as she braced herself for whatever would happen next.

sixty-six

DUKE DROVE five miles down the road.

Ranger knew as every minute passed, the helicopter was getting closer. When it arrived, the pilot could take Simmy anywhere. He might not ever find her again.

But he'd never stop trying.

He couldn't stomach the thought of anything happening to her.

He searched the skies for any sign of the copter. He hadn't seen it yet.

"Daddy . . ." Anastasia said beside him.

Ranger forced himself to look more relaxed as he glanced down at her. "Yes, sweetie?"

"I like your friend Simmy. Is she going to be okay?"

His throat tightened. "I'm doing everything in my power to make sure she's okay."

"What happens after that? What will we do? I get to stay with you, right? Not Mother?"

"I'd never send you to live with anyone but me. When this is over, I'll take you somewhere safe. It will be you and me. Forever."

She grinned, but her smile faltered with a touch of confusion. "Not Simmy?"

Surprise raced through him. "Would you like that?"

She nodded. "She's nice. She makes me feel warm and fuzzy inside, especially when she gives me a hug."

Ranger knew the feeling well.

He liked that idea also. Liked the thought of him, Anastasia, and Simmy all being a family. Living together and taking care of each other.

There was no one else he would truly trust with his daughter. No one who had the kind of capacity for love that Simmy did.

Even after everything she'd been through, she was the real warrior.

"What about Karen?" Anastasia asked. "She was my nanny, and I'm worried about her."

"How long ago did she leave?" Ranger asked.

"About a week."

Ranger hoped Vivian hadn't taken any drastic measures with the woman. But he wouldn't put it past Vivian either.

"I'll look for Karen," he promised. "I'll figure out where she is."

Duke pulled off to the side of the road. They didn't want to get too close and announce their arrival, so they'd go the rest of the way on foot.

And by "they," Ranger meant him and Duke. Anastasia needed to stay far away from this confrontation, and he needed Blaze and Andi to stay with her.

He ran the plan past everyone, and they agreed.

Then he and Duke climbed out and walked toward the hangar.

There was still no sign of that helicopter. Did that mean they were in the wrong place?

But if Simmy wasn't here, Ranger didn't know where she would be.

And that simply wasn't acceptable.

———

SIMMY CONTINUED to stare at Vivian and Mark as they held guns on each other.

Vivian sneered at Mark. "I should have killed you when I had the chance. I saw you in my house, walking around like you belonged there. You messed up my plans."

Somehow, Mark had tracked Simmy to Vivian's place. Then he must have waited, hoping she'd return. It was the only place that made sense.

Had he killed Vivian's guards? Or had Vivian, for some reason, done it?

Simmy supposed it didn't really matter.

"How did you know we'd go back to your house?" Simmy asked Vivian. "How did you know we'd find Anastasia?"

Vivian shrugged as if annoyed by the question. "I

know Ranger. I knew he'd find his precious daughter. As far as the house . . . well, I figured as much. It's shelter—and there's not much else around. There's food there too."

"Were you the one who stole our keys and food?" Simmy continued to try to put the pieces together.

"That would be me." Mark sounded smug at the admission. "And my men. We were waiting for just the right opportunity to grab you, but it never came. So we made the best with what we had. Figured it would buy us some time. Without your keys and food, your options were limited. Sorry about the little girl, though. Didn't really mean for her to get involved with this, but it couldn't be helped."

Mark was such a jerk. Simmy had no idea what she had seen in him. Then again, he was good at fooling people. Good at seeming upright and kind.

But since she'd found out who he really was—*what* he really was—she could see right through him.

Whatever happened, she couldn't go with him. She had to find a way to escape.

Had Ranger realized she was missing yet? How would he find her? Besides, he had his daughter to take care of. The girl should be his priority. Not Simmy.

Did she have anyone else who would come for her? That was the question she'd asked herself so many times.

She thought her father had left—though he really hadn't known of her existence.

Her mother had never loved her.

She'd thought she had Mark, but that relationship had also been a mistake.

Then she and Ranger had bonded. But now with Anastasia in the picture, Simmy wasn't sure where they would stand. Or if they *should* stand. With his daughter in the picture, Simmy wasn't sure she'd have a place with him. His priorities would shift—as they should.

Again, that feeling of being all alone in this world hit her.

But she wasn't alone.

The same book that had brought her so much comfort when she escaped from Mark brought her comfort now.

The Bible.

Simmy had read in those pages that she was never alone. Not when God was by her side.

He was even with her now.

She closed her eyes and lifted a prayer for protection. Not only for herself, but for Ranger and Anastasia and the rest of the gang as well.

When she opened her eyes again, a new sense of peace washed over her.

Simmy's gaze met Vivian's. "You came into the trading post."

Vivian smirked again. "I was looking for Ranger and hoped you might have some information. Unfortunately, you were tightlipped."

Relief filled Simmy. She hadn't shared anything of value. She'd feared so deeply that she was the one who'd given away Ranger's location. That she'd set this in motion somehow.

"I've also been doing some business up in the oil fields," Vivian continued.

"You mentioned that a time or two." Simmy's heart pounded harder as a thought occurred.

Could this have anything to do with Victor Goodman? Andi had been investigating the man, trying to bring him down. What if Vivian was connected somehow? The thought only hit her now.

"Do you know Victor Goodman?" Simmy didn't want to miss the opportunity to ask the question.

Something flashed in Vivian's gaze. "Victor? Maybe. Do you know him?"

Simmy shrugged. "I heard he was brokering a deal up near Prudhoe Bay."

Vivian's gaze remained on her as if ascertaining Simmy's end game.

Just then, a shadow passed over the door.

Someone else was here, she realized.

What Simmy didn't know was . . . if that person was a friend or a foe.

sixty-seven

RANGER LINGERED NEAR THE DOOR, peering through a small crack.

Voices drifted outward, but he could barely make out the conversation.

However, he heard enough to put the pieces together.

The situation was worse than he'd imagined.

Vivian was inside, her gun raised.

A man—Knave, Ranger would guess—also stood with his gun pointed toward Vivian.

Simmy wasn't in the middle of the standoff, but she was definitely in the line of fire.

Ranger could insert himself into the scene, but that wouldn't help any of them.

At least he had his wildcard—Duke.

He circled the building, found his friend at the back, and paused. Two men were dead on the ground. The two men who'd been after them in the woods.

Duke shook his head as he glanced down at the men. "They were like this when I found them."

Ranger clenched his jaw. Vivian must have taken them out.

"Anyone else back here?" he asked.

"I haven't seen anyone."

"Simmy is inside." Ranger explained the situation with Vivian and the other man. "We need a plan to get her out."

"That's going to be tricky given the setup."

"I know." Ranger's jaw hardened as his thoughts raced through various ideas and plans. Finally, one settled in his mind. "I have an idea that might work."

Just then, a helicopter chopped through the air in the distance.

The chopper should be here at any minute. When that happened, Ranger had to make sure that Simmy didn't get onboard.

He gripped his gun and prepared himself for battle.

———

SIMMY'S THROAT tightened as she watched Mark and Vivian continue to face off.

She had no idea how this would end, but it didn't look good.

When all the different scenarios had played out in her mind, none of them ended with her walking away from this situation alive.

Regret filled her. More than anything, she wanted to tell Ranger how much he meant to her. She loved him enough to stay or walk away—whatever he thought was best.

He made her feel safe for the first time in her life. Even with the danger around her, she'd known that Ranger would be there.

That was something she'd been searching for her entire life.

Would she ever have the chance?

Just then, the entire hangar went black.

Mark gripped her arm more tightly. "What . . . ?"

"Who did that?" Vivian glanced around, the edges of her eyes crinkled with irritation.

"Maybe your guy," Mark suggested.

"My guy isn't that stupid," she snipped back.

The doors flung open, and two men flooded the space.

Ranger and Duke. They were here!

Relief filled Simmy—but only for a moment.

Then she remembered how dire the situation was. People could get hurt—or worse, they could get killed.

Ranger aimed his gun at Vivian and Duke's was on Mark.

"Put your guns down," Ranger commanded. "This is over."

"This isn't over until I say it's over." Vivian kept her gun on Mark. "And thank you so much for coming. I was hoping to see you again." She said the words as if she were an actress in a movie and this was merely a casual conversation.

Simmy almost wanted to roll her eyes. *Almost.* The situation was too serious to warrant that response.

"You just don't give up, do you?" Mark held Simmy with one hand and his gun with the other.

Unlike the others, he kept swerving his weapon from person to person.

He might be a vile businessman. But he wasn't a trained fighter.

"I was trying to make it easy and leave with Simmy," Mark continued, glaring at Ranger. "I figured it couldn't hurt to keep you alive and wondering. But I can see now that I was wrong."

"You can say that again," Ranger muttered.

"Just leave us alone." Mark's voice climbed higher. "No one has to get hurt. All I want is Simmy."

"You're not going anywhere with Simmy," Ranger said.

Simmy's heart beat harder.

She wasn't alone, was she? Not when Ranger was here. Now that she realized that, she never wanted to let him go.

"She's not yours," Mark retorted.

"She's not yours either." Ranger narrowed his eyes as he stared at the man.

"What's so special about her? Can we just concentrate on me for a moment?" Vivian had the nerve to let out a sigh. "I have needs also."

In different circumstances, Simmy would have rolled her eyes.

Talk about being a narcissist.

Above them, the copter sounded louder. It was almost here.

Simmy had no idea how this would turn out. But no matter what, she was *not* getting in that helicopter with Mark.

sixty-eight

RANGER WAS GROWING IMPATIENT. Yet the situation was fragile. Each move had to be purposeful.

"Listen," Ranger started. "If either of you pull the trigger, then Duke and I will take you both down in two seconds flat. It's a no-win situation for either of you. So you need to listen closely. Put your guns on the floor. Now."

Neither Mark nor Vivian moved.

"I'm going to give you another three seconds to think this through and to see how neither of you are walking away from this," Ranger continued. "Drop your weapons."

The two of them looked at each other another moment. Then Vivian let out another sigh, as if his request annoyed her.

But finally, she rolled her eyes and put the gun on the floor before raising her hands in the air.

Ranger grabbed it and motioned to Duke. "Zip ties are in my backpack."

His friend grabbed some ties and secured her wrists and ankles. As he did that, Ranger kept his gun aimed on Mark.

He waited for Mark to do the same. Instead, the man stared defiantly, as if trying to come up with a backup plan.

"I've waited too long to find my wife. Now that I've found her, I'm not giving her up," Mark stated. Sweat poured down the sides of his face, and the gun trembled in his hands as he swung it around and aimed at Ranger.

The next moment, a bullet split the air.

———

SIMMY SUCKED in a breath when she heard the gunshot.

Who . . . ? What . . . ?

Everything seemed to turn to gel around her, moving in slow motion.

She glanced around.

Took a quick inventory of herself.

Glanced at Ranger, who still stood with his gun raised.

Then Mark collapsed to the floor.

Her gaze jerked up.

Who had shot him? Ranger? Vivian?

But no. He'd been shot in the back. How . . . ?

She slowly turned.

Another figure appeared.

Apollo.

Apollo had pulled the trigger?

Simmy's lungs froze as she tried to put things together.

Had Apollo been protecting Ranger? Or . . . ?

Another theory hit her with enough intensity to knock the air out of her.

Was Apollo working for Vivian?

In an instant, Ranger turned toward his friend, gun raised. Duke pointed his weapon at the man also.

But Apollo's gun was already trained on Ranger.

Mark moaned on the floor beside her, still alive—for now. Gone was his cockiness, and now he reminded her of a little boy as his face crumpled with pain.

Her gaze shifted.

Mark's gun had slid across the floor, probably five feet away. If Simmy needed to grab it, she could. But she didn't want to make any sudden moves.

She'd have to time it just right.

"Help . . . me . . ." Mark looked up at her, his gaze pleading.

Simmy shook her head.

There was no way she'd help him. Not after all the pain he'd caused.

Besides, any movement might put Ranger in danger.

"Put your guns on the floor, or I'll pull the trigger," Apollo appeared beside Simmy and shoved his gun to her head.

The breath left her lungs as she froze.

"You were working for Vivian?" Ranger spit out the words Simmy had been thinking.

Apollo raised a shoulder, not a hint of remorse in his gaze. "It wasn't exactly what I wanted, but Vivian, as the saying goes, made me an offer I couldn't refuse. Cut those ties. Now."

Duke glanced at him, and Ranger nodded.

Duke took a knife from his pocket and released the woman's wrists and ankles.

"How could you?" Ranger stared at Apollo and shook his head. "We worked together. Had each other's backs."

"I know, and that did make this more difficult. But Vivian found me and asked me questions about you. Offered me a nice paycheck if I could track you down and lead you to her. Unfortunately, she was unsuccessful on her own."

"So that's what you did." Anger simmered in Ranger's voice. "Are you the one who sent that picture of Anastasia to me?"

Apollo grinned. "I knew it was the perfect way to lure you back."

"What do you even want?" Ranger remained bristled, his muscles hard and his jaw set. "Certainly, I'm not the husband you were always looking for."

Vivian snorted at his words. "Oh goodness, no. What woman in her right mind really wants a husband?"

Mark moaned on the floor again, losing more blood.

Simmy's gaze wandered to the gun. If only she could grab it . . .

But Apollo's gun continued to dig into her temple.

She cringed but tried to remain still, to not set the man off.

"I need to know names." Vivian paced closer to Ranger. "Apollo said he didn't have that information. That he was merely a handler."

Ranger didn't deny her words. But he didn't offer any information either.

Vivian continued. "The only way I can get back into my family's good graces is to present them with information on your colleagues. I need to know who is undercover in Russia trying to obtain information for the US government."

Ranger shook his head. "You know I'm not going to tell you that."

"If you want to live, and if you want your precious *Simmy*," she said the name with disdain, "to live, then you will."

Oh, no, Simmy thought. There was no way she would be a bargaining chip in this.

It wouldn't be for her sake that Ranger gave up the names of good men and women who worked for the CIA.

How could Simmy ensure that didn't happen?

sixty-nine

RANGER'S THROAT TIGHTENED.

He couldn't give up the names of his former colleagues.

But he couldn't let Simmy be shot either.

His throat swelled as he considered his options.

None of them ensured everyone would be okay.

He scowled at his former colleague. How could Apollo betray him like this? Were there any good people left out there who would keep their integrity instead of taking a payout?

He knew there were.

The members of the murder club. Though he'd been skeptical about some of them at first, he'd come to learn they were good people. He needed good people in his life. People he could believe in.

People who were nothing like Vivian.

Right now, the woman paced the space as if she owned it.

No surprise.

Meanwhile, Duke stood on guard. Simmy had her hands raised in the air. Knave—Ranger assumed that was who the man was—moaned on the floor near her feet.

Blaze was still outside with Andi and Anastasia. Ranger hoped he wouldn't leave them.

The helicopter would land at any time now. Even though Mark wouldn't be getting inside, Ranger could easily see Vivian commandeering it and forcing the pilot to take her wherever she demanded.

He could envision her leaving this place, dead bodies in her wake.

Including his.

How could he have ever fallen for this woman?

It was a question he asked himself all the time. He'd been so lost at that time in his life. He'd desperately wanted purpose. Meaning.

And Vivian had made him feel like a million bucks. He'd been so blinded by her beauty and his own lack of moral compass that he'd given in. If only he could go back in time and talk some sense into his old self.

"So, what's it going to be?" Vivian stared at Ranger. "Give me the names or she dies. It's pretty simple."

Apollo kept his gun on Simmy.

Ranger let out a long and low rumbling grunt. "You don't have to do this."

"Of course I do." Vivian shook her head back and

forth in a diva-like manner. "This is what you signed up for when you decided to betray the people who trusted you."

"I never wanted to betray you," he told her. "I was doing my job."

"And I'm only doing my job now," Vivian said. "The government would very much like to know who should be executed next. Who is betraying them. And you have that information."

"It's not that simple."

"We can make it that simple." Vivian's gaze locked on his, vengeance dripping from her eyes. "I did really care about you, you know. Then you had to go and take Anastasia from me."

"You never loved her."

"Of course, I did. In my own way, at least." Her words didn't sound convincing. Even Vivian had to know that.

"This isn't what love looks like." If Ranger's eyes could burn lasers into Vivian, she'd be burnt to a crisp right now. "And I think you know that. You don't have the capacity to love."

She sneered at him as his words seemed to hit her like a slap.

Then she raised her gun. "Maybe I'll just do away with you instead and forget about all of this."

Before she could pull the trigger, another bang sounded.

Then Vivian collapsed.

———

THE GUN TREMBLED in Simmy's hands.

What had she just done?

All she knew was Vivian was about to shoot Ranger. To kill him.

She couldn't let that happen.

So she'd ducked.

Grabbed Mark's gun.

Aimed.

Fired.

All before Apollo knew what was happening.

As more gunfire sounded, everything blurred around her.

Apollo collapsed.

Duke raced toward Vivian.

Ranger rushed to Simmy.

He took the gun from her and tucked it into his waistband. Put his hands on both sides of her arms. Stared her in the eye.

"It's okay, Simmy," he murmured. "It's going to be okay."

Simmy collapsed into his arms as sobs escaped from her.

Memories of when she'd shot Mark filled her mind. For years, she'd lived with guilt, thinking she'd taken his life.

She'd never willingly kill someone.

That was why Simmy had only shot Vivian's knee.

The woman writhed and moaned on the floor. Blood covered the cement.

Then the sirens sounded.

Were the police on their way? Could it be possible they were already close?

Could all of this really be over?

She dared to hope that could be true.

"It's going to be okay," Ranger murmured. "Thank you."

"For what?" Simmy's voice quivered.

"For saving my life."

"I thought . . ." She couldn't finish her statement. Couldn't tell Ranger she'd thought he was going to die. Saying the words out loud was too painful.

Ranger held her tighter and stroked her head. "I know. I know."

As the police flooded the hangar, Ranger didn't let go of Simmy.

She knew they had a lot of explaining to do.

But maybe the nightmare was finally behind them.

seventy

TWO WEEKS LATER, everything still felt like a blur.

Simmy couldn't believe how things had unfolded.

Mark was dead, and Knave had been arrested back in New York. Simmy had provided those documents she'd printed from Mark's office all those years ago. She'd saved copies, just in case.

The police back in New York hadn't taken her seriously, but the FBI certainly did. That information would now be used as evidence in the trial against Knave.

Simmy would most likely be summoned as a witness. She was okay with that. In a small way, it would help her make things right.

Meanwhile, Vivian and Apollo were in custody. The government would figure out what to do with them, but they'd probably be going away for a long time.

Ranger had been interviewed by the FBI and CIA

several times about everything that had happened. It appeared he could now put that part of his past to rest.

This nightmare was finally over.

Ranger had recently rented a small, three-bedroom house in Fairbanks in a neighborhood with a big yard and lots of other children around for Anastasia to play with.

Anastasia now lived with her dad, and Simmy had never seen Ranger look so happy.

Currently, Simmy—she'd decided to stick with her new name in favor of this new life of hers—stood in the kitchen, fixing some coffee and sandwiches.

As she did, Mr. Knightly wagged his tail beside her.

Yes, Mr. Knightly. Nathaniel had insisted they keep the dog if they wanted him.

And Anastasia unequivocally had wanted the canine.

He belonged here.

Simmy grabbed a dog bone and gave it to Mr. Knightly before rubbing his head. "You're such a good boy."

"Spoiling that dog again?"

She looked up at Ranger as he walked into the room, his hair wet and his face freshly shaven.

Her throat went dry at the sight of him.

"Would you expect anything less?" she forced herself to say.

"Of course not."

He peered into the living room, where Anastasia sat on the couch reading a book.

As he did that, Simmy poured him a cup of coffee.

Ranger paced closer and wrapped his arms around her waist. "I'm glad you're here."

Simmy smiled up at him as warmth filled her. "Me too."

She wasn't living at Ranger's place. But she might one day. The two of them had had many talks about their future. About marriage. About forever.

But, for now, Simmy and Andi were roommates.

Simmy had given up her job at the trading post and moved down to Fairbanks. She'd found a job working hospitality at a local motel until she could figure out something else.

At least she didn't have to worry about Mark or Knave anymore. It would take time to come to terms with the part she'd played in the surrogacy scheme.

She wanted to believe she was innocent. But the truth was, she could have asked more questions. She'd been so desperately seeking a stable life that she'd ignored many of the warning signs at the start.

If she could go back, she would do things differently. *A lot* differently.

But going back wasn't a privilege she had.

She nestled her head against Ranger's chest, and they held each other a moment.

They both had things to work through, but Ranger was different than any other man she'd ever been with. He put her first instead of himself.

And Simmy had never been treated like that before.

Knowing he had her back and truly believed in her made her feel alive.

As did having Anastasia in her life.

She and Simmy had bonded quickly. Now Simmy couldn't wait until she saw Anastasia each day so they could spend time together. In many ways, the girl felt like the daughter she'd never had.

A knock sounded at the door, and Simmy stepped away from Ranger. Mr. Knightly barked and ran toward the sound.

"Someone's here?" She glanced up at him, a wrinkle forming on her brow.

Ranger nodded and took her hand, not looking the least bit surprised. "I think you'll like this."

She had no idea who it might be.

When he opened the door, a stout sixty-something woman with a halo of graying brown hair stood there. Simmy had never seen the woman before.

She had no idea what was going on.

The next instant, Anastasia rose from the couch and darted by them. "Ms. Karen!"

Anastasia flew into the woman's arms. Karen beamed at the girl's attention and held her equally as tight.

Karen . . . Anastasia's nanny.

The one person who'd been a constant in the girl's life over the past two years.

"I've been searching and asking around," Ranger whispered to Simmy. "I finally found her. Vivian forced Karen to leave on the spot. She still hasn't found a job so she was more than happy to come here to help with Anastasia."

"That's wonderful," Simmy murmured.

And it was. Because Ranger still had to work. Simmy hoped that maybe they would keep investigating their cold cases for *The Round Table* podcast. The team had a few things to work out first.

She let Karen and Anastasia have their reunion.

Simmy had some reunions of her own to plan.

First of all, she'd tracked down her half-sister. It was something she'd wanted to do ever since she learned of the woman's existence.

Georgina was Craig Rogers' daughter—Craig, the man Simmy had discovered to be her father. Georgina lived in Florida, and Simmy had begun corresponding with her via email. The two hoped to meet someday.

She also wanted to track down Lexi. Wanted to see the girl for herself. She needed to know that those children she'd birthed had turned out okay.

She squeezed Ranger's hand tighter.

He'd come to mean so much to her.

If people's actions in life were transactions, then what existed between her and Ranger was a fair exchange. The give and take was equal. It was respectful.

They both had their own demons from the past. Their own mistakes—mistakes they'd learned from.

But being with Ranger felt like being at home, a feeling she wouldn't trade.

More than anything, she looked forward to their future together.

~~~

Thank you for reading **The End of the Road**. If you enjoyed this book, please consider leaving a review.

Coming next: **The Secrets She Kept.**

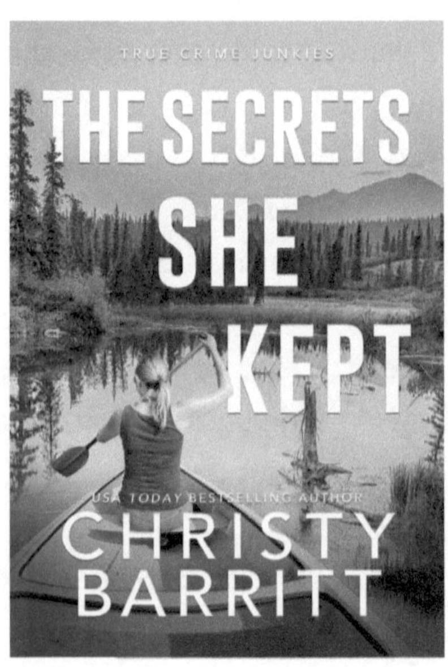
~~~

you also might enjoy: fog lake suspense

Edge of Peril

When evil descends like fog on a mountain community, no one feels safe. After hearing about a string of murders in a Smoky Mountain town, journalist Harper Jennings realizes a startling truth. She knows who may be responsible—the same person who tried to kill her three years ago. Now Harper must convince the cops to believe her before the killer strikes again. Sheriff Luke Wilder returned to his hometown, determined to keep the promise he made to his dying father. The sleepy tourist area with a tragic past hadn't seen a murder in decades—until now. Keeping the community safe seems impossible as darkness edges closer, threatening to consume everything in its path. As The Watcher grows desperate, Harper and Luke must work together in order to defeat him. But the peril around them escalates, making it clear the killer will stop at nothing to get what he wants.

Margin of Error

Some secrets have deadly consequences. Brynlee Parker thought her biggest challenge would be hiking to Dead Man's Bluff and fulfilling her dad's last wishes. She never thought she'd witness two men being viciously murdered while on a mountainous trail. Even worse, the deadly predator is now hunting her. Boone Wilder wants nothing to do with Dead Man's Bluff, not after his wife died there. But he can't seem to mind his own business when a mysterious out-of-towner burst into his camp store in a frenzied panic. Something—or someone— deadly is out there. The killer's hunger for blood seems to be growing at a brutal pace. Can Brynlee and Boone figure out who's behind these murders? Or will the hurts and secrets from their past not allow for even a margin of error?

Brink of Danger

Ansley Wilder has always lived life on the wild side, using thrills to numb the pain from her past and escape her mistakes. But a near-death experience two years ago changed everything. When another incident nearly claims her life, she turns her thrill-seeking ways into a fight for survival. Ryan Philips left Fog Lake to chase adventure far from home. Now he's returned as the new fire chief in town, but the slower paced life he seeks is nowhere to be found. Not only is a wildfire blazing out of control, but a malicious killer known as "The Woodsman" is enacting crimes that appear accidental. Plus, there seems to be a strange connection with these incidents and his best friend's little sister, Ansley Wilder. As a killer watches their every move and the forest fire threatens to destroy their scenic town, both Ryan and Ansley hover on the brink of danger. One wrong move could send them tumbling over the edge . . . permanently.

Line of Duty

Jaxon Wilder didn't plan on returning home to Fog Lake, Tennessee, following his tour of duty in Iraq. But after a gut-wrenching failure during his stint in the Army, he now faces a new challenge: his family. Abby Brennan always did her best to be the good girl and to live by the rules. When a wrong decision changes her entire life, she tries to hide from the world. However, a madman known as the Executioner is determined to find her and enact his own brand of justice. When Jaxon and Abby are thrown together in the killer's crosshairs, they're forced to depend on one another to survive. Will Jaxon's sense of duty be enough to help keep Abby safe? Or will deadly secrets lead to the penalty of death?

Legacy of Lies

The justice system failed her family—and so did her hometown. Madison Colson knows deep down that her father—a convicted serial killer—is innocent. But believing it and proving it are two entirely different things. Unable to help her father, Madison has spent most of her adult life overcompensating by helping others. When her aunt dies unexpectantly, duty calls her back to Fog Lake, Tennessee, a beautiful but painful place she'd rather forget. Terrifying events begin to unfold once she arrives, unleashing her worst nightmares. The Good Samaritan Killer—or a copycat—is back, and now Madison Colson is his target. FBI Special Agent Shane Townsend is determined to stop the deadly rampage that has sent the tightknit community into a frenzy. But he needs to earn Madison's trust first. The task feels impossible, especially considering his father is the one who put her dad in prison. With the whole town on edge and pointing fingers, tension escalates out of control. Madison and Shane must sort the facts from the lies—and fight for a legacy of truth—before The Good Samaritan Killer has the final say.

Secrets of Shame

A killer has a promise to keep . . . Attorney Isaac Colson only wants to put his tumultuous past in Fog Lake behind him and return to his life in Memphis. But when an ominous text threatens that he must come back or there will be deadly consequences, he knows he can't take any chances. Rebecca Moreno has only ever loved one man—her high school sweetheart, Isaac Colson. But when his dad went to prison for murder, Rebecca's father forbade them from seeing each other again. Years later, Isaac is back in town and old feelings are stirring. But Rebecca is harboring a secret that could change everything. When The Good Samaritan Killer strikes again, guilt pummels her. She has to tell Isaac the truth. But as events unfold, she has more to lose than ever. Isaac and Rebecca must find answers—their lives depend on it. But everyone seems to have secrets, each that forms an obstacle to finding the truth . . . and to staying alive.

Refuge of Redemption

Home is a place of refuge—unless it's a killer's playground. For years, Bear Colson has been known as the serial killer's son. But now, someone else is behind bars for the crimes his father was accused of committing. Bear wants to believe hope for a brighter future is in sight, but he has reason to suspect more than one killer was involved. Forensic photographer Piper Stephens' career crashed and burned when she trusted the wrong man. Now, after discovering an alarming secret about the infamous Good Samaritan Killer, she sets out to find both answers and redemption. But things go awry when her assistant becomes the next victim. As fear batters Fog Lake residents once again, Bear and Piper join forces to track down the truth. But the killer is determined to remain in the shadows—and he'll destroy anyone who stands in his way.

complete book list

Squeaky Clean Mysteries:

#1 Hazardous Duty

Half Witted (Squeaky Clean In Between Mysteries Book 1, novella)

#2 Suspicious Minds

#2.5 It Came Upon a Midnight Crime (novella)

#3 Organized Grime

#4 Dirty Deeds

#5 The Scum of All Fears

#6 To Love, Honor and Perish

#7 Mucky Streak

#8 Foul Play

#9 Broom & Gloom

#10 Dust and Obey

#11 Thrill Squeaker

#11.5 Swept Away (novella)

#12 Cunning Attractions

#13 Cold Case: Clean Getaway

#14 Cold Case: Clean Sweep

#15 Cold Case: Clean Break

#16 Cleans to an End

While You Were Sweeping, A Riley Thomas Spinoff

The Sierra Files:

#1 Pounced

#2 Hunted

#3 Pranced

#4 Rattled

The Gabby St. Claire Diaries (a Tween Mystery series):

#1 The Curtain Call Caper

#2 The Disappearing Dog Dilemma

#3 The Bungled Bike Burglaries

The Worst Detective Ever

#1 Ready to Fumble

#2 Reign of Error

#3 Safety in Blunders

#4 Join the Flub

#5 Blooper Freak

#6 Flaw Abiding Citizen

#7 Gaffe Out Loud

#8 Joke and Dagger

#9 Wreck the Halls

#10 Glitch and Famous

#11 Not on My Botch

Raven Remington
Relentless

Holly Anna Paladin Mysteries:
#1 Random Acts of Murder
#2 Random Acts of Deceit
#2.5 Random Acts of Scrooge
#3 Random Acts of Malice
#4 Random Acts of Greed
#5 Random Acts of Fraud
#6 Random Acts of Outrage
#7 Random Acts of Iniquity

Lantern Beach Mysteries
#1 Hidden Currents
#2 Flood Watch
#3 Storm Surge
#4 Dangerous Waters
#5 Perilous Riptide
#6 Deadly Undertow

Lantern Beach Romantic Suspense
#1 Tides of Deception
#2 Shadow of Intrigue
#3 Storm of Doubt
#4 Winds of Danger
#5 Rains of Remorse

#6 Torrents of Fear

Lantern Beach P.D.
#1 On the Lookout
#2 Attempt to Locate
#3 First Degree Murder
#4 Dead on Arrival
#5 Plan of Action

Lantern Beach Escape
Afterglow (a novelette)

Lantern Beach Blackout
#1 Dark Water
#2 Safe Harbor
#3 Ripple Effect
#4 Rising Tide

Lantern Beach Guardians
#1 Hide and Seek
#2 Shock and Awe
#3 Safe and Sound

Lantern Beach Blackout: The New Recruits
#1 Rocco
#2 Axel
#3 Beckett
#4 Gabe

Lantern Beach Mayday
#1 Run Aground
#2 Dead Reckoning
#3 Tipping Point

Lantern Beach Blackout: Danger Rising
#1 Brandon
#2 Dylan
#3 Maddox
#4 Titus

Lantern Beach Christmas
Silent Night

Crime á la Mode
#1 Dead Man's Float
#2 Milkshake Up
#3 Bomb Pop Threat
#4 Banana Split Personalities

Beach Bound Books and Beans Mysteries
#1 Bound by Murder
#2 Bound by Disaster
#3 Bound by Mystery
#4 Bound by Trouble
#5 Bound by Mayhem

Vanishing Ranch
#1 Forgotten Secrets

#2 Necessary Risk

#3 Risky Ambition

#4 Deadly Intent

#5 Lethal Betrayal

#6 High Stakes Deception

#7 Fatal Vendetta

#8 Troubled Tidings

#9 Narrow Escape

#10 Desperate Rescue

The Sidekick's Survival Guide

#1 The Art of Eavesdropping

#2 The Perks of Meddling

#3 The Exercise of Interfering

#4 The Practice of Prying

#5 The Skill of Snooping

#6 The Craft of Being Covert

Saltwater Cowboys

#1 Saltwater Cowboy

#2 Breakwater Protector

#3 Cape Corral Keeper

#4 Seagrass Secrets

#5 Driftwood Danger

#6 Unwavering Security

Beach House Mysteries

#1 The Cottage on Ghost Lane

#2 The Inn on Hanging Hill

#3 The House on Dagger Point

School of Hard Rocks Mysteries
#1 The Treble with Murder
#2 Crime Strikes a Chord
#3 Tone Death

Carolina Moon Series
#1 Home Before Dark
#2 Gone By Dark
#3 Wait Until Dark
#4 Light the Dark
#5 Taken By Dark

Suburban Sleuth Mysteries:
Death of the Couch Potato's Wife

Fog Lake Suspense:
#1 Edge of Peril
#2 Margin of Error
#3 Brink of Danger
#4 Line of Duty
#5 Legacy of Lies
#6 Secrets of Shame
#7 Refuge of Redemption

Cape Thomas Series:
#1 Dubiosity
#2 Disillusioned

#3 Distorted

Standalone Romantic Mystery:
The Good Girl

Suspense:
Imperfect
The Wrecking

Sweet Christmas Novella:
Home to Chestnut Grove

Standalone Romantic-Suspense:
Keeping Guard
The Last Target
Race Against Time
Ricochet
Key Witness
Lifeline
High-Stakes Holiday Reunion
Desperate Measures
Hidden Agenda
Mountain Hideaway
Dark Harbor
Shadow of Suspicion
The Baby Assignment
The Cradle Conspiracy
Trained to Defend
Mountain Survival

Dangerous Mountain Rescue

Nonfiction:
Characters in the Kitchen
Changed: True Stories of Finding God through Christian Music (out of print)
The Novel in Me: The Beginner's Guide to Writing and Publishing a Novel (out of print)

about the author

USA Today has called Christy Barritt's books "scary, funny, passionate, and quirky."

Christy writes both mystery and romantic suspense novels that are clean with underlying messages of faith. Her books have sold more than four million copies and have won the Daphne du Maurier Award for Excellence in Suspense and Mystery, have been twice nominated for the Romantic Times Reviewers' Choice Award, and have finaled for both a Carol Award and Foreword Magazine's Book of the Year.

She is married to her Prince Charming, a man who thinks she's hilarious—but only when she's not trying to be. Christy is a self-proclaimed klutz, an avid music lover who's known for spontaneously bursting into song, and a road trip aficionado.

When she's not working or spending time with her family, she enjoys singing, playing the guitar, and exploring small,

unsuspecting towns where people have no idea how acci-
dent-prone she is.

Find Christy online at:
    www.christybarritt.com
    www.facebook.com/christybarritt
    www.twitter.com/cbarritt

Sign up for Christy's newsletter to get information on all of her latest releases here: **www.christybarritt.com/ newsletter-sign-up/**

 facebook.com/AuthorChristyBarritt

 x.com/christybarritt

 instagram.com/cebarritt